# THE SINGING BONE (THE ADVENTURES OF DR.THORNDYKE)

## LECTOR HOUSE PUBLIC DOMAIN WORKS

THE SINGING BONE
(THE ADVENTURES OF DR. THORNDYKE)

RICHARD AUSTIN FREEMAN

ISBN: 978-93-5344-634-5

First Published: 1912



LECTOR HOUSE

LECTOR HOUSE LLP
E-MAIL: lectorpublishing@gmail.com

# THE SINGING BONE
# (THE ADVENTURES OF
# DR. THORNDYKE)

BY

R. AUSTIN FREEMAN

Published in
UK: 1912
US: 1923

Reprinted in 1947 as
"The Adventures of Dr. Thorndyke"

# PREFACE

THE peculiar construction of the first four stories in the present collection will probably strike both reader and critic and seem to call for some explanation, which I accordingly proceed to supply.

In the conventional "detective story" the interest is made to focus on the question, "Who did it?" The identity of the criminal is a secret that is jealously guarded up to the very end of the book, and its disclosure forms the final climax.

This I have always regarded as somewhat of a mistake. In real life, the identity of the criminal is a question of supreme importance for practical reasons; but in fiction, where no such reasons exist, I conceive the interest of the reader to be engaged chiefly by the demonstration of unexpected consequences of simple actions, of unsuspected causal connections, and by the evolution of an ordered train of evidence from a mass of facts apparently incoherent and unrelated. The reader's curiosity is concerned not so much with the question "Who did it?" as with the question "How was the discovery achieved?" That is to say, the ingenious reader is interested more in the intermediate action than in the ultimate result.

The offer by a popular author of a prize to the reader who should identify the criminal in a certain "detective story," exhibiting as it did the opposite view, suggested to me an interesting question.

Would it be possible to write a detective story in which from the outset the reader was taken entirely into the author's confidence, was made an actual witness of the crime and furnished with every fact that could possibly be used in its detection? Would there be any story left when the reader had all the facts? I believed that there would; and as an experiment to test the justice of my belief, I wrote "The Case of Oscar Brodski." Here the usual conditions are reversed; the reader knows everything, the detective knows nothing, and the interest focuses on the unexpected significance of trivial circumstances.

By excellent judges on both sides of the Atlantic—including the editor of 'Pearson's Magazine'—this story was so far approved of that I was invited to produce others of the same type.

Three more were written and are here included together with one of the more orthodox characters, so that the reader can judge of the respective merits of the two methods of narration.

Nautical readers will observe that I have taken the liberty (for obvious reasons connected with the law of libel) of planting a screw-pile lighthouse on the Girdler Sand in place of the light-vessel. I mention the matter to forestall criticism and save readers the trouble of writing to point out the error.

R. A. F,

Gravesend

# CONTENTS

# CHAPTER I.

## THE CASE OF OSCAR BRODSKI

### PART I.
### THE MECHANISM OF CRIME

A SURPRISING amount of nonsense has been talked about conscience. On the one hand remorse (or the "again-bite," as certain scholars of ultra-Teutonic leanings would prefer to call it); on the other hand "an easy conscience": these have been accepted as the determining factors of happiness or the reverse.

Of course there is an element of truth in the "easy conscience" view, but it begs the whole question. A particularly hardy conscience may be quite easy under the most unfavourable conditions—conditions in which the more feeble conscience might be severely afflicted with the "again-bite." And, then, it seems to be the fact that some fortunate persons have no conscience at all; a negative gift that raises them above the mental vicissitudes of the common herd of humanity.

Now, Silas Hickler was a case in point. No one, looking into his cheerful, round face, beaming with benevolence and wreathed in perpetual smiles, would have imagined him to be a criminal. Least of all, his worthy, high-church housekeeper, who was a witness to his unvarying amiability, who constantly heard him carolling light-heartedly about the house and noted his appreciative zest at meal-times.

Yet it is a fact that Silas earned his modest, though comfortable, income by the gentle art of burglary. A precarious trade and risky withal, yet not so very hazardous if pursued with judgment and moderation. And Silas was eminently a man of judgment. He worked invariably alone. He kept his own counsel. No confederate had he to turn King's Evidence at a pinch; no one he knew would bounce off in a fit of temper to Scotland Yard. Nor was he greedy and thriftless, as most criminals are. His "scoops" were few and far between, carefully planned, secretly executed, and the proceeds judiciously invested in "weekly property."

In early life Silas had been connected with the diamond industry, and he still did a little rather irregular dealing. In the trade he was suspected of transactions with I.D.B.'s, and one or two indiscreet dealers had gone so far as to whisper the ominous word "fence." But Silas smiled a benevolent smile and went his way. He knew what he knew, and his clients in Amsterdam were not inquisitive.

Such was Silas Hickler. As he strolled round his garden in the dusk of an October evening, he seemed the very type of modest, middle-class prosperity. He was dressed in the travelling suit that he wore on his little continental trips; his bag was packed and stood in readiness on the sitting-room sofa. A parcel of diamonds (purchased honestly, though without impertinent questions, at Southampton) was in the inside pocket of his waistcoat, and another more valuable parcel was stowed in a cavity in the heel of his right boot. In an hour and a half it would be time for him to set out to catch the boat train at the junction; meanwhile there was nothing to do but to stroll round the fading garden and consider how he should invest the proceeds of the impending deal. His housekeeper had gone over to Welham for the week's shopping, and would probably not be back until eleven o'clock. He was alone in the premises and just a trifle dull.

He was about to turn into the house when his ear caught the sound of footsteps on the unmade road that passed the end of the garden. He paused and listened. There was no other dwelling near, and the road led nowhere, fading away into the waste land beyond the house. Could this be a visitor? It seemed unlikely, for visitors were few at Silas Hickler's house. Meanwhile the footsteps continued to approach, ringing out with increasing loudness on the hard, stony path.

Silas strolled down to the gate, and, leaning on it, looked out with some curiosity. Presently a glow of light showed him the face of a man, apparently lighting his pipe; then a dim figure detached itself from the enveloping gloom, advanced towards him and halted opposite the garden. The stranger removed a cigarette from his mouth and, blowing out a cloud of smoke, asked—

"Can you tell me if this road will take me to Badsham Junction?"

"No," replied Hickler, "but there is a footpath farther on that leads to the station."

"Footpath!" growled the stranger. "I've had enough of footpaths. I came down from town to Catley intending to walk across to the junction. I started along the road, and then some fool directed me to a short cut, with the result that I have been blundering about in the dark for the last half-hour. My sight isn't very good, you know," he added.

"What train do you want to catch?" asked Hickler.

"Seven fifty-eight," was the reply.

"I am going to catch that train myself," said Silas, "but I shan't be starting for another hour. The station is only three-quarters of a mile from here. If you like to come in and take a rest, we can walk down together and then you'll be sure of not missing your way."

"It's very good of you," said the stranger, peering, with spectacled eyes, at the dark house, "but—I think—?"

"Might as well wait here as at the station," said Silas in his genial way, holding the gate open, and the stranger, after a momentary hesitation, entered and, flinging away his cigarette, followed him to the door of the cottage.

The sitting-room was in darkness, save for the dull glow of the expiring fire, but, entering before his guest, Silas applied a match to the lamp that hung from the ceiling. As the flame leaped up, flooding the little interior with light, the two men regarded one another with mutual curiosity.

"Brodski, by Jingo!" was Hickler's silent commentary, as he looked at his guest. "Doesn't know me, evidently—wouldn't, of course, after all these years and with his bad eyesight. Take a seat, sir," he added aloud. "Will you join me in a little refreshment to while away the time?"

Brodski murmured an indistinct acceptance, and, as his host turned to open a cupboard, he deposited his hat (a hard, grey felt) on a chair in a corner, placed his bag on the edge of the table, resting his umbrella against it, and sat down in a small arm-chair.

"Have a biscuit?" said Hickler, as he placed a whisky-bottle on the table together with a couple of his best star-pattern tumblers and a siphon.

"Thanks, I think I will," said Brodski. "The railway journey and all this confounded tramping about, you know—?"

"Yes," agreed Silas. "Doesn't do to start with an empty stomach. Hope you don't mind oat-cakes; I see they're the only biscuits I have."

Brodski hastened to assure him that oat-cakes were his special and peculiar fancy, and in confirmation, having mixed himself a stiff jorum, he fell to upon the biscuits with evident gusto.

Brodski was a deliberate feeder, and at present appeared to be somewhat sharp set. His measured munching being unfavourable to conversation, most of the talking fell to Silas; and, for once, that genial transgressor found the task embarrassing. The natural thing would have been to discuss his guest's destination and perhaps the object of his journey; but this was precisely what Hickler avoided doing. For he knew both, and instinct told him to keep his knowledge to himself.

Brodski was a diamond merchant of considerable reputation, and in a large way of business. He bought stones principally in the rough, and of these he was a most excellent judge. His fancy was for stones of somewhat unusual size and value, and it was well known to be his custom, when he had accumulated a sufficient stock, to carry them himself to Amsterdam and supervise the cutting of the rough stones. Of this Hickler was aware, and he had no doubt that Brodski was now starting on one of his periodical excursions; that somewhere in the recesses of his rather shabby clothing was concealed a paper packet possibly worth several thousand pounds.

Brodski sat by the table munching monotonously and talking little. Hickler sat opposite him, talking nervously and rather wildly at times, and watching his guest with a growing fascination. Precious stones, and especially diamonds, were Hickler's specialty. "Hard stuff"—silver plate—he avoided entirely; gold, excepting in the form of specie, he seldom touched; but stones, of which he could carry off a whole consignment in the heel of his boot and dispose of with absolute safety, formed the staple of his industry. And here was a man sitting opposite him with a parcel in his pocket containing the equivalent of a dozen of his most successful "scoops;" stones worth perhaps—? Here he pulled himself up short and began to talk rapidly, though without much coherence. For, even as he talked, other Words, formed subconsciously, seemed to insinuate themselves into the interstices of the sentences, and to carry on a parallel train of thought.

"Gets chilly in the evenings now, doesn't it?" said Hickler.

"It does indeed," Brodski agreed, and then resumed his slow munching, breathing audibly through his nose.

"Five thousand at least," the subconscious train of thought resumed; "probably six or seven, perhaps ten." Silas fidgeted in his chair and endeavoured to concentrate his ideas on some topic of interest. He was growing disagreeably conscious of a new and unfamiliar state of mind.

"Do you take any interest in gardening?", he asked. Next to diamonds and weekly "property," his besetting weakness was fuchsias.

Brodski chuckled sourly. "Hatton Garden is the nearest approach—?" He broke off suddenly, and then added, "I am a Londoner, you know."

The abrupt break in the sentence was not unnoticed by Silas, nor had he any difficulty in interpreting it. A man who carries untold wealth upon his person must needs be wary in his speech.

"Yes," he answered absently, "it's hardly a Londoner's hobby." And then, half consciously, he began a rapid calculation. Put it at five thousand pounds. What would that represent in weekly property? His last set of houses had cost two hundred and fifty pounds apiece, and he had let them at ten shillings and sixpence a week. At that rate, five thousand pounds represented twenty houses at ten and sixpence a week—say ten pounds a week—one pound eight shillings a day—five hundred and twenty pounds a year—for life. It was a competency. Added to what he already had, it was wealth. With that income he could fling the tools of his trade into the river and live out the remainder of his life in comfort and security.

He glanced furtively at his guest across the table, and then looked away quickly as he felt stirring within him an impulse the nature of which he could not mistake. This must be put an end to. Crimes against the person he had always looked upon as sheer insanity. There was, it is true, that little affair of the Weybridge policeman, but that was unforeseen and unavoidable, and it was the constable's doing after all. And there was the old housekeeper at Epsom, too, but, of course, if the old idiot would shriek in that insane fashion—well, it was an accident, very regrettable, to be sure, and no one could be more sorry for the mishap than himself. But deliberate homicide!—robbery from the person! It was the act of a stark lunatic.

Of course, if he had happened to be that sort of person, here was the opportunity of a lifetime. The immense booty, the empty house, the solitary neighbourhood, away from the main road and from other habitations; the time, the darkness—but, of course, there was the body to be thought of; that was always the difficulty. What to do with the body? Here he caught the shriek of the up express, rounding the curve in the line that ran past the waste land at the back of the house.

The sound started a new train of thought, and, as he followed it out, his eyes fixed themselves on the unconscious and taciturn Brodski, as he sat thoughtfully sipping his whisky. At length, averting his gaze with an effort, he rose suddenly from his chair and turned to look at the clock on the mantelpiece, spreading out his hands before the dying fire. A tumult of strange sensations warned him to leave the house. He shivered slightly, though he was rather hot than chilly, and, turning his head, looked at the door.

"Seems to be a confounded draught," he said, with another slight shiver; "did I shut the door properly, I wonder?" He strode across the room and, opening the door wide, looked out into the dark garden. A desire, sudden and urgent, had come over him to get out into the open air, to be on the road and have done with this madness that was knocking at the door of his brain.

"I wonder if it is worth while to start yet," he said, with a yearning glance at the murky, starless sky.

Brodski roused himself and looked round. "Is your clock right?" he asked.

Silas reluctantly admitted that it was.

"How long will it take us to walk to the station?" inquired Brodski.

"Oh, about twenty-five minutes to half-an-hour," replied Silas, unconsciously exaggerating the distance.

"Well," said Brodski, "we've got more than an hour yet, and it's more comfortable here than hanging about the station. I don't see the use of starting before we need."

"No; of course not," Silas agreed. A wave of strange emotion, half-regretful, half-triumphant, surged through his brain. For some moments he remained standing on the threshold, looking out dreamily into the night. Then he softly closed the door; and, seemingly without the exercise of his volition, the key turned noiselessly in the lock.

He returned to his chair and tried to open a conversation with the taciturn Brodski, but the words came faltering and disjointed. He felt his face growing hot, his brain full and intense, and there was a faint, high-pitched singing in his ears. He was conscious of watching his guest with a new and fearful interest, and, by sheer force of will, turned away his eyes; only to find them a moment later involuntarily returning to fix the unconscious man with yet more horrible intensity. And ever through his mind walked, like a dreadful procession, the thoughts of what that other man—the man of blood and violence—would do in these circumstances. Detail by detail the hideous synthesis fitted together the parts of the imagined crime, and arranged them in due sequence until they formed a succession of events, rational, connected and coherent.

He rose uneasily from his chair, with his eyes still riveted upon his guest. He could not sit any longer opposite that man with his hidden store of precious gems. The impulse that he recognized with fear and wonder was growing more ungovernable from moment to moment. If he stayed it would presently overpower him, and then? He shrank with horror from the dreadful thought, but his fingers itched to handle the diamonds. For Silas was, after all, a criminal by nature and habit. He was a beast of prey. His livelihood had never been earned; it had been taken by stealth or, if necessary, by force. His instincts were predacious, and the proximity of unguarded valuables suggested to him, as a logical consequence, their abstraction or seizure. His unwillingness to let these diamonds go away beyond his reach was fast becoming overwhelming.

But he would make one more effort to escape. He would keep out of Brodski's actual presence until the moment for starting came.

"If you'll excuse me," he said, "I will go and put on a thicker pair of boots. After all this dry weather we may get a change, and damp feet are very uncomfortable when you are travelling."

"Yes; dangerous too," agreed Brodski.

Silas walked through into the adjoining kitchen, where, by the light of the little lamp that was burning there, he had seen his stout, country boots placed, cleaned and in readiness, and sat down upon a chair to make the change. He did not, of course, intend to wear the country boots, for the diamonds were concealed in those he had on. But he would make the change and then alter his mind; it would all help to pass the time. He took a deep breath. It was a relief, at any rate, to be out of that room. Perhaps if he stayed away, the temptation would pass. Brodski would go on his way—he wished that he was going alone—and the danger would be over—at least—and the opportunity would have gone—the diamonds—?

He looked up as he slowly unlaced his boot. From where he sat he could see Brodski sitting by the table with his back towards the kitchen door. He had finished eating, now, and was composedly rolling a cigarette. Silas breathed heavily, and, slipping off his boot, sat for a while motionless, gazing steadily at the other man's back. Then he unlaced the other boot, still staring abstractedly at his unconscious guest, drew it off, and laid it very quietly on the floor.

Brodski calmly finished rolling his cigarette, licked the paper, put away his pouch, and, having dusted the crumbs of tobacco from his knees, began to search his pockets for a match. Suddenly, yielding to an uncontrollable impulse, Silas stood up and began stealthily to creep along the passage to the sitting-room. Not a sound came from his stockinged feet. Silently as a cat he stole forward, breathing softly with parted lips, until he stood at the threshold of the room. His face flushed duskily, his eyes, wide and staring, glittered in the lamplight, and the racing blood hummed in his ears.

Brodski struck a match—Silas noted that it was a wooden vesta—lighted his cigarette, blew out the match and flung it into the fender. Then he replaced the box in his pocket and commenced to smoke.

Slowly and without a sound Silas crept forward into the room, step by step, with catlike stealthiness, until he stood close behind Brodski's chair—so close that he had to turn his head that his breath might not stir the hair upon the other man's head. So, for half-a-minute, he stood motionless, like a symbolical statue of Murder, glaring down with horrible, glittering eyes upon the unconscious diamond merchant, while his quick breath passed without a sound through his open mouth and his fingers writhed slowly like the tentacles of a giant hydra. And then, as noiselessly as ever, he backed away to the door, turned quickly and walked back into the kitchen.

He drew a deep breath. It had been a near thing. Brodski's life had hung upon a thread For it had been so easy. Indeed, if he had happened, as he stood behind the man's chair, to have a weapon—a hammer, for instance, or even a stone?

He glanced round the kitchen and his eyes lighted on a bar that had been left by the workmen who had put up the new greenhouse. It was an odd piece cut off from a square, wrought-iron stanchion, and was about a foot long and perhaps three-quarters of an inch thick. Now, if he had had that in his hand a minute ago—

He picked the bar up, balanced it in his hand and swung it round his head. A formidable weapon this: silent, too. And it fitted the plan that had passed through his brain. Bah! He had better put the thing down.

But he did not. He stepped over to the door and looked again at Brodski, sitting, as before, meditatively smoking, with his back towards the kitchen.

Suddenly a change came over Silas. His face flushed, the veins of his neck stood out and a sullen scowl settled on his face. He drew out his watch, glanced at it earnestly and replaced it. Then he strode swiftly but silently along the passage into the sitting-room.

A pace away from his victim's chair he halted and took deliberate aim. The bar swung aloft, but not without some faint rustle of movement, for Brodski looked round quickly even as the iron whistled through the air. The movement disturbed the murderer's aim, and the bar glanced off his victim's head, making only a trifling wound. Brodski sprang up with a tremulous, bleating cry, and clutched his assailant's arms with the tenacity of mortal terror.

Then began a terrible struggle, as the two men, locked in a deadly embrace, swayed to and fro and trampled backwards and forwards. The chair was overturned, an empty glass swept from the table and, with Brodski's spectacles, crushed beneath stamping feet. And thrice that dreadful, pitiful, bleating cry rang out into the night, filling Silas, despite his murderous frenzy, with terror lest some chance wayfarer should hear it. Gathering his great strength for a final effort, he forced his victim backwards onto the table and, snatching up a corner of the tablecloth, thrust it into his face and crammed it into his mouth as it opened to utter another shriek. And thus they remained for a full two minutes, almost motionless, like some dreadful group of tragic allegory. Then, when the last faint twitchings had died away, Silas relaxed his grasp and let the limp body slip softly onto the floor.

It was over. For good or for evil, the thing was done. Silas stood up, breathing heavily, and, as he wiped the sweat from his face, he looked at the clock. The hands stood at one minute to seven. The whole thing had taken a little over three minutes. He had nearly an hour in which to finish his task The goods train that entered into his scheme came by at twenty minutes past, and it was only three hundred yards to the line. Still, he must not waste time. He was now quite composed, and only disturbed by the thought that Brodski's cries might have been heard. If no one had heard them it was all plain sailing.

He stooped, and, gently disengaging the table-cloth from the dead man's teeth, began a careful search of his pockets. He was not long finding what he sought, and, as he pinched the paper packet and felt the little hard bodies grating on one another inside, his faint regrets for what had happened were swallowed up in self-congratulations.

He now set about his task with business-like briskness and an attentive eye on the clock. A few large drops of blood had fallen on the table-cloth, and there was a small bloody smear on the carpet by the dead man's head. Silas fetched from the kitchen some water, a nail-brush and a dry cloth, and, having washed out the stains from the table-cover—not forgetting the deal table-top underneath—and cleaned away the smear from the carpet and rubbed the damp places dry, he slipped a sheet of paper under the head of the corpse to prevent further contamination. Then he set the tablecloth straight, stood the chair upright, laid the broken spectacles on the table and picked up the cigarette, which had been trodden flat in the struggle, and flung it under the grate. Then there was the broken glass, which he swept up into a dust-pan. Part of it was the remains of the shattered tumbler, and the rest the fragments of the broken spectacles. He turned it out onto a sheet of paper and looked it over carefully, picking out the larger recognizable pieces of the spectacle-glasses and putting them aside on a separate slip of paper, together with a sprinkling of the minute fragments. The remainder he shot back into the dust-pan and, having hurriedly put on his boots, carried it out to the rubbish-heap at the back of the house.

It was now time to start. Hastily cutting off a length of string from his string-box—for Silas was an orderly man and despised the oddments of string with which many people make shift—he tied it to the dead man's bag and umbrella and slung them from his shoulder. Then he folded up the paper of broken glass, and, slipping it and the spectacles into his pocket, picked up the body and threw it over his shoulder. Brodski was a small, spare man, weighing not more than nine stone; not a very formidable burden for a big, athletic man like Silas.

The night was intensely dark, and, when Silas looked out of the back gate over the waste land that stretched from his house to the railway, he could hardly see twenty yards ahead. After listening cautiously and hearing no sound, he went out, shut the gate softly behind him and set forth at a good pace, though carefully, over the broken ground. His progress was not as silent as he could have wished for, though.

The scanty turf that covered the gravelly land was thick enough to deaden his footfalls, the swinging bag and umbrella made an irritating noise; indeed, his movements were more hampered by them than by the weightier burden.

The distance to the line was about three hundred yards. Ordinarily he would have walked it in from three to four minutes, but now, going cautiously with his burden and stopping now and again to listen, it took him just six minutes to reach the three-bar fence that separated the waste land from the railway. Arrived here he halted for a moment and once more listened attentively, peering into the darkness on all sides. Not a living creature was to be seen or heard in this desolate spot, but far away, the shriek of an engine's whistle warned him to hasten.

Lifting the corpse easily over the fence, he carried it a few yards farther to a point where the line curved sharply.

Here he laid it face downwards, with the neck over the near rail. Drawing out his pocket-knife, he cut through the knot that fastened the umbrella to the string and also secured the bag; and when he had flung the bag and umbrella on the track beside the body, he carefully pocketed the string, excepting the little loop that had fallen to the ground when the knot was cut.

The quick snort and clanking rumble of an approaching goods train began now to be clearly audible. Rapidly, Silas; drew from his pockets the battered spectacles and the packet of broken glass. The former he threw down by the dead man's head, and then, emptying the packet into his hand, sprinkled the fragments of glass around the spectacles.

He was none too soon. Already the quick, laboured puffing of the engine sounded close at hand. His impulse was to stay and watch; to witness the final catastrophe that should convert the murder into an accident or suicide. But it was hardly safe: it would be better that he should not be near lest he should not be able to get away without being seen. Hastily he climbed back over the fence and strode away across the rough fields, while the train came snorting and clattering towards the curve.

He had nearly reached his back gate when a sound from the line brought him to a sudden halt; it was a prolonged whistle accompanied by the groan of brakes and the loud clank of colliding trucks. The snorting of the engine had ceased and was replaced by the penetrating hiss of escaping steam.

The train had stopped!

For one brief moment Silas stood with bated breath and mouth agape like one petrified; then he strode forward quickly to the gate, and, letting himself in, silently slid the bolt. He was undeniably alarmed. What could have happened on the line? It was practically certain that the body had been seen; but what was happening now? and would they come to the house? He entered the kitchen, and having paused again to listen—for somebody might come and knock at the door at any moment—he walked through the sitting-room and looked round. All seemed in order there. There was the bar, though, lying where he had dropped it in the scuffle. He picked it up and held it under the lamp. There was no blood on it; only one or two hairs. Somewhat absently he wiped it with the table-cover, and then, running out through the kitchen into the back garden, dropped it over the wall into a bed of nettles. Not that there was anything incriminating in the bar, but, since he had used it as a weapon, it had somehow acquired a sinister aspect to his eye.

He now felt that it would be well to start for the station at once. It was not time yet, for it was barely twenty-five minutes past seven; but he did not wish to be found in the house if any one should come. His soft hat was on the sofa with his bag, to which his umbrella was strapped. He put on the hat, caught up the bag and stepped over to the door; then he came back to turn down the lamp. And it was at this moment, when he stood with his hand raised to the burner, that his eyes, travelling by chance into the dim corner of the room, lighted on Brodski's grey felt hat, reposing on the chair where the dead man had placed it when he entered the house.

Silas stood for a few moments as if petrified, with the chilly sweat of mortal fear standing in beads upon his forehead. Another instant and he would have turned the lamp down and gone on his way; and then—? He strode over to the chair, snatched up the hat and looked inside it. Yes, there was the name, "Oscar Brodski," written plainly on the lining. If he had gone away, leaving it to be discovered, he would have been lost; indeed, even now, if a search-party should come to the house, it was enough to send him to the gallows.

His limbs shook with horror at the thought, but in spite of his panic he did not lose his self-possession. Darting through into the kitchen, he grabbed up a handful of the dry brush-wood that was kept for lighting fires and carried it to the sitting-room grate where he thrust it on the extinct, but still hot, embers, and crumpling up the paper that he had placed under Brodski's head—on which paper he now noticed, for the first time, a minute bloody smear—he poked it in under the wood, and striking a wax match, set light to it. As the wood flared up, he hacked at the hat with his pocket knife and threw the ragged strips into the blaze.

And all the while his heart was thumping and his hands a-tremble with the dread of discovery. The fragments of felt were far from inflammable, tending rather to fuse into cindery masses that smoked and smouldered than to burn away into actual ash. Moreover, to his dismay, they emitted a powerful resinous stench mixed with the odour of burning hair, so that he had to open the kitchen window (since he dared not unlock the front door) to disperse the reek. And still, as he fed the fire with small cut fragments, he strained his ears to catch, above the crackling of the wood, the sound of the dreaded footsteps, the knock on the door that should be as the summons of Fate.

The time, too, was speeding on. Twenty-one minutes to eight! In a few minutes more he must set out or he would miss the train. He dropped the dismembered hat-brim on the blazing wood and ran upstairs to open a window, since he must close that in the kitchen before he left. When he came back, the brim had already curled up into a black, clinkery mass that bubbled and hissed as the fat, pungent smoke rose from it sluggishly to the chimney.

Nineteen minutes to eight! It was time to start. He took up the poker and carefully beat the cinders into small particles, stirring them into the glowing embers of the wood and coal. There was nothing unusual in the appearance of the grate. It was his constant custom to burn letters and other discarded articles in the sitting-room fire: his housekeeper would notice nothing out of the common. Indeed, the cinders would probably be reduced to ashes before she returned. He had been careful to notice that there were no metallic fittings of any kind in the hat, which might have escaped burning.

Once more he picked up his bag, took a last look round, turned down the lamp and, unlocking the door, held it open for a few moments. Then he went out, locked the door, pocketed the key (of which his housekeeper had a duplicate) and set off at a brisk pace for the station.

He arrived in good time after all, and, having taken his ticket, strolled through onto the platform. The train was not yet signalled, but there seemed to be an unusual stir in the place. The passengers were collected in a group at one end of the platform, and were all looking in one direction down the line; and, even as he walked towards them, with a certain tremulous, nauseating curiosity, two men emerged from the darkness and ascended the slope to the platform, carrying a stretcher covered with a tarpaulin. The passengers parted to let the bearers pass, turning fascinated eyes upon the shape that showed faintly through the rough pall; and, when the stretcher had been borne into the lamp-room, they fixed their attention upon a porter who followed carrying a hand-bag and an umbrella.

Suddenly one of the passengers started forward with an exclamation.

"Is that his umbrella?" he demanded.

"Yes, sir," answered the porter, stopping and holding it out for the speaker's inspection.

"My God!" ejaculated the passenger; then, turning sharply to a tall man who stood close by, he said excitedly: "That's Brodski's umbrella. I could swear to it. You remember Brodski?" The tall man nodded, and the passenger, turning once more to the porter, said: "I identify that umbrella. It belongs to a gentleman named Brodski. If you look in his hat you will see his name written in it. He always writes his name in his hat."

"We haven't found his hat yet," said the porter; "but here is the station-master coming up the line." He awaited the arrival of his superior and then announced: "This gentleman, sir, has identified the umbrella."

"Oh," said the station-master, "you recognize the umbrella, sir, do you? Then perhaps you would step into the lamp-room and see if you can identify the body."

"Is it—is he—very much injured?" the passenger asked tremulously.

"Well, yes," was the reply. "You see, the engine and six of the trucks went over him before they could stop the train. Took his head clean off, in fact."

"Shocking! shocking!" gasped the passenger. "I think, if you don't mind—I'd—I'd rather not. You don't think it's necessary, doctor, do you?"

"Yes, I do," replied the tall man. "Early identification may be of the first importance."

"Then I suppose I must," said the passenger.

Very reluctantly he allowed himself to be conducted by the station-master to the lamp-room, as the clang of the bell announced the approaching train. Silas Hickler followed and took his stand with the expectant crowd outside the closed door. In a few moments the passenger burst out, pale and awe-stricken, and rushed up to his tall friend. "It is!" he exclaimed breathlessly. "It's Brodski! Poor old Brodski! Horrible! horrible! He was to have met me here and come on with me to Amsterdam."

"Had he any—merchandize about him?" the tall man asked; and Silas strained his ears to catch the reply.

"He had some stones, no doubt, but I don't know what.

His clerk will know, of course. By the way, doctor, could you watch the case for me? Just to be sure it was really an accident or—you know what. We were old friends, you know, fellow townsmen, too; we were both born in Warsaw. I'd like you to give an eye to the case."

"Very well," said the other. "I will satisfy myself that—there is nothing more than appears, and let you have a report. Will that do?"

"Thank you. It's excessively good of you, doctor. Ah! here comes the train. I hope it won't inconvenience you to stay and see to this matter."

"Not in the least," replied the doctor. "We are not due at Warmington until to-morrow afternoon, and I expect we can find out all that is necessary to know before that."

Silas looked long and curiously at the tall, imposing man who was, as it were, taking his seat at the chessboard, to play against him for his life. A formidable antagonist he looked, with his keen, thoughtful face, so resolute and calm. As Silas stepped into his carriage he thought with deep discomfort of Brodski's hat, and hoped that he had made no other oversight.

## PART II.
## THE MECHANISM OF DETECTION
## (RELATED BY CHRISTOPHER JERVIS, M.D.)

THE singular circumstances that attended the death of Mr. Oscar Brodski, the well-known diamond merchant of Hatton Garden, illustrated very forcibly the importance of one or two points in medico-legal practice which Thorndyke was accustomed to insist were not sufficiently appreciated. What those points were, I shall leave my friend and teacher to state at the proper place; and meanwhile, as the case is in the highest degree instructive, I shall record the incidents in the order of their occurrence.

The dusk of an October evening was closing in as Thorndyke and I, the sole occupants of a smoking compartment, found ourselves approaching the little station of Ludham; and, as the train slowed down, we peered out at the knot of country, people who were waiting on the platform. Suddenly Thorndyke exclaimed in a tone of surprise: "Why, that is surely Boscovitch!" and almost at the same moment a brisk, excitable little man darted at the door of our compartment and literally tumbled in.

"I hope I don't intrude on this learned conclave," he said, shaking hands genially and banging his Gladstone with impulsive violence into the rack; "but I saw your faces at the window, and naturally jumped at the chance of such pleasant companionship."

"You are very flattering," said Thorndyke; "so flattering that you leave us nothing to say. But what in the name of fortune are you doing at—what's the name of the place—Ludham?"

"My brother has a little place a mile or so from here, and I have been spending a couple of days with him," Mr. Boscovitch explained. "I shall change at Badsham Junction and catch the boat train for Amsterdam. But whither are you two bound? I see you have your mysterious little green box up on the hat-rack, so I infer that you are on some romantic quest, eh? Going to unravel some dark and intricate crime?"

"No," replied Thorndyke. "We are bound for Warmington on a quite prosaic errand. I am instructed to watch the proceedings at an inquest there to-morrow on behalf of the Griffin Life Insurance Office, and we are travelling down to-night as it is rather a cross-country journey."

"But why the box of magic?" asked Boscovitch, glancing up at the hat-rack.

"I never go away from home without it," answered Thorndyke. "One never knows what may turn up; the trouble of carrying it is small when set off against the comfort of having appliances at hand in an emergency."

Boscovitch continued to stare up at the little square case covered with Willesden canvas. Presently he remarked: "I often used to wonder what you had in it when you were down at Chelmsford in connection with that bank murder—what an amazing case that was, by the way, and didn't your methods of research astonish the police!" As he still looked up wistfully at the case, Thorndyke good-naturedly lifted it down and unlocked it. As a matter of fact he was rather proud of his "portable laboratory," and certainly it was a triumph of condensation, for, small as it was—only a foot square by four inches deep—it contained a fairly complete outfit for a preliminary investigation.

"Wonderful!" exclaimed Boscovitch, when the case lay open before him, displaying its rows of little re-agent bottles, tiny test-tubes, diminutive spirit-lamp, dwarf microscope and assorted instruments on the same Lilliputian scale; "it's like a doll's house—everything looks as if it was seen through the wrong end of a telescope. But are these tiny things really efficient? That microscope now—?"

"Perfectly efficient at low and moderate magnifications," said Thorndyke. "It looks like a toy, but it isn't one; the lenses are the best that can be had. Of course a full-sized instrument would be infinitely more convenient—but I shouldn't have it with me, and should have to make shift with a pocket-lens. And so with the rest of the under-sized appliances; they are the alternative to no appliances."

Boscovitch pored over the case and its contents, fingering the instruments delicately and asking questions innumerable about their uses; indeed, his curiosity was but half appeased when, half-an-hour later, the train began to slow down.

"By Jove!" he exclaimed, starting up and seizing his bag, "here we are at the junction already. You change here too, don't you?"

"Yes," replied Thorndyke. "We take the branch train on to Warmington."

As we stepped out onto the platform, we became aware that something unusual was happening or had happened. All the passengers and most of the porters and supernumeraries were gathered at one end of the station, and all were looking intently into the darkness down the line.

"Anything wrong?" asked Mr. Boscovitch, addressing the station-inspector.

"Yes, sir," the official replied; "a man has been run over by the goods train about a mile down the line. The station-master has gone down with a stretcher to bring him in, and I expect that is his lantern that you see coming this way."

As we stood watching the dancing light grow momentarily brighter, flashing fitful reflections from the burnished rails, a man came out of the booking-office and joined the group of onlookers. He attracted my attention, as I afterwards remembered, for two reasons: in the first place his round, jolly face was excessively pale and bore a strained and wild expression, and, in the second, though he stared into the darkness with eager curiosity he asked no questions.

The swinging lantern continued to approach, and then suddenly two men came into sight bearing a stretcher covered with a tarpaulin, through which the shape of a human figure was dimly discernible. They ascended the slope to the platform, and proceeded with their burden to the lamp-room, when the inquisitive gaze of the passengers was transferred to a porter who followed carrying a handbag and umbrella and to the station-master who brought up the rear with his lantern.

As the porter passed, Mr. Boscovitch started forward with sudden excitement.

"Is that his umbrella?" he asked.

"Yes, sir," answered the porter, stopping and holding it out for the speaker's inspection.

"My God!" ejaculated Boscovitch; then, turning sharply to Thorndyke, he exclaimed: "That's Brodski's umbrella. I could swear to it. You remember Brodski?"

Thorndyke nodded, and Boscovitch, turning once more to the porter, said: "I identify that umbrella. It belongs to a gentleman named Brodski. If you look in his hat, you will see his name written in it. He always writes his name in his hat."

"We haven't found his hat yet," said the porter; "but here is the station-master." He turned to his superior and announced: "This gentleman, sir, has identified the umbrella."

"Oh," said the station-master, "you recognize the umbrella, sir, do you? Then perhaps you would step into the lamp-room and see if you can identify the body."

Mr. Boscovitch recoiled with a look of alarm. "Is it? is he—very much injured?" he asked nervously.

"Well, yes," was the reply. "You see, the engine and six of the trucks went over him before they could stop the train. Took his head clean off, in fact."

"Shocking! shocking!" gasped Boscovitch. "I think? if you don't mind—I'd—

I'd rather not. You don't think it necessary, doctor, do you?"

"Yes, I do," replied Thorndyke. "Early identification may be of the first importance."

"Then I suppose I must," said Boscovitch; and, with extreme reluctance, he followed the station-master to the lamp-room, as the loud ringing of the bell announced the approach of the boat train. His inspection must have been of the briefest, for, in a few moments, he burst out, pale and awe-stricken, and rushed up to Thorndyke.

"It is!" he exclaimed breathlessly. "It's Brodski! Poor" old Brodski! Horrible! horrible! He was to have met me here and come on with me to Amsterdam."

"Had he any—merchandize about him?" Thorndyke asked; and, as he spoke, the stranger whom I had previously noticed edged up closer as if to catch the reply.

"He had some stones, no doubt," answered Boscovitch, "but I don't know what they were. His clerk will know, of course. By the way, doctor, could you watch the case for me? Just to be sure it was really an accident or—you know what. We were old friends, you know, fellow townsmen, too; we were both born in Warsaw. I'd like you to give an eye to the case."

"Very well," said Thorndyke. "I will satisfy myself that there is nothing more than appears, and let you have a report. Will that do?"

"Thank you," said Boscovitch. "It's excessively good of you, doctor. Ah, here comes the train. I hope it won't inconvenience you to stay and see to the matter."

"Not in the least," replied Thorndyke. "We are not due at Warmington until to-morrow afternoon, and I expect we can find out all that is necessary to know and still keep our appointment."

As Thorndyke spoke, the stranger, who had kept close to us with the evident purpose of hearing what was said, bestowed on him a very curious and attentive look; and it was only when the train had actually come to rest by the platform that he hurried away to find a compartment.

No sooner had the train left the station than Thorndyke sought out the station-master and informed him of the instructions that he had received from Boscovitch. "Of course," he added, in conclusion, "we must not move in the matter until the police arrive. I suppose they have been informed?"

"Yes," replied the station-master; "I sent a message at once to the Chief Constable, and I expect him or an inspector at any moment. In fact, I think I will slip out to the approach and see if he is coming." He evidently wished to have a word in private with the police officer before committing himself to any statement.

As the official departed, Thorndyke and I began to pace the now empty platform, and my friend, as was his wont, when entering on a new inquiry, meditatively reviewed the features of the problem.

"In a case of this kind," he remarked, "we have to decide on one of three possible explanations: accident, suicide or homicide; and our decision will be determined by inferences from three sets of facts: first, the general facts of the case; second, the special data obtained by examination of the body, and, third, the special data obtained by examining the spot on which the body was found. Now the only general facts at present in our possession are that the deceased was a diamond merchant making a journey for a specific purpose and probably having on his person property of small bulk and great value. These facts are somewhat against the hypothesis of suicide and somewhat favourable to that of homicide. Facts relevant to the question of accident would be the existence or otherwise of a level crossing, a road or path leading to the line, an enclosing fence with or without a gate, and any other facts rendering probable or otherwise the accidental presence of the deceased at the spot where the body was found. As we do not possess these facts, it is desirable that we extend our knowledge."

"Why not put a few discreet questions to the porter who brought in the bag and umbrella?" I suggested. "He is at this moment in earnest conversation with the ticket collector and would, no doubt, be glad of a new listener."

"An excellent suggestion, Jervis," answered Thorndyke. "Let us see what he has to tell us." We approached the porter and found him, as I had anticipated, bursting to unburden himself of the tragic story.

"The way the thing happened, sir, was this," he said, in answer to Thorndyke's question: "There's a sharpish bend in the road just at that place, and the goods train was just rounding the curve when the driver suddenly caught sight of something lying across the rails. As the engine turned, the head-lights shone on it and then he saw it was a man. He shut off steam at once, blew his whistle, and put the brakes down hard, but, as you know, sir, a goods train takes some stopping; before they could bring her up, the engine and half-a-dozen trucks had gone over the poor beggar."

"Could the driver see how the man was lying?" Thorndyke asked.

"Yes, he could see him quite plain, because the headlights were full on him. He was lying on his face with his neck over the near rail on the downside. His head was in the four-foot and his body by the side of the track. It looked as if he had laid himself out a-purpose."

"Is there a level crossing thereabouts?" asked Thorndyke.

"No, sir. No crossing, no road, no path, no nothing," said the porter, ruthlessly sacrificing grammar to emphasis. "He must have come across the fields and climbed over the fence to get onto the permanent way. Deliberate suicide is what it looks like."

"How did you learn all this?" Thorndyke inquired.

"Why, the driver, you see, sir, when him and his mate had lifted the body off the track, went on to the next signal-box and sent in his report by telegram. The station-master told me all about it as we walked down the line."

Thorndyke thanked the man for his information, and, as we strolled back towards the lamp-room, discussed the bearing of these new facts.

"Our friend is unquestionably right in one respect," he said; "this was not an accident. The man might, if he were near-sighted, deaf or stupid, have climbed over the fence and got knocked down by the train. But his position, lying across the rails, can only be explained by one of two hypotheses: either it was, as the porter says, deliberate suicide, or else the man was already dead or insensible. We must leave it at that until we have seen the body, that is, if the police will allow us to see it. But here comes the station-master and an officer with him. Let us hear what they have to say."

The two officials had evidently made up their minds to decline any outside assistance. The divisional surgeon would make the necessary examination, and information could be obtained through the usual channels. The production of Thorndyke's card, however, somewhat altered the situation. The police inspector hummed and hawed irresolutely, with the card in his hand, but finally agreed to allow us to view the body, and we entered the lamp-room together, the station-master leading the way to turn up the gas.

The stretcher stood on the floor by one wall, its grim burden still hidden by the tarpaulin, and the hand-bag and umbrella lay on a large box, together with the battered frame of a pair of spectacles from which the glasses had fallen out.

"Were these spectacles found by the body?" Thorndyke inquired.

"Yes," replied the station-master. "They were close to the head and the glass was scattered about on the ballast."

Thorndyke made a note in his pocket-book, and then, as the inspector removed the tarpaulin, he glanced down on the corpse, lying limply on the stretcher and looking grotesquely horrible with its displaced head and distorted limbs. For fully a minute he remained silently stooping over the uncanny object, on which the inspector was now throwing the light of a large lantern; then he stood up and said quietly to me: "I think we can eliminate two out of the three hypotheses."

The inspector looked at him quickly, and was about to ask a question, when his attention was diverted by the travelling-case which Thorndyke had laid on a shelf and now opened to abstract a couple of pairs of dissecting forceps.

"We've no authority to make a post mortem, you know," said the inspector.

"No, of course not," said Thorndyke. "I am merely going to look into the mouth." With one pair of forceps he turned back the lip and, having scrutinized its inner surface, closely examined the teeth.

"May I trouble you for your lens, Jervis?" he said; and, as I handed him my doublet ready opened, the inspector brought the lantern close to the dead face and leaned forward eagerly. In his usual systematic fashion, Thorndyke slowly passed the lens along the whole range of sharp, uneven teeth, and then, bringing it back to the centre, examined with more minuteness the upper incisors. At length, very delicately, he picked out with his forceps some minute object from between two of the upper front teeth and held it in the focus of the lens. Anticipating his next move, I took a labelled microscope-slide from the case and handed it to him together with a dissecting needle, and, as he transferred the object to the slide and spread it out with the needle, I set up the little microscope on the shelf.

"A drop of Farrant and a cover-glass, please, Jervis," said Thorndyke.

I handed him the bottle, and, when he had let a drop of the mounting fluid fall gently on the object and put on the cover-slip, he placed the slide on the stage of the microscope and examined it attentively.

Happening to glance at the inspector, I observed on his countenance a faint grin, which he politely strove to suppress when he caught my eye.

"I was thinking, sir," he said apologetically, "that it's a bit off the track to be finding out what he had for dinner. He didn't die of unwholesome feeding."

Thorndyke looked up with a smile. "It doesn't do, inspector, to assume that anything is off the track in an inquiry of this kind. Every fact must have some significance, you know."

"I don't see any significance in the diet of a man who has had his head cut off," the inspector rejoined defiantly.

"Don't you?" said Thorndyke. "Is there no interest attaching to the last meal of a man who has met a violent death? These crumbs, for instance, that are scattered over the dead man's waistcoat. Can we learn nothing from them?"

"I don't see what you can learn," was the dogged rejoinder.

Thorndyke picked off the crumbs, one by one, with his forceps, and having deposited them on a slide, inspected them, first with the lens and then through the microscope.

"I learn," said he, "that shortly before his death, the deceased partook of some kind of whole-meal biscuits, apparently composed partly of oatmeal."

"I call that nothing," said the inspector. "The question that we have got to settle is not what refreshments had the deceased been taking, but what was the cause of his death: did he commit suicide? was he killed by accident? or was there any foul play?"

"I beg your pardon," said Thorndyke, "the questions that remain to be settled are, who killed the deceased and with what motive? The others are already answered as far as I am, concerned."

The inspector stared in sheer amazement not unmixed with incredulity.

"You haven't been long coming to a conclusion, sir," he said.

"No, it was a pretty obvious case of murder," said Thorndyke. "As to the motive, the deceased was a diamond merchant and is believed to have had a quantity of stones about his person. I should suggest that you search the body."

The inspector gave vent to an exclamation of disgust. "I see," he said. "It was just a guess on your part. The dead man was a diamond merchant and had valuable property about him; therefore he was murdered." He drew himself up, and, regarding Thorndyke with stern reproach, added: "But you must understand, sir, that this is a judicial inquiry, not a prize competition in a penny paper. And, as to searching the body, why, that is what I principally came for." He ostentatiously turned his back on us and proceeded systematically to turn out the dead man's pockets, laying the articles, as he removed them, on the box by the side of the hand-bag and umbrella.

While he was thus occupied, Thorndyke looked over the body generally, paying special attention to the soles of the boots, which, to the inspector's undissembled amusement, he very thoroughly examined with the lens.

"I should have thought, sir, that his feet were large enough to be seen with the naked eye," was his comment; "but perhaps," he added, with a sly glance at the station-master, "you're a little near-sighted."

Thorndyke chuckled good-humouredly, and, while the officer continued his search, he looked over the articles that had already been laid on the box. The purse and pocket-book he naturally left for the inspector to open, but the reading-glasses, pocket-knife and card-case and other small pocket articles were subjected to a searching scrutiny. The inspector watched him out of the corner of his eye with furtive amusement; saw him hold up the glasses to the light to estimate their refractive power, peer into the tobacco pouch, open the cigarette book and examine the watermark of the paper, and even inspect the contents of the silver match-box.

"What might you have expected to find in his tobacco pouch?" the officer asked, laying down a bunch of keys from the dead man's pocket.

"Tobacco," Thorndyke replied stolidly; "but I did not expect to find fine-cut Latakia. I don't remember ever having seen pure Latakia smoked in cigarettes."

"You do take an interest in things, sir," said the inspector, with a side glance at the stolid station-master.

"I do," Thorndyke agreed; "and I note that there are no diamonds among this collection."

"No, and we don't know that he had any about him; but there's a gold watch and chain, a diamond scarf-pin, and a purse containing"—he opened it and tipped out its contents into his hand—"twelve pounds in gold. That doesn't look much like robbery, does it? What do you say to the murder theory now?"

"My opinion is unchanged," said Thorndyke, "and I should like to examine the spot where the body was found. Has the engine been inspected?" he added, addressing the station-master.

"I telegraphed to Bradfield to have it examined," the official answered. "The report has probably come in by now. I'd better see before we start down the line."

We emerged from the lamp-room and, at the door, found the station-inspector waiting with a telegram. He handed it to the station-master, who read it aloud.

"The engine has been carefully examined by me. I find small smear of blood on near leading wheel and smaller one on next wheel following. No other marks." He glanced questioningly at Thorndyke, who nodded and remarked: "It will be interesting to see if the line tells the same tale."

The station-master looked puzzled and was apparently about to ask for an explanation; but the inspector, who had carefully pocketed the dead man's property, was impatient to start and, accordingly, when Thorndyke had repacked his case and had, at his own request, been furnished with a lantern, we set off down the permanent way, Thorndyke carrying the light and I the indispensable green case.

"I am a little in the dark about this affair," I said, when we had allowed the two officials to draw ahead out of earshot; "you came to a conclusion remarkably quickly. What was it that so immediately determined the opinion of murder as against suicide?"

"It was a small matter but very conclusive," replied Thorndyke. "You noticed a small scalp-wound above the left temple? It was a glancing wound, and might easily have been made by the engine. But the wound had bled; and it had bled for an appreciable time. There were two streams of blood from it, and in both the blood was firmly clotted and partially dried. But the man had been decapitated; and this wound, if inflicted by the engine, must have been made after the decapitation, since it was on the side most distant from the engine as it approached. Now, a decapitated head does not bleed. Therefore, this wound was inflicted before the decapitation.

"But not only had the wound bled: the blood had trickled down in two streams at right angles to one another. First, in the order of time as shown by the appearance of the stream, it had trickled down the side of the face and dropped on the collar. The second stream ran from the wound to the back of the head. Now, you know, Jervis, there are no exceptions to the law of gravity. If the blood ran down the face towards the chin, the face must have been upright at the time; and if the blood trickled from the front to the back of the head, the head must have been horizontal and face upwards. But the man when he was seen by the engine-driver, was lying face downwards. The only possible inference is that when the wound was inflicted, the man was in the upright position—standing or sitting; and that subsequently, and while he was still alive, he lay on his back for a sufficiently long time for the blood to have trickled to the back of his head."

"I see. I was a duffer not to have reasoned this out for myself," I remarked contritely.

"Quick observation and rapid inference come by practice," replied Thorndyke. "What did you notice about the face?"

"I thought there was a strong suggestion of asphyxia."

"Undoubtedly," said Thorndyke. "It was the face of a suffocated man. You must have noticed, too, that the tongue was very distinctly swollen and that on the inside of the upper lip were deep indentations made by the teeth, as well as one or two slight wounds, obviously caused by heavy pressure on the mouth. And now observe how completely these facts and inferences agree with those from the scalp wound. If we knew that the deceased had received a blow on the head, had struggled with his assailant and been finally borne down and suffocated, we should look for precisely those signs which we have found."

"By the way, what was it that you found wedged between the teeth? I did not get a chance to look through the microscope."

"Ah!" said Thorndyke, "there we not only get confirmation, but we carry our inferences a stage further. The object was a little tuft of some textile fabric. Under the microscope I found it to consist of several different fibres, differently dyed. The bulk of it consisted of wool fibres dyed crimson, but there were also cotton fibres dyed blue and a few which looked like jute, dyed yellow. It was obviously a parti-coloured fabric and might have been part of a woman's dress, though the presence of the jute is much more suggestive of a curtain or rug of inferior quality."

"And its importance?"

"Is that, if it is not part of an article of clothing, then it must have come from an article of furniture, and furniture suggests a habitation."

"That doesn't seem very conclusive," I objected.

"It is not; but it is valuable corroboration."

"Of what?"

"Of the suggestion offered by the soles of the dead man's boots. I examined them most minutely and could find no trace of sand, gravel or earth, in spite of the fact that he must have crossed fields and rough land to reach the place where he was found. What I did find was fine tobacco ash, a charred mark as if a cigar or cigarette had been trodden on, several crumbs of biscuit, and, on a projecting brad, some coloured fibres, apparently from a carpet. The manifest suggestion is that the man was killed in a house with a carpeted floor, and carried from thence to the railway."

I was silent for some moments. Well as I knew Thorndyke, I was completely taken by surprise; a sensation, indeed, that I experienced anew every time that I accompanied him on one of his investigations. His marvellous power of co-ordinating apparently insignificant facts, of arranging them into an ordered sequence and making them tell a coherent story, was a phenomenon that I never got used to; every exhibition of it astonished me afresh.

"If your inferences are correct," I said, "the problem is practically solved. There must be abundant traces inside the house. The only question is, which house is it?"

"Quite so," replied Thorndyke; "that is the question, and a very difficult question it is. A glance at that interior would doubtless clear up the whole mystery. But how are we to get that glance? We cannot enter houses speculatively to see if they present traces of a murder. At present, our clue breaks off abruptly. The other end of it is in some unknown house, and, if we cannot join up the two ends, our problem remains unsolved. For the question is, you remember, Who killed Oscar Brodski?"

"Then what do you propose to do?" I asked.

"The next stage of the inquiry is to connect some particular house with this crime. To that end, I can only gather up all available facts and consider each in all its possible bearings. If I cannot establish any such connection, then the inquiry will have failed and we shall have to make a fresh start—say, at Amsterdam, if it turns out that Brodski really had diamonds on his person, as I have no doubt he had."

Here our conversation was interrupted by our arrival at the spot where the body had been found. The station-master had halted, and he and the inspector were now examining the near rail by the light of their lanterns.

"There's remarkably little blood about," said the former. "I've seen a good many accidents of this kind and there has always been a lot of blood, both on the engine and on the road. It's very curious."

Thorndyke glanced at the rail with but slight attention: that question had ceased to interest him. But the light of his lantern flashed onto the ground at the side of the track—a loose, gravelly soil mixed with fragments of chalk—and from thence to the soles of the inspector's boots, which were displayed as he knelt by the rail.

"You observe, Jervis?" he said in a low voice, and I nodded. The inspector's boot-soles were covered with adherent particles of gravel and conspicuously marked by the chalk on which he had trodden.

"You haven't found the hat, I suppose?" Thorndyke asked, stooping to pick up a short piece of string that lay on the ground at the side of the track.

"No," replied the inspector, "but it can't be far off. You seem to have found another clue, sir," he added, with a grin, glancing at the piece of string.

"Who knows," said Thorndyke. "A short end of white twine with a green strand in it. It may tell us something later. At any rate we'll keep it," and, taking from his pocket a small tin box containing, among other things, a number of seed envelopes, he slipped the string into one of the latter and scribbled a note in pencil on the outside. The inspector watched his proceedings with an indulgent smile, and then returned to his examination of the track, in which Thorndyke now joined.

"I suppose the poor chap was near-sighted," the officer remarked, indicating the remains of the shattered spectacles; "that might account for his having strayed onto the line."

"Possibly," said Thorndyke. He had already noticed the fragments scattered over a sleeper and the adjacent ballast, and now once more produced his "collecting-box," from which he took another seed envelope. "Would you hand me a pair of forceps, Jervis," he said; "and perhaps you wouldn't mind taking a pair yourself and helping me to gather up these fragments."

As I complied, the inspector looked up curiously.

"There isn't any doubt that these spectacles belonged to the deceased, is there?" he asked. "He certainly wore spectacles, for I saw the mark on his nose."

"Still, there is no harm in verifying the fact," said Thorndyke, and he added to me in a lower tone, "Pick up every particle you can find, Jervis. It may be most important."

"I don't quite see how," I said, groping amongst the shingle by the light of the lantern in search of the tiny splinters of glass.

"Don't you?" returned Thorndyke. "Well, look at these fragments; some of them are a fair size, but many of these on the sleeper are mere grains. And consider their number. Obviously, the condition of the glass does not agree with the circumstances in which we find it. These are thick concave spectacle-lenses broken into a great number of minute fragments. Now how were they broken? Not merely by falling, evidently: such a lens, when it is dropped, breaks into a small number of large pieces. Nor were they broken by the wheel passing over them, for they would then have been reduced to fine powder, and that powder would have been visible on the rail, which it is not. The spectacle-frames, you may remember, presented the same incongruity: they were battered and damaged more than they would have been by falling, but not nearly so much as they would have been if the wheel had passed over them."

"What do you suggest, then?" I asked.

"The appearances suggest that the spectacles had been trodden on. But, if the body was carried here the probability is that the spectacles were carried here too, and that they were then already broken; for it is more likely that they were trodden on during the struggle than that the murderer trod on them after bringing them here. Hence the importance of picking up every fragment."

"But why?" I inquired, rather foolishly, I must admit.

"Because, if, when we have picked up every fragment that we can find, there still remains missing a larger portion of the lenses than we could reasonably expect, that would tend to support our hypothesis and we might find the missing remainder elsewhere. If, on the other hand, we find as much of the lenses as we could expect to find, we must conclude that they were broken on this spot."

While we were conducting our search, the two officials were circling around with their lanterns in quest of the missing hat; and, when we had at length picked up the last fragment, and a careful search, even aided by a lens, failed to reveal any other, we could see their lanterns moving, like will-o'-the-wisps, some distance down the line.

"We may as well see what we have got before our friends come back," said Thorndyke, glancing at the twinkling lights. "Lay the case down on the grass by the fence; it will serve for a table."

I did so, and Thorndyke, taking a letter from his pocket, opened it, spread it out flat on the case, securing it with a couple of heavy stones, although the night was quite calm. Then he tipped the contents of the seed envelope out on the paper, and carefully spreading out the pieces of glass, looked at them for some moments in silence. And, as he looked, there stole over his face a very curious expression; with sudden eagerness he began picking out the large fragments and laying them on two visiting-cards which he had taken from his card-case. Rapidly and with wonderful deftness he fitted the pieces together, and, as the reconstituted lenses began gradually to take shape on their cards I looked on with growing excitement, for something in my colleague's manner told me that we were on the verge of a discovery.

At length the two ovals of glass lay on their respective cards, complete save for one or two small gaps; and the little heap that remained consisted of fragments so minute as to render further reconstruction impossible. Then Thorndyke leaned back and laughed softly.

"This is certainly an unlooked-for result," said he.

"What is?" I asked.

"Don't you see, my dear fellow? There's too much glass. We have almost completely built up the broken lenses, and the fragments that are left over are considerably more than are required to fill up the gaps."

I looked at the little heap of small fragments and saw at once that it was as he had said. There was a surplus of small pieces.

"This is very extraordinary," I said. "What do you think can be the explanation?"

"The fragments will probably tell us," he replied, "if we ask them intelligently."

He lifted the paper and the two cards carefully onto the ground, and, opening the case, took out the little microscope, to which he fitted the lowest-power objective and eye-piece—having a combined magnification of only ten diameters. Then he transferred the minute fragments of glass to a slide, and, having arranged the lantern as a microscope-lamp, commenced his examination.

"Ha!" he exclaimed presently. "The plot thickens. There is too much glass and yet too little; that is to say, there are only one or two fragments here that belong to the spectacles; not nearly enough to complete the building up of the lenses. The remainder consists of a soft, uneven, moulded glass, easily distinguished from the clear, hard optical glass. These foreign fragments are all curved, as if they had formed part of a cylinder, and are, I should say, portions of a wine-glass or tumbler." He moved the slide once or twice, and then continued: "We are in luck, Jervis. Here is a fragment with two little diverging lines etched on it, evidently the points of an eight-rayed star—and here is another with three points—the ends of three rays. This enables us to reconstruct the vessel perfectly. It was a clear, thin glass—probably a tumbler—decorated with scattered stars; I dare say you know the pattern. Sometimes there is an ornamented band in addition, but generally the stars form the only decoration. Have a look at the specimen."

I had just applied my eye to the microscope when the station-master and the inspector came up. Our appearance, seated on the ground with the microscope between us, was too much for the police officer's gravity, and he laughed long and joyously.

"You must excuse me, gentlemen," he said apologetically, "but really, you know, to an old hand, like myself, it does look a little—well—you understand—I dare say a microscope is a very interesting and amusing thing, but it doesn't get you much forwarder in a case like this, does it?"

"Perhaps not," replied Thorndyke. "By the way, where did you find the hat, after all?"

"We haven't found it," the inspector replied.

"Then we must help you to continue the search," said Thorndyke. "If you will wait a few moments, we will come with you." He poured a few drops of xylol balsam on the cards to fix the reconstituted lenses to their supports and then, packing them and the microscope in the case, announced that he was ready to start.

"Is there any village or hamlet near?" he asked the station-master.

"None nearer than Corfield. That is about half-a-mile from here."

"And where is the nearest road?"

"There is a half-made road that runs past a house about three hundred yards from here. It belonged to a building estate that was never built. There is a footpath from it to the station."

"Are there any other houses near?"

"No. That is the only house for half-a-mile round, and there is no other road near here."

"Then the probability is that Brodski approached the railway from that direction, as he was found on that side of the permanent way."

The inspector agreeing with this view, we all set off slowly towards the house, piloted by the station-master and searching the ground as we went. The waste land over which we passed was covered with patches of docks and nettles, through each of which the inspector kicked his way, searching with feet and lantern for the missing hat. A walk of three hundred yards brought us to a low wall enclosing a garden, beyond which we could see a small house; and here we halted while the inspector waded into a large bed of nettles beside the wall and kicked vigorously. Suddenly there came a clinking sound mingled with objurgations, and the inspector hopped out holding one foot and soliloquizing profanely.

"I wonder what sort of a fool put a thing like that into a bed of nettles!" he exclaimed, stroking the injured foot. Thorndyke picked the object up and held it in the light of the lantern, displaying a piece of three-quarter inch rolled iron bar about a foot long. "It doesn't seem to have been there very long," he observed, examining it closely, "there is hardly any rust on it."

"It has been there long enough for me," growled the inspector, "and I'd like to bang it on the head of the blighter that put it there."

Callously indifferent to the inspector's sufferings, Thorndyke continued calmly to examine the bar. At length, resting his lantern on the wall, he produced his pocket-lens, with which he resumed his investigation, a proceeding that so exasperated the inspector that that afflicted official limped off in dudgeon, followed by the station-master, and we heard him, presently, rapping at the front door of the house.

"Give me a slide, Jervis, with a drop of Farrant on it," said Thorndyke. "There are some fibres sticking to this bar."

I prepared the slide, and, having handed it to him together with a cover-glass, a pair of forceps and a needle, set up the microscope on the wall.

"I'm sorry for the inspector," Thorndyke remarked, with his eye applied to the little instrument, "but that was a lucky kick for us. Just take a look at the specimen."

I did so, and, having moved the slide about until I had seen the whole of the object, I gave my opinion. "Red wool fibres, blue cotton fibres and some yellow vegetable fibres that look like jute."

"Yes," said Thorndyke; "the same combination of fibres as that which we found on the dead man's teeth and probably from the same source. This bar has probably been wiped on that very curtain or rug with which poor Brodski was stifled. We will place it on the wall for future reference, and meanwhile, by hook or by crook, we must get into that house. This is much too plain a hint to be disregarded."

Hastily repacking the case, we hurried to the front of the house, where we found the two officials looking rather vaguely up the unmade road.

"There's a light in the house," said the inspector, "but there's no one at home. I have knocked a dozen times and got no answer. And I don't see what we are hanging about here for at all. The hat is probably close to where the body was found, and we shall find it in the morning."

Thorndyke made no reply, but, entering the garden, stepped up the path, and having knocked gently at the door, stooped and listened attentively at the keyhole.

"I tell you there's no one in the house, sir," said the inspector irritably; and, as Thorndyke continued to listen, he walked away, muttering angrily. As soon as he was gone, Thorndyke flashed his lantern over the door, the threshold, the path and the small flower-beds; and, from one of the latter, I presently saw him stoop and pick something up.

"Here is a highly instructive object, Jervis," he said, coming out to the gate, and displaying a cigarette of which only half-an-inch had been smoked.

"How instructive?" I asked. "What do you learn from it?"

"Many things," he replied. "It has been lit and thrown away unsmoked; that indicates a sudden change of purpose. It was thrown away at the entrance to the house, almost certainly by someone entering it. That person was probably a stranger, or he would have taken it in with him. But he had not expected to enter the house, or he would not have lit it. These are the general suggestions; now as to the particular ones. The paper of the cigarette is of the kind known as the 'Zig-Zag' brand; the very conspicuous water-mark is quite easy to see. Now Brodski's cigarette book was a 'Zig-Zag' book—so called from the way in which the papers pull out. But let us see what the tobacco is like." With a pin from his coat, he hooked out from the unburned end a wisp of dark, dirty brown tobacco, which he held out for my inspection.

"Fine-cut Latakia," I pronounced, without hesitation.

"Very well," said Thorndyke. "Here is a cigarette made of an unusual tobacco similar to that in Brodski's pouch and wrapped in an unusual paper similar to those in Brodski's cigarette book. With due regard to the fourth rule of the syllogism, I suggest that this cigarette was made by Oscar Brodski. But, nevertheless, we will look for corroborative detail."

"What is that?" I asked.

"You may have noticed that Brodski's match-box contained round wooden vestas—which are also rather unusual. As he must have lighted the cigarette within a few steps of the gate, we ought to be able to find the match with which he lighted it. Let us try up the road in the direction from which he would probably have approached."

We walked very slowly up the road, searching the ground with the lantern, and we had hardly gone a dozen paces when I espied a match lying on the rough path and eagerly picked it up. It was a round wooden vesta.

Thorndyke examined it with interest and having deposited it, with the cigarette, in his "collecting-box," turned to retrace his steps. "There is now, Jervis, no reasonable doubt that Brodski was murdered in that house. We have succeeded in connecting that house with the crime, and now we have got to force an entrance and join up the other clues." We walked quickly back to the rear of the premises, where we found the inspector conversing disconsolately with the station-master.

"I think, sir," said the former, "we had better go back now; in fact, I don't see what we came here for, but—here! I say, sir, you mustn't do that!" For Thorndyke, without a word of warning, had sprung up lightly and thrown one of his long legs over the wall.

"I can't allow you to enter private premises, sir," continued the inspector; but Thorndyke quietly dropped down on the inside and turned to face the officer over the wall.

"Now, listen to me, inspector," said he. "I have good reasons for believing that the dead man, Brodski, has been in this house, in fact, I am prepared to swear an information to that effect. But time is precious; we must follow the scent while it is hot. And I am not proposing to break into the house off-hand. I merely wish to examine the dust-bin."

"The dust-bin!" gasped the inspector. "Well, you really are a most extraordinary gentleman! What do you expect to find in the dust-bin?"

"I am looking for a broken tumbler or wine-glass. It is a thin glass vessel decorated with a pattern of small, eight-pointed stars. It may be in the dust-bin or it may be inside the house."

The inspector hesitated, but Thorndyke's confident manner had evidently impressed him.

"We can soon see what is in the dust-bin," he said, "though what in creation a broken tumbler has to do with the case is more than I can understand. However, here goes." He sprang up onto the wall, and, as he dropped down into the garden, the station-master and I followed.

Thorndyke lingered a few moments by the gate examining the ground, while the two officials hurried up the path. Finding nothing of interest, however, he walked towards the house, looking keenly about him as he went; but we were hardly half-way up the path when we heard the voice of the inspector calling excitedly.

"Here you are, sir, this way," he sang out, and, as we hurried forward, we suddenly came on the two officials standing over a small rubbish-heap and looking the picture of astonishment. The glare of their lanterns illuminated the heap, and showed us the scattered fragments of a thin glass, star-pattern tumbler.

"I can't imagine how you guessed it was here, sir," said the inspector, with a new-born respect in his tone, "nor what you're going to do with it now you have found it."

"It is merely another link in the chain of evidence," said Thorndyke, taking a pair of forceps from the case and stooping over the heap. "Perhaps we shall find something else." He picked up several small fragments of glass, looked at them closely and dropped them again. Suddenly his eye caught a small splinter at the base of the heap. Seizing it with the forceps, he held it close to his eye in the strong lamplight, and, taking out his lens, examined it with minute attention. "Yes," he said at length, "this is what I was looking for. Let me have those two cards, Jervis."

I produced the two visiting-cards with the reconstructed lenses stuck to them, and, laying them on the lid of the case, threw the light of the lantern on them. Thorndyke looked at them intently for some time, and from them to the fragment that he held. Then, turning to the inspector, he said: "You saw me pick up this splinter of glass?"

"Yes, sir," replied the officer.

"And you saw where we found these spectacle-glasses and know whose they were?"

"Yes, sir. They are the dead man's spectacles, and you found them where the body had been."

"Very well," said Thorndyke; "now observe;" and, as the two officials craned forward with parted lips, he laid the little splinter in a gap in one of the lenses and then gave it a gentle push forward, when it occupied the gap perfectly, joining edge to edge with the adjacent fragments and rendering that portion of the lens complete.

"My God!" exclaimed the inspector. "How on earth did you know?"

"I must explain that later," said Thorndyke. "Meanwhile we had better have a look inside the house. I expect to find there a cigarette—or possibly a cigar—which has been trodden on, some whole-meal biscuits, possibly a wooden vesta, and perhaps even the missing hat."

At the mention of the hat, the inspector stepped eagerly to the back door, but, finding it bolted, he tried the window. This also was securely fastened and, on Thorndyke's advice, we went round to the front door.

"This door is locked too," said the inspector. "I'm afraid we shall have to break in. It's a nuisance, though."

"Have a look at the window," suggested Thorndyke.

The officer did so, struggling vainly to undo the patent catch with his pocket-knife.

"It's no go," he said, coming back to the door. "We shall have to—?" He broke off with an astonished stare, for the door stood open and Thorndyke was putting something in his pocket.

"Your friend doesn't waste much time—even in picking a lock," he remarked to me, as we followed Thorndyke into the house; but his reflections were soon merged in a new surprise. Thorndyke had preceded us into a small sitting-room dimly lighted by a hanging lamp turned down low.

As we entered he turned up the light and glanced about the room. A whisky-bottle was on the table, with a siphon, a tumbler and a biscuit-box. Pointing to the latter, Thorndyke said to the inspector: "See what is in that box."

The inspector raised the lid and peeped in, the station-master peered over his shoulder, and then both stared at Thorndyke.

"How in the name of goodness did you know that there were whole-meal biscuits in the house, sir?" exclaimed the station-master.

"You'd be disappointed if I told you," replied Thorndyke. "But look at this." He pointed to the hearth, where lay a flattened, half-smoked cigarette and a round wooden vesta. The inspector gazed at these objects in silent wonder, while, as to the station-master, he continued to stare at Thorndyke with what I can only describe as superstitious awe.

"You have the dead man's property with you, I believe?" said my colleague.

"Yes," replied the inspector; "I put the things in my pocket for safety."

"Then," said Thorndyke, picking up the flattened cigarette, "let us have a look at his tobacco-pouch."

As the officer produced and opened the pouch, Thorndyke neatly cut open the cigarette with his sharp pocket-knife. "Now," said he, "what kind of tobacco is in the pouch?"

The inspector took out a pinch, looked at it and smelt it distastefully. "It's one of those stinking tobaccos," he said, "that they put in mixtures—Latakia, I think."

"And what is this?" asked Thorndyke, pointing to the open cigarette.

"Same stuff, undoubtedly," replied the inspector.

"And now let us see his cigarette papers," said Thorndyke.

The little book, or rather packet—for it consisted of separated papers—was produced from the officer's pocket and a sample paper abstracted. Thorndyke laid the half-burnt paper beside it, and the inspector, having examined the two, held them up to the light.

"There isn't much chance of mistaking that 'Zig-Zag' watermark," he said. "This cigarette was made by the deceased; there can't be the shadow of a doubt."

"One more point," said Thorndyke, laying the burnt wooden vesta on the table. "You have his match-box?"

The inspector brought forth the little silver casket, opened it and compared the wooden vestas that it contained with the burnt end. Then he shut the box with a snap.

"You've proved it up to the hilt," said he. "If we could only find the hat, we should have a complete case."

"I'm not sure that we haven't found the hat," said Thorndyke. "You notice that something besides coal has been burned in the grate."

The inspector ran eagerly to the fire-place and began with feverish hands, to pick out the remains of the extinct fire. "The cinders are still warm," he said, "and they are certainly not all coal cinders. There has been wood burned here on top of the coal, and these little black lumps are neither coal nor wood. They may quite possibly be the remains of a burnt hat, but, lord! who can tell? You can put together the pieces of broken spectacle-glasses, but you can't build up a hat out of a few cinders." He held out a handful of little, black, spongy cinders and looked ruefully at Thorndyke, who took them from him and laid them out on a sheet of paper.

"We can't reconstitute the hat, certainly," my friend agreed, "but we may be able to ascertain the origin of these remains. They may not be cinders of a hat, after all." He lit a wax match and, taking up one of the charred fragments, applied the flame to it. The cindery mass fused at once with a crackling, seething sound, emitting a dense smoke, and instantly the air became charged with a pungent, resinous odour mingled with the smell of burning animal matter.

"Smells like varnish," the station-master remarked.

"Yes. Shellac," said Thorndyke; "so the first test gives a positive result. The next test will take more time."

He opened the green case and took from it a little flask, fitted for Marsh's arsenic test, with a safety funnel and escape tube, a small folding tripod, a spirit lamp and a disc of asbestos to serve as a sand-bath. Dropping into the flask several of the cindery masses, selected after careful inspection, he filled it up with alcohol and placed it on the disc, which he rested on the tripod. Then he lighted the spirit lamp underneath and sat down to wait for the alcohol to boil.

"There is one little point that we may as well settle," he said presently, as the bubbles began to rise in the flask. "Give me a slide with a drop of Farrant on it, Jervis."

I prepared the slide while Thorndyke, with a pair of forceps, picked out a tiny wisp from the table-cloth. "I fancy we have seen this fabric before," he remarked, as he laid the little pinch of fluff in the mounting fluid and slipped the slide onto the stage of the microscope. "Yes," he continued, looking into the eye-piece, "here are our old acquaintances, the red wool fibres, the blue cotton and the yellow jute. We must label this at once or we may confuse it with the other specimens."

"Have you any idea how the deceased met his death?" the inspector asked.

"Yes," replied Thorndyke. "I take it that the murderer enticed him into this room and gave him some refreshments. The murderer sat in the chair in which you are sitting, Brodski sat in that small arm-chair. Then I imagine the murderer attacked him with that iron bar that you found among the nettles, failed to kill him at the first stroke, struggled with him and finally suffocated him with the table-cloth. By the way, there is just one more point. You recognize this piece of string?" He took from his "collecting-box" the little end of twine that had been picked up by the line. The inspector nodded. "Look behind you, you will see where it came from."

The officer turned sharply and his eye lighted on a string-box on the mantel-piece. He lifted it down, and Thorndyke drew out from it a length of white twine with one green strand, which he compared with the piece in his hand. "The green strand in it makes the identification fairly certain," he said. "Of course the string was used to secure the umbrella and hand-bag. He could not have carried them in his hand, encumbered as he was with the corpse. But I expect our other specimen is ready now." He lifted the flask off the tripod, and, giving it a vigorous shake, examined the contents through his lens. The alcohol had now become dark-brown in colour, and was noticeably thicker and more syrupy in consistence.

"I think we have enough here for a rough test," said he, selecting a pipette and a slide from the case. He dipped the former into the flask and, having sucked up a few drops of the alcohol from the bottom, held the pipette over the slide on which he allowed the contained fluid to drop.

Laying a cover-glass on the little pool of alcohol, he put the slide on the microscope stage and examined it attentively, while we watched him in expectant silence.

At length he looked up, and, addressing the inspector, asked: "Do you know what felt hats are made of?"

"I can't say that I do, sir," replied the officer.

"Well, the better quality hats are made of rabbits' and hares' wool—the soft under-fur, you know—cemented together with shellac. Now there is very little doubt that these cinders contain shellac, and with the microscope I find a number of small hairs of a rabbit. I have, therefore, little hesitation in saying that these cinders are the remains of a hard felt hat; and, as the hairs do not appear to be dyed, I should say it was a grey hat."

At this moment our conclave was interrupted by hurried footsteps on the garden path and, as we turned with one accord, an elderly woman burst into the room.

She stood for a moment in mute astonishment, and then, looking from one to the other, demanded: "Who are you? and what are you doing here?"

The inspector rose. "I am a police officer, madam," said he. "I can't give you any further information just now, but, if you will excuse me asking, who are you?"

"I am Mr. Hickler's housekeeper," she replied.

"And Mr. Hickler; are you expecting him home shortly?"

"No, I am not," was the curt reply. "Mr. Hickler is away from home just now. He left this evening by the boat train."

"For Amsterdam?" asked Thorndyke.

"I believe so, though I don't see what business it is of yours," the housekeeper answered.

"I thought he might, perhaps, be a diamond broker or merchant," said Thorndyke. "A good many of them travel by that train."

"So he is," said the woman, "at least, he has something to do with diamonds."

"Ah. Well, we must be going, Jervis," said Thorndyke, "we have finished here, and we have to find an hotel or inn. Can I have a word with you, inspector?"

The officer, now entirely humble and reverent, followed us out into the garden to receive Thorndyke's parting advice.

"You had better take possession of the house at once, and get rid of the housekeeper. Nothing must be removed. Preserve those cinders and see that the rubbish-heap is not disturbed, and, above all, don't have the room swept. An officer will be sent to relieve you."

With a friendly "good-night" we went on our way, guided by the station-master; and here our connection with the case came to an end. Hickler (whose Christian name turned out to be Silas) was, it is true, arrested as he stepped ashore from the steamer, and a packet of diamonds, subsequently identified as the property of Oscar Brodski, found upon his person. But he was never brought to trial, for on the return voyage he contrived to elude his guards for an instant as the ship was approaching the English coast, and it was not until three days later, when a handcuffed body was cast up on the lonely shore by Orfordness, that the authorities knew the fate of Silas Hickler.

"An appropriate and dramatic end to a singular and yet typical case," said Thorndyke, as he put down the newspaper. "I hope it has enlarged your knowledge, Jervis, and enabled you to form one or two useful corollaries."

"I prefer to hear you sing the medico-legal doxology," I answered, turning upon him like the proverbial worm and grinning derisively (which the worm does not).

"I know you do," he retorted, with mock gravity, "and I lament your lack of mental initiative. However, the points that this case illustrates are these: First, the danger of delay; the vital importance of instant action before that frail and fleeting thing that we call a clue has time to evaporate. A delay of a few hours would have left us with hardly a single datum. Second, the necessity of pursuing the most trivial clue to an absolute finish, as illustrated by the spectacles. Third, the urgent need of a trained scientist to aid the police; and, last," he concluded, with a smile, "we learn never to go abroad without the invaluable green case."

# CHAPTER II.

## A CASE OF PREMEDITATION

### PART I.
### THE ELIMINATION OF MR. PRATT

THE wine merchant who should supply a consignment of petit vin to a customer who had ordered, and paid for, a vintage wine, would render himself subject to unambiguous comment. Nay! more; he would be liable to certain legal penalties. And yet his conduct would be morally indistinguishable from that of the railway company which, having accepted a first-class fare, inflicts upon the passenger that kind of company which he has paid to avoid. But the corporate conscience, as Herbert Spencer was wont to explain, is an altogether inferior product to that of the individual.

Such were the reflections of Mr. Rufus Pembury when, as the train was about to move out of Maidstone (West) station, a coarse and burly man (clearly a denizen of the third-class) was ushered into his compartment by the guard. He had paid the higher fare, not for cushioned seats, but for seclusion or, at least, select companionship. The man's entry had deprived him of both, and he resented it.

But if the presence of this stranger involved a breach of contract, his conduct was a positive affront—an indignity; for, no sooner had the train started than he fixed upon Mr. Pembury a gaze of impertinent intensity, and continued thereafter to regard him with a stare as steady and unwinking as that of a Polynesian idol.

It was offensive to a degree, and highly disconcerting withal. Mr. Pembury fidgeted in his seat with increasing discomfort and rising temper. He looked into his pocket-book, read one or two letters and sorted a collection of visiting-cards. He even thought of opening his umbrella. Finally, his patience exhausted and his wrath mounting to boiling-point, he turned to the stranger with frosty remonstrance.

"I imagine, sir, that you will have no difficulty in recognizing me, should we ever meet again—which God forbid."

"I should recognize you among ten thousand," was the reply, so unexpected as to leave Mr. Pembury speechless.

"You see," the stranger continued impressively, "I've got the gift of faces. I never forget."

"That must be a great consolation," said Pembury.

"It's very useful to me," said the stranger, "at least, it used to be, when I was a warder at Portland—you remember me, I dare say: my name is Pratt. I was assistant-warder in your time. God-forsaken hole, Portland, and mighty glad I was when they used to send me up to town on reckernizing duty. Holloway was the house of detention then, you remember; that was before they moved to Brixton."

Pratt paused in his reminiscences, and Pembury, pale and gasping with astonishment, pulled himself together.

"I think," said he, "you must be mistaking me for someone else."

"I don't," replied Pratt. "You're Francis Dobbs, that's who you are. Slipped away from Portland one evening about twelve years ago. Clothes washed up on the Bill next day. No trace of fugitive. As neat a mizzle as ever I heard of. But there are a couple of photographs and a set of fingerprints at the Habitual Criminals Register. P'r'aps you'd like to come and see 'em?"

"Why should I go to the Habitual Criminals Register?" Pembury demanded faintly.

"Ah! Exactly. Why should you? When you are a man of means, and a little judiciously invested capital would render it unnecessary?"

Pembury looked out of the window, and for a minute or more preserved a stony silence. At length he turned suddenly to Pratt. "How much?" he asked.

"I shouldn't think a couple of hundred a year would hurt you," was the calm reply.

Pembury reflected awhile. "What makes you think I am a man of means?" he asked presently.

Pratt smiled grimly. "Bless you, Mr. Pembury," said he, "I know all about you. Why, for the last six months I have been living within half-a-mile of your house."

"The devil you have!"

"Yes. When I retired from the service, General O'Gorman engaged me as a sort of steward or caretaker of his little place at Baysford—he's very seldom there himself—and the very day after I came down, I met you and spotted you, but, naturally, I kept out of sight myself. Thought I'd find out whether you were good for anything before I spoke, so I've been keeping my ears open and I find you are good for a couple of hundred."

There was an interval of silence, and then the ex-warder resumed—"That's what comes of having a memory for faces. Now there's Jack Ellis, on the other hand; he must have had you under his nose for a couple of years, and yet he's never twigged—he never will either," added Pratt, already regretting the confidence into which his vanity had led him.

"Who is Jack Ellis?" Pembury demanded sharply.

"Why, he's a sort of supernumerary at the Baysford Police Station; does odd jobs; rural detective, helps in the office and that sort of thing. He was in the Civil Guard at Portland, in your time, but he got his left forefinger chopped off, so they pensioned him, and, as he was a Baysford man, he got this billet. But he'll never reckernize you, don't you fear."

"Unless you direct his attention to me," suggested Pembury.

"There's no fear of that," laughed Pratt. "You can trust me to sit quiet on my own nest-egg. Besides, we're not very friendly. He came nosing round our place after the parlourmaid—him a married man, mark you! But I soon boosted him out, I can tell you; and Jack Ellis don't like me now."

"I see," said Pembury reflectively; then, after a pause, he asked: "Who is this General O'Gorman? I seem to know the name."

"I expect you do," said Pratt. "He was governor of Dartmoor when I was there—that was my last billet—and, let me tell you, if he'd been at Portland in your time, you'd never have got away."

"How is that?"

"Why, you see, the general is a great man on bloodhounds. He kept a pack at Dartmoor and, you bet, those lags knew it. There were no attempted escapes in those days. They wouldn't have had a chance."

"He has the pack still, hasn't he?" asked Pembury.

"Rather. Spends any amount of time on training 'em, too. He's always hoping there'll be a burglary or a murder in the neighbourhood so as he can try 'em, but he's never got a chance yet. P'r'aps the crooks have heard about 'em. But, to come back to our little arrangement: what do you say to a couple of hundred, paid quarterly, if you like?"

"I can't settle the matter off-hand," said Pembury. "You must give me time to think it over."

"Very well," said Pratt. "I shall be back at Baysford to-morrow evening. That will give you a clear day to think it over. Shall I look in at your place to-morrow night?"

"No," replied Pembury; "you'd better not be seen at my house, nor I at yours. If I meet you at some quiet spot, where we shan't be seen, we can settle our business without any one knowing that we have met. It won't take long, and we can't be too careful."

"That's true," agreed Pratt. "Well, I'll tell you what. There's an avenue leading up to our house; you know it, I expect. There's no lodge, and the gates are always ajar, excepting at night. Now I shall be down by the six-thirty at Baysford. Our place is a quarter of an hour from the station. Say you meet me in the avenue at a quarter to seven."

"That will suit me," said Pembury; "that is, if you are sure the bloodhounds won't be straying about the grounds."

"Lord bless you, no!" laughed Pratt. "D'you suppose the general lets his precious hounds stray about for any casual crook to feed with poisoned sausage? No, they're locked up safe in the kennels at the back of the house. Hallo! This'll be Swanley, I expect. I'll change into a smoker here and leave you time to turn the matter over in your mind. So long. To-morrow evening in the avenue at a quarter to seven. And, I say, Mr. Pembury, you might as well bring the first installment with you—fifty, in small notes or gold."

"Very well," said Mr. Pembury. He spoke coldly enough, but there was a flush on his cheeks and an angry light in his eyes, which, perhaps, the ex-warder noticed; for when he had stepped out and shut the door, he thrust his head in at the window and said threateningly—

"One more word, Mr. Pembury-Dobbs: no hanky-panky, you know. I'm an old hand and pretty fly, I am. So don't you try any chickery-pokery on me. That's all." He withdrew his head and disappeared, leaving Pembury to his reflections.

The nature of those reflections—if some telepathist transferring his attention for the moment from hidden courtyards or missing thimbles to more practical matters—could have conveyed them into the mind of Mr. Pratt, would have caused that quondam official some surprise and, perhaps, a little disquiet. For long experience of the criminal, as he appears when in durance, had produced some rather misleading ideas as to his behaviour when at large. In fact, the ex-warder had considerably under-estimated the ex-convict.

Rufus Pembury, to give his real name—for Dobbs was literally a nom de guerre—was a man of strong character and intelligence. So much so that, having tried the criminal career and found it not worth pursuing, he had definitely abandoned it. When the cattle-boat that picked him up off Portland Bill had landed him at an American port, he brought his entire ability and energy to bear on legitimate commercial pursuits, and with such success that, at the end of ten years, he was able to return to England with a moderate competence. Then he had taken a modest house near the little town of Baysford, where he had lived quietly on his savings for the last two years, holding aloof without much difficulty from the rather exclusive local society; and here he might have lived out the rest of his life in peace but for the unlucky chance that brought the man Pratt into the neighbourhood. With the arrival of Pratt his security was utterly destroyed.

There is something eminently unsatisfactory about a blackmailer. No arrangement with him has any permanent validity. No undertaking that he gives is binding. The thing which he has sold remains in his possession to sell over again. He pockets the price of emancipation, but retains the key of the fetters. In short, the blackmailer is a totally impossible person.

Such were the considerations that had passed through the mind of Rufus Pembury, even while Pratt was making his proposals; and those proposals he had never for an instant entertained. The ex-warder's advice to him to "turn the matter over in his mind" was unnecessary. For his mind was already made up. His decision was arrived at in the very moment when Pratt had disclosed his identity. The conclusion was self-evident. Before Pratt appeared he was living in peace and security. While Pratt remained, his liberty was precarious from moment to moment. If Pratt should disappear, his peace and security would return. Therefore Pratt must be eliminated.

It was a logical consequence.

The profound meditations, therefore, in which Pembury remained immersed for the remainder of the journey, had nothing whatever to do with the quarterly allowance; they were concerned exclusively with the elimination of ex-warder Pratt.

Now Rufus Pembury was not a ferocious man. He was not even cruel. But he was gifted with a certain magnanimous cynicism which ignored the trivialities of sentiment and regarded only the main issues. If a wasp hummed over his tea-cup, he would crush that wasp; but not with his bare hand. The wasp carried the means of aggression. That was the wasp's look-out. His concern was to avoid being stung.

So it was with Pratt. The man had elected, for his own profit, to threaten Pembury's liberty. Very well. He had done it at his own risk. That risk was no concern of Pembury's. His concern was his own safety.

When Pembury alighted at Charing Cross, he directed his steps (after having watched Pratt's departure from the station) to Buckingham Street, Strand, where he entered a quiet private hotel. He was apparently expected, for the manageress greeted him by his name as she handed him his key.

"Are you staying in town, Mr. Pembury?" she asked.

"No," was the reply. "I go back to-morrow morning, but I may be coming up again shortly. By the way, you used to have an encyclopaedia in one of the rooms. Could I see it for a moment?"

"It is in the drawing-room," said the manageress. "Shall I show you—but you know the way, don't you?"

Certainly Mr. Pembury knew the way. It was on the first floor; a pleasant old-world room looking on the quiet old street; and on a shelf, amidst a collection of novels, stood the sedate volumes of Chambers's Encyclopaedia.

That a gentleman from the country should desire to look up the subject of "hounds" would not, to a casual observer, have seemed unnatural. But when from hounds the student proceeded to the article on blood, and thence to one devoted to perfumes, the observer might reasonably have felt some surprise; and this surprise might have been augmented if he had followed Mr. Pembury's subsequent proceedings, and specially if he had considered them as the actions of a man whose immediate aim was the removal of a superfluous unit of the population.

Having deposited his bag and umbrella in his room, Pembury set forth from the hotel as one with a definite purpose; and his footsteps led, in the first place, to an umbrella shop on the Strand, where he selected a thick rattan cane. There was nothing remarkable in this, perhaps; but the cane was of an uncomely thickness and the salesman protested. "I like a thick cane," said Pembury.

"Yes, sir; but for a gentleman of your height" (Pembury was a small, slightly-built man) "I would venture to suggest—?"

"I like a thick cane," repeated Pembury. "Cut it down to the proper length and don't rivet the ferrule on. I'll cement it on when I get home."

His next investment would have seemed more to the purpose, though suggestive of unexpected crudity of method. It was a large Norwegian knife. But not content with this he went on forthwith to a second cutler's and purchased a second knife, the exact duplicate of the first. Now, for what purpose could he want two identically similar knives? And why not have bought them both at the same shop? It was highly mysterious.

Shopping appeared to be a positive mania with Rufus Pembury. In the course of the next half-hour he acquired a cheap hand-bag, an artist's black-japanned brush-case, a three-cornered file, a stick of elastic glue and a pair of iron crucible-tongs. Still insatiable, he repaired to an old-fashioned chemist's shop in a by-street, where he further enriched himself with a packet of absorbent cotton-wool and an ounce of permanganate of potash; and, as the chemist wrapped up these articles, with the occult and necromantic air peculiar to chemists, Pembury watched him impassively.

"I suppose you don't keep musk?" he asked carelessly.

The chemist paused in the act of heating a stick of sealing-wax, and appeared as if about to mutter an incantation. But he merely replied: "No, sir. Not the solid musk; it's so very costly. But I have the essence."

"That isn't as strong as the pure stuff, I suppose?"

"No," replied the chemist, with a cryptic smile, "not so strong, but strong enough. These animal perfumes are so very penetrating, you know; and so lasting. Why, I venture to say that if you were to sprinkle a table-spoonful of the essence in the middle of St. Paul's, the place would smell of it six months hence."

"You don't say so!" said Pembury. "Well, that ought to be enough for anybody. I'll take a small quantity, please, and, for goodness' sake, see that there isn't any on the outside of the bottle. The stuff isn't for myself, and I don't want to go about smelling like a civet cat."

"Naturally you don't, sir," agreed the chemist. He then produced an ounce bottle, a small glass funnel and a stoppered bottle labelled "Ess. Moschi," with which he proceeded to perform a few trifling feats of legerdemain.

"There, sir," said he, when he had finished the performance, "there is not a drop on the outside of the bottle, and, if I fit it with a rubber cork, you will be quite secure."

Pembury's dislike of musk appeared to be excessive, for, when the chemist had retired into a secret cubicle as if to hold converse with some familiar spirit (but actually to change half-a-crown), he took the brush-case from his bag, pulled off its lid, and then, with the crucible-tongs, daintily lifted the bottle off the counter, slid it softly into the brush-case, and, replacing the lid, returned the case and tongs to the bag. The other two packets he took from the counter and dropped into his pocket, and, when the presiding wizard, having miraculously transformed a single half-crown into four pennies, handed him the product, he left the shop and walked thoughtfully back towards the Strand. Suddenly a new idea seemed to strike him. He halted, considered for a few moments and then strode away northward to make the oddest of all his purchases.

The transaction took place in a shop in the Seven Dials, whose strange stock-in-trade ranged the whole zoological gamut, from water-snails to Angora cats. Pembury looked at a cage of guinea-pigs in the window and entered the shop.

"Do you happen to have a dead guinea-pig?" he asked.

"No; mine are all alive," replied the man, adding, with a sinister grin: "But they're not immortal, you know."

Pembury looked at the man distastefully. There is an appreciable difference between a guinea-pig and a blackmailer. "Any small mammal would do," he said.

"There's a dead rat in that cage, if he's any good," said the man. "Died this morning, so he's quite fresh."

"I'll take the rat," said Pembury; "he'll do quite well."

The little corpse was accordingly made into a parcel and deposited in the bag, and Pembury, having tendered a complimentary fee, made his way back to the hotel.

After a modest lunch he went forth and spent the remainder of the day transacting the business which had originally brought him to town. He dined at a restaurant and did not return to his hotel until ten o'clock, when he took his key, and tucking under his arm a parcel that he had brought in with him, retired for the night. But before undressing—and after locking his door—he did a very strange and unaccountable thing. Having pulled off the loose ferrule from his newly-purchased cane, he bored a hole in the bottom of it with the spike end of the file. Then, using the latter as a broach, he enlarged the hole until only a narrow rim of the bottom was left. He next rolled up a small ball of cottonwool and pushed it into the ferrule; and having smeared the end of the cane with elastic glue, he replaced the ferrule, warming it over the gas to make the glue stick.

When he had finished with the cane, he turned his attention to one of the Norwegian knives. First, he carefully removed with the file most of the bright, yellow varnish from the wooden case or handle.

Then he opened the knife, and, cutting the string of the parcel that he had brought in, took from it the dead rat which he had bought at the zoologist's. Laying the animal on a sheet of paper, he cut off its head, and, holding it up by the tail, allowed the blood that oozed from the neck to drop on the knife, spreading it over both sides of the blade and handle with his finger.

Then he laid the knife on the paper and softly opened the window. From the darkness below came the voice of a cat, apparently perfecting itself in the execution of chromatic scales; and in that direction Pembury flung the body and head of the rat, and closed the window. Finally, having washed his hands and stuffed the paper from the parcel into the fire-place, he went to bed.

But his proceedings in the morning were equally mysterious. Having breakfasted betimes, he returned to his bedroom and locked himself in. Then he tied his new cane, handle downwards, to the leg of the dressing-table. Next, with the crucible-tongs, he drew the little bottle of musk from the brush-case, and, having assured himself, by sniffing at it, that the exterior was really free from odour, he withdrew the rubber cork. Then, slowly and with infinite care, he poured a few drops—perhaps half-a-teaspoonful—of the essence on the cotton-wool that bulged through the hole in the ferrule, watching the absorbent material narrowly as it soaked up the liquid. When it was saturated he proceeded to treat the knife in the same fashion, letting fall a drop of the essence on the wooden handle—which soaked it up readily. This done, he slid up the window and looked out. Immediately below was a tiny yard in which grew, or rather survived, a couple of faded laurel bushes. The body of the rat was nowhere to be seen; it had apparently been spirited away in the night. Holding out the bottle, which he still held, he dropped it into the bushes, flinging the rubber cork after it.

His next proceeding was to take a tube of vaseline from his dressing-bag and squeeze a small quantity onto his fingers. With this he thoroughly smeared the shoulder of the brush-case and the inside of the lid, so as to ensure an air-tight joint. Having wiped his fingers, he picked the knife up with the crucible-tongs, and, dropping it into the brush-case, immediately pushed on the lid. Then he heated the tips of the tongs in the gas flame to destroy the scent, packed the tongs and brush-case in the bag, untied the cane—carefully avoiding contact with the ferrule—and, taking up the two bags, went out, holding the cane by its middle.

There was no difficulty in finding an empty compartment, for first-class passengers were few at that time in the morning. Pembury waited on the platform until the guard's whistle sounded, when he stepped into the compartment, shut the door and laid the cane on the seat with its ferrule projecting out of the off-side window, in which position it remained until the train drew up in Baysford station.

Pembury left his dressing-bag at the cloak-room, and, still grasping the cane by its middle, he sallied forth. The town of Baysford lay some half-a-mile to the east of the station; his own house was a mile along the road to the west; and halfway between his house and the station was the residence of General O'Gorman. He knew the place well. Originally a farmhouse, it stood on the edge of a great expanse of flat meadows and communicated with the road by an avenue, nearly three hundred yards long, of ancient trees. The avenue was shut off from the road by a pair of iron gates, but these were merely ornamental, for the place was unenclosed and accessible from the surrounding meadows—indeed, an indistinct footpath crossed the meadows and intersected the avenue about half-way up.

On this occasion Pembury, whose objective was the avenue, elected to approach it by the latter route; and at each stile or fence that he surmounted, he paused to survey the country. Presently the avenue arose before him, lying athwart the narrow track, and, as he entered it between two of the trees, he halted and looked about him.

He stood listening for a while. Beyond the faint rustle of leaves no sound was to be heard. Evidently there was no one about, and, as Pratt was at large, it was probable that the general was absent.

And now Pembury began to examine the adjacent trees with more than a casual interest. The two between which he had entered were respectively an elm and a great pollard oak, the latter being an immense tree whose huge, warty bole divided about seven feet from the ground into three limbs, each as large as a fair-sized tree, of which the largest swept outward in a great curve half-way across the avenue. On this patriarch Pembury bestowed especial attention, walking completely round it and finally laying down his bag and cane (the latter resting on the bag with the ferrule off the ground) that he might climb up, by the aid of the warty outgrowths, to examine the crown; and he had just stepped up into the space between the three limbs, when the creaking of the iron gates was followed by a quick step in the avenue. Hastily he let himself down from the tree, and, gathering up his possessions, stood close behind the great bole.

"Just as well not to be seen," was his reflection, as he hugged the tree closely and waited, peering cautiously round the trunk. Soon a streak of moving shadow heralded the stranger's approach, and he moved round to keep the trunk between himself and the intruder. On the footsteps came, until the stranger was abreast of the tree; and when he had passed Pembury peeped round at the retreating figure. It was only the postman, but then the man knew him, and he was glad he had kept out of sight.

Apparently the oak did not meet his requirements, for he stepped out and looked up and down the avenue. Then, beyond the elm, he caught sight of an ancient pollard hornbeam—a strange, fantastic tree whose trunk widened out trumpet-like above into a broad crown, from the edge of which multitudinous branches uprose like the limbs of some weird hamadryad.

That tree he approved at a glance, but he lingered behind the oak until the postman, returning with brisk step and cheerful whistle, passed down the avenue and left him once more in solitude. Then he moved on with a resolute air to the hornbeam.

The crown of the trunk was barely six feet from the ground. He could reach it easily, as he found on trying. Standing the cane against the tree—ferrule downwards, this time—he took the brush-case from the bag, pulled off the lid, and, with the crucible-tongs, lifted out the knife and laid it on the crown of the tree, just out of sight, leaving the tongs also invisible—still grasping the knife. He was about to replace the brush-case in the bag, when he appeared to alter his mind. Sniffing at it, and finding it reeking with the sickly perfume, he pushed the lid on again and threw the case up into the tree, where he heard it roll down into the central hollow of the crown. Then he closed the bag, and, taking the cane by its handle, moved slowly away in the direction whence he had come, passing out of the avenue between the elm and the oak.

His mode of progress was certainly peculiar. He walked with excessive slowness, trailing the cane along the ground, and every few paces he would stop and press the ferrule firmly against the earth, so that, to any one who should have observed him, he would have appeared to be wrapped in an absorbing reverie.

Thus he moved on across the fields, not, however, returning to the high road, but crossing another stretch of fields until he emerged into a narrow lane that led out into the High Street. Immediately opposite to the lane was the police station, distinguished from the adjacent cottages only by its lamp, its open door and the notices pasted up outside. Straight across the road Pembury walked, still trailing the cane, and halted at the station door to read the notices, resting his cane on the doorstep as he did so. Through the open doorway he could see a man writing at a desk. The man's back was towards him, but, presently, a movement brought his left hand into view, and Pembury noted that the forefinger was missing. This, then, was Jack Ellis, late of the Civil Guard at Portland.

Even while he was looking the man turned his head, and Pembury recognized him at once. He had frequently met him on the road between Baysford and the adjoining village of Thorpe, and always at the same time. Apparently Ellis paid a daily visit to Thorpe—perhaps to receive a report from the rural constable—and he started between three and four and returned between seven and a quarter past.

Pembury looked at his watch. It was a quarter past three. He moved away thoughtfully (holding his cane, now, by the middle), and began to walk slowly in the direction of Thorpe—westward.

For a while he was deeply meditative, and his face wore a puzzled frown. Then, suddenly, his face cleared and he strode forward at a brisker pace. Presently he passed through a gap in the hedge, and, walking in a field parallel with the road, took out his purse—a small pigskin pouch.

Having frugally emptied it of its contents, excepting a few shillings, he thrust the ferrule of his cane into the small compartment ordinarily reserved for gold or notes.

And thus he continued to walk on slowly, carrying the cane by the middle and the purse jammed on the end.

At length he reached a sharp double curve in the road whence he could see back for a considerable distance; and here opposite a small opening, he sat down to wait. The hedge screened him effectually from the gaze of passers-by—though these were few enough—without interfering with his view.

A quarter of an hour passed. He began to be uneasy. Had he been mistaken? Were Ellis's visits only occasional instead of daily, as he had thought? That would be tiresome though not actually disastrous. But at this point in his reflections a figure came into view, advancing along the road with a steady swing. He recognized the figure. It was Ellis.

But there was another figure advancing from the opposite direction: a labourer, apparently. He prepared to shift his ground, but another glance showed him that the labourer would pass first. He waited. The labourer came on and, at length, passed the opening, and, as he did so, Ellis disappeared for a moment in a bend of the road. Instantly Pembury passed his cane through the opening in the hedge, shook off the purse and pushed it into the middle of the foot-way. Then he crept forward, behind the hedge, towards the approaching official, and again sat down to wait. On came the steady tramp of the unconscious Ellis, and, as it passed, Pembury drew aside an obstructing branch and peered out at the retreating figure. The question now was, would Ellis see the purse? It was not a very conspicuous object.

The footsteps stopped abruptly. Looking out, Pembury saw the police official stoop, pick up the purse, examine its contents and finally stow it in his trousers pocket. Pembury heaved a sigh of relief; and, as the dwindling figure passed out of sight round a curve in the road, he rose, stretched himself and strode away briskly.

Near the gap was a group of ricks, and, as he passed them, a fresh idea suggested itself. Looking round quickly he passed to the farther side of one and, thrusting his cane deeply into it, pushed it home with a piece of stick that he picked up near the rick, until the handle was lost among the straw. The bag was now all that was left, and it was empty—for his other purchases were in the dressing-bag, which, by the way, he must fetch from the station. He opened it and smelt the interior, but, though he could detect no odour, he resolved to be rid of it if possible.

As he emerged from the gap a wagon jogged slowly past. It was piled high with sacks, and the tail-board was down. Stepping into the road, he quickly overtook the wagon, and, having glanced round, laid the bag lightly on the tail-board. Then he set off for the station.

On arriving home he went straight up to his bedroom, and, ringing for his housekeeper, ordered a substantial meal. Then he took off his clothes and deposited them, even to his shirt, socks and necktie, in a trunk, wherein his summer clothing was stored with a plentiful sprinkling of naphthol to preserve it from the moth. Taking the packet of permanganate of potash from his dressing-bag, he passed into the adjoining bathroom, and, tipping the crystals into the bath, turned on the water. Soon the bath was filled with a pink solution of the salt, and into this he plunged, immersing his entire body and thoroughly soaking his hair. Then he emptied the bath and rinsed himself in clear water, and, having dried himself, returned to the bedroom and dressed himself in fresh clothing. Finally he took a hearty meal, and then lay down on the sofa to rest until it should be time to start for the rendezvous.

Half-past six found him lurking in the shadow by the station-approach, within sight of the solitary lamp. He heard the train come in, saw the stream of passengers emerge, and noted one figure detach itself from the throng and turn on to the Thorpe road. It was Pratt, as the lamplight showed him; Pratt, striding forward to the meeting-place with an air of jaunty satisfaction and an uncommonly creaky pair of boots.

Pembury followed him at a safe distance, and rather by sound than sight, until he was well past the stile at the entrance to the footpath. Evidently he was going on to the gates. Then Pembury vaulted over the stile and strode away swiftly across the dark meadows.

When he plunged into the deep gloom of the avenue, his first act was to grope his way to the hornbeam and slip his hand up onto the crown and satisfy himself that the tongs were as he had left them. Reassured by the touch of his fingers on the iron loops, he turned and walked slowly down the avenue. The duplicate knife—ready opened—was in his left inside breast-pocket, and he fingered its handle as he walked.

Presently the iron gate squeaked mournfully, and then the rhythmical creak of a pair of boots was audible, coming up the avenue. Pembury walked forward slowly until a darker smear emerged from the surrounding gloom, when he called out—

"Is that you, Pratt?"

"That's me," was the cheerful, if ungrammatical response, and, as he drew nearer, the ex-warder asked: "Have you brought the rhino, old man?"

The insolent familiarity of the man's tone was agreeable to Pembury: it strengthened his nerve and hardened his heart. "Of course," he replied; "but we must have a definite understanding, you know."

"Look here," said Pratt, "I've got no time for jaw. The General will be here presently; he's riding over from Bingfield with a friend. You hand over the dibs and we'll talk some other time."

"That is all very well," said Pembury, "but you must understand—?" He paused abruptly and stood still. They were now close to the hornbeam, and, as he stood, he stared up into the dark mass of foliage.

"What's the matter?" demanded Pratt. "What are you staring at?" He, too, had halted and stood gazing intently into the darkness.

Then, in an instant, Pembury whipped out the knife and drove it, with all his strength, into the broad back of the ex-warder, below the left shoulder-blade.

With a hideous yell Pratt turned and grappled with his assailant. A powerful man and a competent wrestler, too, he was far more than a match for Pembury unarmed, and, in a moment, he had him by the throat. But Pembury clung to him tightly, and, as they trampled to and fro and round and round, he stabbed again and again with the viciousness of a scorpion, while Pratt's cries grew more gurgling and husky. Then they fell heavily to the ground, Pembury underneath. But the struggle was over. With a last bubbling groan, Pratt relaxed his hold and in a moment grew limp and inert. Pembury pushed him off and rose, trembling and breathing heavily.

But he wasted no time. There had been more noise than he had bargained for. Quickly stepping up to the hornbeam, he reached up for the tongs. His fingers slid into the looped handles; the tongs grasped the knife, and he lifted it out from its hiding-place and carried it to where the corpse lay, depositing it on the ground a few feet from the body. Then he went back to the tree and carefully pushed the tongs over into the hollow of the crown.

At this moment a woman's voice sounded shrilly from the top of the avenue.

"Is that you, Mr. Pratt?" it called.

Pembury started and then stepped back quickly, on tiptoe, to the body. For there was the duplicate knife. He must take that away at all costs.

The corpse was lying on its back. The knife was underneath it, driven in to the very haft. He had to use both hands to lift the body, and even then he had some difficulty in disengaging the weapon. And, meanwhile, the voice, repeating its question, drew nearer.

At length he succeeded in drawing out the knife and thrust it into his breast-pocket. The corpse fell back, and he stood up gasping.

"Mr. Pratt! Are you there?" The nearness of the voice startled Pembury, and, turning sharply, he saw a light twinkling between the trees. And then the gates creaked loudly and he heard the crunch of a horse's hoofs on the gravel.

He stood for an instant bewildered—utterly taken by surprise. He had not reckoned on a horse. His intended flight across the meadows towards Thorpe was now impracticable. If he were overtaken he was lost, for he knew there was blood on his clothes and his hands were wet and slippery—to say nothing of the knife in his pocket.

But his confusion lasted only for an instant. He remembered the oak tree; and, turning out of the avenue, he ran to it, and, touching it as little as he could with his bloody hands, climbed quickly up into the crown. The great horizontal limb was nearly three feet in diameter, and, as he lay out on it, gathering his coat closely round him, he was quite invisible from below.

He had hardly settled himself when the light which he had seen came into full view, revealing a woman advancing with a stable lantern in her hand. And, almost at the same moment, a streak of brighter light burst from the opposite direction. The horseman was accompanied by a man on a bicycle.

The two men came on apace, and the horseman, sighting the woman, called out: "Anything the matter, Mrs. Parton?" But, at that moment, the light of the bicycle lamp fell full on the prostrate corpse. The two men uttered a simultaneous cry of horror; the woman shrieked aloud: and then the horseman sprang from the saddle and ran forward to the body.

"Why," he exclaimed, stooping over it, "it's Pratt;" and, as the cyclist came up and the glare of his lamp shone on a great pool of blood, he added: "There's been foul play here, Hanford."

Hanford flashed his lamp around the body, lighting up the ground for several yards.

"What is that behind you, O'Gorman?" he said suddenly; "isn't it a knife?" He was moving quickly towards it when O'Gorman held up his hand.

"Don't touch it!" he exclaimed. "We'll put the hounds onto it. They'll soon track the scoundrel, whoever he is. By God! Hanford, this fellow has fairly delivered himself into our hands." He stood for a few moments looking down at the knife with something uncommonly like exultation, and then, turning quickly to his friend, said: "Look here, Hanford; you ride off to the police station as hard as you can pelt. It is only three-quarters of a mile; you'll do it in five minutes. Send or bring an officer and I'll scour the meadows meanwhile. If I haven't got the scoundrel when you come back, we'll put the hounds onto this knife and run the beggar down."

"Right," replied Hanford, and without another word he wheeled his machine about, mounted and rode away into the darkness.

"Mrs. Parton," said O'Gorman, "watch that knife. See that nobody touches it while I go and examine the meadows."

"Is Mr. Pratt dead, sir?" whimpered Mrs. Parton.

"Gad! I hadn't thought of that," said the general. "You'd better have a look at him; but mind! nobody is to touch that knife or they will confuse the scent."

He scrambled into the saddle and galloped away across the meadows in the direction of Thorpe; and, as Pembury listened to the diminuendo of the horse's hoofs, he was glad that he had not attempted to escape; for that was the direction in which he had meant to go, and he would surely have been overtaken.

As soon as the general was gone, Mrs. Parton, with many a terror-stricken glance over her shoulder, approached the corpse and held the lantern close to the dead face. Suddenly she stood up, trembling violently, for footsteps were audible coming down the avenue. A familiar voice reassured her.

"Is anything wrong, Mrs. Parton?" The question proceeded from one of the maids who had come in search of the elder woman, escorted by a young man, and the pair now came out into the circle of light.

"Good God!" ejaculated the man. "Who's that?"

"It's Mr. Pratt," replied Mrs. Parton. "He's been murdered."

The girl screamed, and then the two domestics approached on tiptoe, staring at the corpse with the fascination of horror.

"Don't touch that knife," said Mrs. Parton, for the man was about to pick it up. "The general's going to put the bloodhounds onto it."

"Is the general here, then?" asked the man; and, as he spoke, the drumming of hoofs, growing momentarily louder, answered him from the meadow.

O'Gorman reined in his horse as he perceived the group of servants gathered about the corpse. "Is he dead, Mrs. Parton?" he asked.

"I am afraid so, sir," was the reply.

"Ha! Somebody ought to go for the doctor; but not you, Bailey. I want you to get the hounds ready and wait with them at the top of the avenue until I call you."

He was off again into the Baysford meadows, and Bailey hurried away, leaving the two women staring at the body and talking in whispers.

Pembury's position was cramped and uncomfortable. He dared not move, hardly dared to breathe, for the women below him were not a dozen yards away; and it was with mingled feelings of relief and apprehension that he presently saw from his elevated station a group of lights approaching rapidly along the road from Baysford. Presently they were hidden by the trees, and then, after a brief interval, the whirr of wheels sounded on the drive and streaks of light on the tree-trunks announced the new arrivals. There were three bicycles, ridden respectively by Mr. Hanford, a police inspector and a sergeant; and, as they drew up, the general came thundering back into the avenue.

"Is Ellis with you?" he asked, as he pulled up.

"No, sir," was the reply. "He hadn't come in from Thorpe when we left. He's rather late to-night."

"Have you sent for a doctor?"

"Yes, sir, I've sent for Dr. Hills," said the inspector, resting his bicycle against the oak. Pembury could smell the reek of the lamp as he crouched. "Is Pratt dead?"

"Seems to be," replied O'Gorman, "but we'd better leave that to the doctor. There's the murderer's knife. Nobody has touched it. I'm going to fetch the bloodhounds now."

"Ah! that's the thing," said the inspector. "The man can't be far away." He rubbed his hands with a satisfied air as O'Gorman cantered away up the avenue.

In less than a minute there came out from the darkness the deep baying of a hound followed by quick footsteps on the gravel. Then into the circle of light emerged three sinister shapes, loose-limbed and gaunt, and two men advancing at a shambling trot.

"Here, inspector," shouted the general, "you take one; I can't hold 'em both."

The inspector ran forward and seized one of the leashes, and the general led his hound up to the knife, as it lay on the ground. Pembury, peering cautiously round the bough, watched the great brute with almost impersonal curiosity; noted its high poll, its wrinkled forehead and melancholy face as it stooped to snuff suspiciously at the prostrate knife.

For some moments the hound stood motionless, sniffing at the knife; then it turned away and walked to and fro with its muzzle to the ground. Suddenly it lifted its head, bayed loudly, lowered its muzzle and started forward between the oak and the elm, dragging the general after it at a run.

The inspector next brought his hound to the knife, and was soon bounding away to the tug of the leash in the general's wake.

"They don't make no mistakes, they don't," said Bailey, addressing the gratified sergeant, as he brought forward the third hound; "you'll see—?" But his remark was cut short by a violent jerk of the leash, and the next moment he was flying after the others, followed by Mr. Hanford.

The sergeant daintily picked the knife up by its ring, wrapped it in his handkerchief and bestowed it in his pocket. Then he ran off after the hounds.

Pembury smiled grimly. His scheme was working out admirably in spite of the unforeseen difficulties. If those confounded women would only go away, he could come down and take himself off while the course was clear. He listened to the baying of the hounds, gradually growing fainter in the increasing distance, and cursed the dilatoriness of the doctor. Confound the fellow! Didn't he realize that this was a case of life or death?

Suddenly his ear caught the tinkle of a bicycle bell; a fresh light appeared coming up the avenue and then a bicycle swept up swiftly to the scene of the tragedy, and a small elderly man jumped down by the side of the body. Giving his machine to Mrs. Parton, he stooped over the dead man, felt the wrist, pushed back an eyelid, held a match to the eye and then rose. "This is a shocking affair, Mrs. Parton," said he. "The poor fellow is quite dead. You had better help me to carry him to the house. If you two take the feet I will take the shoulders."

Pembury watched them raise the body and stagger away with it up the avenue. He heard their shuffling steps die away and the door of the house shut. And still he listened. From far away in the meadows came, at intervals, the baying of the hounds. Other sounds there was none. Presently the doctor would come back for his bicycle, but, for the moment, the coast was clear. Pembury rose stiffly. His hands had stuck to the tree where they had pressed against it, and they were still sticky and damp. Quickly he let himself down to the ground, listened again for a moment, and then, making a small circuit to avoid the lamplight, softly crossed the avenue and stole away across the Thorpe meadows.

The night was intensely dark, and not a soul was stirring in the meadows. He strode forward quickly, peering into the darkness and stopping now and again to listen; but no sound came to his ears, save the now faint baying of the distant hounds. Not far from his house, he remembered, was a deep ditch spanned by a wooden bridge, and towards this he now made his way; for he knew that his appearance was such as to convict him at a glance. Arrived at the ditch, he stooped to wash his hands and wrists; and, as he bent forward, the knife fell from his breast-pocket into the shallow water at the margin. He groped for it, and, having found it, drove it deep into the mud as far out as he could reach. Then he wiped his hands on some water-weed, crossed the bridge and started homewards.

He approached his house from the rear, satisfied himself that his housekeeper was in the kitchen, and, letting himself in very quietly with his key, went quickly up to his bedroom. Here he washed thoroughly—in the bath, so that he could get rid of the discoloured water—changed his clothes and packed those that he took off in a portmanteau.

By the time he had done this the gong sounded for supper. As he took his seat at the table, spruce and fresh in appearance, quietly cheerful in manner, he addressed his housekeeper. "I wasn't able to finish my business in London," he said. "I shall have to go up again to-morrow."

"Shall you come home the same day?" asked the housekeeper.

"Perhaps," was the reply, "and perhaps not. It will depend on circumstances."

He did not say what the circumstances might be, nor did the housekeeper ask. Mr. Pembury was not addicted to confidences. He was an eminently discreet man: and discreet men say little.

## PART II.
## RIVAL SLEUTH-HOUNDS

## (RELATED BY CHRISTOPHER JERVIS, M.D.)

THE half-hour that follows breakfast, when the fire has, so to speak, got into its stride, and the morning pipe throws up its clouds of incense, is, perhaps, the most agreeable in the whole day. Especially so when a sombre sky, brooding over the town, hints at streets pervaded by the chilly morning air, and hoots from protesting tugs upon the river tell of lingering mists, the legacy of the lately-vanished night.

The autumn morning was raw: the fire burned jovially. I thrust my slippered feet towards the blaze and meditated, on nothing in particular, with cat-like enjoyment. Presently a disapproving grunt from Thorndyke attracted my attention, and I looked round lazily. He was extracting, with a pair of office shears, the readable portions of the morning paper, and had paused with a small cutting between his finger and thumb. "Bloodhounds again," said he. "We shall be hearing presently of the revival of the ordeal by fire."

"And a deuced comfortable ordeal, too, on a morning like this," I said, stroking my legs ecstatically. "What is the case?"

He was about to reply when a sharp rat-tat from the little brass knocker announced a disturber of our peace. Thorndyke stepped over to the door and admitted a police inspector in uniform, and I stood up, and, presenting my dorsal aspect to the fire, prepared to combine bodily comfort with attention to business.

"I believe I am speaking to Dr. Thorndyke," said the officer, and, as Thorndyke nodded, he went on: "My name, sir, is Fox, Inspector Fox of the Baysford Police. Perhaps you've seen the morning paper?"

Thorndyke held up the cutting, and, placing a chair by the fire, asked the inspector if he had breakfasted.

"Thank you, sir, I have," replied Inspector Fox. "I came up to town by the late train last night so as to be here early, and stayed at an hotel. You see, from the paper, that we have had to arrest one of our own men. That's rather awkward, you know, sir."

"Very," agreed Thorndyke.

"Yes; it's bad for the force and bad for the public too. But we had to do it. There was no way out that we could see. Still, we should like the accused to have every chance, both for our sake and his own, so the chief constable thought he'd like to have your opinion on the case, and he thought that, perhaps, you might be willing to act for the defence."

"Let us have the particulars," said Thorndyke, taking a writing-pad from a drawer and dropping into his armchair. "Begin at the beginning," he added, "and tell us all you know."

"Well," said the inspector, after a preliminary cough, "to begin with the murdered man: his name is Pratt. He was a retired prison warder, and was employed as steward by General O'Gorman, who is a retired prison governor—you may have heard of him in connection with his pack of bloodhounds. Well, Pratt came down from London yesterday evening by a train arriving at Baysford at six-thirty. He was seen by the guard, the ticket collector and the outside porter. The porter saw him leave the station at six-thirty-seven. General O'Gorman's house is about half-a-mile from the station. At five minutes to seven the general and a gentleman named Hanford and the general's housekeeper, a Mrs. Parton, found Pratt lying dead in the avenue that leads up to the house. He had apparently been stabbed, for there was a lot of blood about, and a knife—a Norwegian knife—was lying on the ground near the body. Mrs. Parton had thought she heard someone in the avenue calling out for help, and, as Pratt was just due, she came out with a lantern. She met the general and Mr. Hanford, and all three seem to have caught sight of the body at the same moment. Mr. Hanford cycled down to us, at once, with the news; we sent for a doctor, and I went back with Mr. Hanford and took a sergeant with me. We arrived at twelve minutes past seven, and then the general, who had galloped his horse over the meadows each side of the avenue without having seen anybody, fetched out his bloodhounds and led them up to the knife. All three hounds took up the scent at once—I held the leash of one of them—and they took us across the meadows without a pause or a falter, over stiles and fences, along a lane, out into the town, and then, one after the other, they crossed the road in a bee-line to the police station, bolted in at the door, which stood open, and made straight for the desk, where a supernumerary officer, named Ellis, was writing. They made a rare to-do, struggling to get at him, and it was as much as we could manage to hold them back. As for Ellis, he turned as pale as a ghost."

"Was any one else in the room?" asked Thorndyke.

"Oh, yes. There were two constables and a messenger. We led the hounds up to them, but the brutes wouldn't take any notice of them. They wanted Ellis."

"And what did you do?"

"Why, we arrested Ellis, of course. Couldn't do anything else—especially with the general there."

"What had the general to do with it?" asked Thorndyke.

"He's a J.P. and a late governor of Dartmoor, and it was his hounds that had run the man down. But we must have arrested Ellis in any case."

"Is there anything against the accused man?"

"Yes, there is. He and Pratt were on distinctly unfriendly terms. They were old comrades, for Ellis was in the Civil Guard at Portland when Pratt was warder there—he was pensioned off from the service because he got his left forefinger chopped off—but lately they had had some unpleasantness about a woman, a parlourmaid of the general's. It seems that Ellis, who is a married man, paid the girl too much attention—or Pratt thought he did—and Pratt warned Ellis off the premises. Since then they had not been on speaking terms."

"And what sort of a man is Ellis?"

"A remarkably decent fellow he always seemed; quiet, steady, good-natured; I should have said he wouldn't have hurt a fly. We all liked him—better than we liked Pratt, in fact; poor Pratt was what you'd call an old soldier—sly, you know, sir—and a bit of a sneak."

"You searched and examined Ellis, of course?"

"Yes. There was nothing suspicious about him except that he had two purses. But he says he picked up one of them? a small, pigskin pouch—on the footpath of the Thorpe road yesterday afternoon; and there's no reason to disbelieve him. At any rate, the purse was not Pratt's."

Thorndyke made a note on his pad, and then asked: "There were no blood-stains or marks on his clothing?"

"No. His clothing was not marked or disarranged in any way."

"Any cuts, scratches or bruises on his person?"

"None whatever," replied the inspector.

"At what time did you arrest Ellis?"

"Half-past seven exactly."

"Have you ascertained what his movements were? Had he been near the scene of the murder?"

"Yes; he had been to Thorpe and would pass the gates of the avenue on his way back. And he was later than usual in returning, though not later than he has often been before."

"And now, as to the murdered man: has the body been examined?"

"Yes; I had Dr. Hills's report before I left. There were no less than seven deep knife-wounds, all on the left side of the back. There was a great deal of blood on the ground, and Dr. Hills thinks Pratt must have bled to death in a minute or two."

"Do the wounds correspond with the knife that was found?"

"I asked the doctor that, and he said 'Yes,' though he wasn't going to swear to any particular knife. However, that point isn't of much importance. The knife was covered with blood, and it was found close to the body."

"What has been done with it, by the way?" asked Thorndyke.

"The sergeant who was with me picked it up and rolled it in his handkerchief to carry in his pocket. I took it from him, just as it was, and locked it in a dispatch-box."

"Has the knife been recognized as Ellis's property?"

"No, sir, it has not."

"Were there any recognizable footprints or marks of a struggle?" Thorndyke asked.

The inspector grinned sheepishly. "I haven't examined the spot, of course, sir," said he, "but, after the general's horse and the bloodhounds and the general on foot and me and the gardener and the sergeant and Mr. Hanford had been over it twice, going and returning, why, you see, sir—?"

"Exactly, exactly," said Thorndyke. "Well, inspector, I shall be pleased to act for the defence; it seems to me that the case against Ellis is in some respects rather inconclusive."

The inspector was frankly amazed. "It certainly hadn't struck me in that light, sir," he said.

"No? Well, that is my view; and I think the best plan will be for me to come down with you and investigate matters on the spot."

The inspector assented cheerfully, and, when we had provided him with a newspaper, we withdrew to the laboratory to consult time-tables and prepare for the expedition.

"You are coming, I suppose, Jervis?" said Thorndyke.

"If I shall be of any use," I replied.

"Of course you will," said he. "Two heads are better than one, and, by the look of things, I should say that ours will be the only ones with any sense in them. We will take the research case, of course, and we may as well have a camera with us. I see there is a train from Charing Cross in twenty minutes."

For the first half-hour of the journey Thorndyke sat in his corner, alternately conning over his notes and gazing with thoughtful eyes out of the window. I could see that the case pleased him, and was careful not to break in upon his train of thought. Presently, however, he put away his notes and began to fill his pipe with a more companionable air, and then the inspector, who had been wriggling with impatience, opened fire.

"So you think, sir, that you see a way out for Ellis?"

"I think there is a case for the defence," replied Thorndyke. "In fact, I call the evidence against him rather flimsy."

The inspector gasped. "But the knife, sir? What about the knife?"

"Well," said Thorndyke, "what about the knife? Whose knife was it? You don't know. It was covered with blood. Whose blood? You don't know. Let us assume, for the sake of argument, that it was the murderer's knife. Then the blood on it was Pratt's blood. But if it was Pratt's blood, when the hounds had smelt it they should have led you to Pratt's body, for blood gives a very strong scent. But they did not. They ignored the body. The inference seems to be that the blood on the knife was not Pratt's blood."

The inspector took off his cap and gently scratched the back of his head. "You're perfectly right, sir," he said. "I'd never thought of that. None of us had."

"Then," pursued Thorndyke, "let us assume that the knife was Pratt's. If so, it would seem to have been used in self-defence. But this was a Norwegian knife, a clumsy tool—not a weapon at all—which takes an appreciable time to open and requires the use of two free hands. Now, had Pratt both hands free? Certainly not after the attack had commenced. There were seven wounds, all on the left side of the back; which indicates that he held the murderer locked in his arms and that the murderer's arms were around him. Also, incidentally, that the murderer is right-handed. But, still, let us assume that the knife was Pratt's. Then the blood on it was that of the murderer. Then the murderer must have been wounded. But Ellis was not wounded. Then Ellis is not the murderer. The knife doesn't help us at all."

The inspector puffed out his cheeks and blew softly. "This is getting out of my depth," he said. "Still, sir, you can't get over the bloodhounds. They tell us distinctly that the knife is Ellis's knife and I don't see any answer to that."

"There is no answer because there has been no statement. The bloodhounds have told you nothing. You have drawn certain inferences from their actions, but those inferences may be totally wrong and they are certainly not evidence."

"You don't seem to have much opinion of bloodhounds," the inspector remarked.

"As agents for the detection of crime," replied Thorndyke, "I regard them as useless. You cannot put a bloodhound in the witness-box. You can get no intelligible statement from it. If it possesses any knowledge, it has no means of communicating it. The fact is," he continued, "that the entire system of using bloodhounds for criminal detection is based on a fallacy. In the American plantations these animals were used with great success for tracking runaway slaves. But the slave was a known individual. All that was required was to ascertain his whereabouts. That is not the problem that is presented in the detection of a crime. The detective is not concerned in establishing the whereabouts of a known individual, but in discovering the identity of an unknown individual. And for this purpose bloodhounds are useless. They may discover such identity, but they cannot communicate their knowledge. If the criminal is unknown, they cannot identify him: if he is known, the police have no need of the bloodhound.

"To return to our present case," Thorndyke resumed, after a pause; "we have employed certain agents—the hounds—with whom we are not en rapport, as the spiritualists would say; and we have no 'medium.' The hound possesses a special sense—the olfactory—which in man is quite rudimentary. He thinks, so to speak, in terms of smell, and his thoughts are untranslatable to beings in whom the sense of smell is undeveloped. We have presented to the hound a knife, and he discovers in it certain odorous properties; he discovers similar or related odorous properties in a tract of land and a human individual—Ellis. We cannot verify his discoveries or ascertain their nature. What remains? All that we can say is that there appears to exist some odorous relation between the knife and the man Ellis. But until we can ascertain the nature of that relation, we cannot estimate its evidential value or bearing. All the other 'evidence' is the product of your imagination and that of the general. There is, at present, no case against Ellis."

"He must have been pretty close to the place when the murder happened," said the inspector.

"So, probably, were many other people," answered Thorndyke; "but had he time to wash and change? Because he would have needed it."

"I suppose he would," the inspector agreed dubiously.

"Undoubtedly. There were seven wounds which would have taken some time to inflict. Now we can't suppose that Pratt stood passively while the other man stabbed him. Indeed, as I have said, the position of the wounds shows that he did not. There was a struggle. The two men were locked together. One of the murderer's hands was against Pratt's back; probably both hands were, one clasping and the other stabbing. There must have been blood on one hand and probably on both. But you say there was no blood on Ellis, and there doesn't seem to have been time or opportunity for him to wash."

"Well, it's a mysterious affair," said the inspector; "but I don't see how you are going to get over the bloodhounds."

Thorndyke shrugged his shoulders impatiently. "The bloodhounds are an obsession," he said. "The whole problem really centres around the knife. The questions are, Whose knife was it? and what was the connection between it and Ellis? There is a problem, Jervis," he continued, turning to me, "that I submit for your consideration. Some of the possible solutions are exceedingly curious."

As we set out from Baysford station, Thorndyke looked at his watch and noted the time. "You will take us the way that Pratt went," he said.

"As to that," said the inspector, "he may have gone by the road or by the footpath; but there's very little difference in the distance."

Turning away from Baysford, we walked along the road westward, towards the village of Thorpe, and presently passed on our right a stile at the entrance to a footpath.

"That path," said the inspector, "crosses the avenue about half-way up. But we'd better keep to the road." A quarter of a mile further on we came to a pair of rusty iron gates one of which stood open, and, entering, we found ourselves in a broad drive bordered by two rows of trees, between the trunks of which a long stretch of pasture meadows could be seen on either hand. It was a fine avenue, and, late in the year as it was, the yellowing foliage clustered thickly overhead.

When we had walked about a hundred and fifty yards from the gates, the inspector halted.

"This is the place," he said; and Thorndyke again noted the time.

"Nine minutes exactly," said he. "Then Pratt arrived here about fourteen minutes to seven, and his body was found at five minutes to seven—nine minutes after his arrival. The murderer couldn't have been far away then."

"No, it was a pretty fresh scent," replied the inspector. "You'd like to see the body first, I think you said, sir?"

"Yes; and the knife, if you please."

"I shall have to send down to the station for that. It's locked up in the office."

He entered the house, and, having dispatched a messenger to the police station, came out and conducted us to the outbuilding where the corpse had been deposited. Thorndyke made a rapid examination of the wounds and the holes in the clothing, neither of which presented anything particularly suggestive. The weapon used had evidently been a thick-backed, single-edged knife similar to the one described, and the discolouration around the wounds indicated that the weapon had a definite shoulder like that of a Norwegian knife, and that it had been driven in with savage violence.

"Do you find anything that throws any light on the case?" the inspector asked, when the examination was concluded.

"That is impossible to say until we have seen the knife," replied Thorndyke; "but while we are waiting for it, we may as well go and look at the scene of the tragedy. These are Pratt's boots, I think?" He lifted a pair of stout laced boots from the table and turned them up to inspect the soles.

"Yes, those are his boots," replied Fox, "and pretty easy they'd have been to track, if the case had been the other way about. Those Blakey's protectors are as good as a trademark."

"We'll take them, at any rate," said Thorndyke; and, the inspector having taken the boots from him, we went out and retraced our steps down the avenue.

The place where the murder had occurred was easily identified by a large dark stain on the gravel at one side of the drive, half-way between two trees—an ancient pollard hornbeam and an elm. Next to the elm was a pollard oak with a squat, warty bole about seven feet high, and three enormous limbs, of which one slanted half-way across the avenue; and between these two trees the ground was covered with the tracks of men and hounds superimposed upon the hoof-prints of a horse.

"Where was the knife found?" Thorndyke asked.

The inspector indicated a spot near the middle of the drive, almost opposite the hornbeam and Thorndyke, picking up a large stone, laid it on the spot. Then he surveyed the scene thoughtfully, looking up and down the drive and at the trees that bordered it, and, finally, walked slowly to the space between the elm and the oak, scanning the ground as he went. "There is no dearth of footprints," he remarked grimly, as he looked down at the trampled earth.

"No, but the question is, whose are they?" said the inspector.

"Yes, that is the question," agreed Thorndyke; "and we will begin the solution by identifying those of Pratt."

"I don't see how that will help us," said the inspector. "We know he was here."

Thorndyke looked at him in surprise, and I must confess that the foolish remark astonished me too, accustomed as I was to the quick-witted officers from Scotland Yard.

"The hue and cry procession," remarked Thorndyke, "seems to have passed out between the elm and the oak; elsewhere the ground seems pretty clear." He walked round the elm, still looking earnestly at the ground, and presently continued: "Now here, in the soft earth bordering the turf, are the prints of a pair of smallish feet wearing pointed boots; a rather short man, evidently, by the size of foot and length of stride, and he doesn't seem to have belonged to the procession. But I don't see any of Pratt's; he doesn't seem to have come off the hard gravel."

He continued to walk slowly towards the hornbeam with his eyes fixed on the ground. Suddenly he halted and stooped with an eager look at the earth; and, as Fox and I approached, he stood up and pointed. "Pratt's footprints—faint and fragmentary, but unmistakable. And now, inspector, you see their importance. They furnish the time factor in respect of the other footprints. Look at this one and then look at that." He pointed from one to another of the faint impressions of the dead man's foot.

"You mean that there are signs of a struggle?" said Fox.

"I mean more than that," replied Thorndyke. "Here is one of Pratt's footprints treading into the print of a small, pointed foot; and there at the edge of the gravel is another of Pratt's nearly obliterated by the tread of a pointed foot. Obviously the first pointed footprint was made before Pratt's, and the second one after his; and the necessary inference is that the owner of the pointed foot was here at the same time as Pratt."

"Then he must have been the murderer!" exclaimed Fox.

"Presumably," answered Thorndyke; "but let us see whither he went. You notice, in the first place, that the man stood close to this tree"—he indicated the hornbeam—"and that he went towards the elm. Let us follow him. He passes the elm, you see, and you will observe that these tracks form a regular series leading from the hornbeam and not mixed up with the marks of the struggle. They were, therefore, probably made after the murder had been perpetrated. You will also notice that they pass along the backs of the trees—outside the avenue, that is; what does that suggest to you?"

"It suggests to me," I said, when the inspector had shaken his head hopelessly, "that there was possibly someone in the avenue when the man was stealing off."

"Precisely," said Thorndyke. "The body was found not more than nine minutes after Pratt arrived here. But the murder must have taken some time. Then the housekeeper thought she heard someone calling and came out with a lantern, and, at the same time, the general and Mr. Hanford came up the drive. The suggestion is that the man sneaked along outside the trees to avoid being seen. However, let us follow the tracks. They pass the elm and they pass on behind the next tree; but wait! There is something odd here." He passed behind the great pollard oak and looked down at the soft earth by its roots. "Here is a pair of impressions much deeper than the rest, and they are not a part of the track since their toes point towards the tree. What do you make of that?" Without waiting for an answer he began closely to scan the bole of the tree and especially a large, warty protuberance about three feet from the ground. On the bark above this was a vertical mark, as if something had scraped down the tree, and from the wart itself a dead twig had been newly broken off and lay upon the ground. Pointing to these marks Thorndyke set his foot on the protuberance, and, springing up, brought his eye above the level of the crown, whence the great boughs branched off.

"Ah!" he exclaimed. "Here is something much more definite." With the aid of another projection, he scrambled up into the crown of the tree, and, having glanced quickly round, beckoned to us. I stepped up on the projecting lump and, as my eyes rose above the crown, I perceived the brown, shiny impression of a hand on the edge. Climbing into the crown, I was quickly followed by the inspector, and we both stood up by Thorndyke between the three boughs. From where we stood we looked on the upper side of the great limb that swept out across the avenue; and there on its lichen-covered surface, we saw the imprints in reddish-brown of a pair of open hands.

"You notice," said Thorndyke, leaning out upon the bough, "that he is a short man; I cannot conveniently place my hands so low. You also note that he has both forefingers intact, and so is certainly not Ellis."

"If you mean to say, sir, that these marks were made by the murderer," said Fox, "I say it's impossible. Why, that would mean that he was here looking down at us when we were searching for him with the hounds. The presence of the hounds proves that this man could not have been the murderer."

"On the contrary," said Thorndyke, "the presence of this man with bloody hands confirms the other evidence, which all indicates that the hounds were never on the murderer's trail at all. Come now, inspector, I put it to you: Here is a murdered man; the murderer has almost certainly blood upon his hands; and here is a man with bloody hands, lurking in a tree within a few feet of the corpse and within a few minutes of its discovery (as is shown by the footprints); what are the reasonable probabilities?"

"But you are forgetting the bloodhounds, sir, and the murderer's knife," urged the inspector.

"Tut, tut, man!" exclaimed Thorndyke; "those bloodhounds are a positive obsession. But I see a sergeant coming up the drive, with the knife, I hope. Perhaps that will solve the riddle for us."

The sergeant, who carried a small dispatch-box, halted opposite the tree in some surprise while we descended, when he came forward with a military salute and handed the box to the inspector, who forthwith unlocked it, and, opening the lid, displayed an object wrapped in a pocket-handkerchief.

"There is the knife, sir," said he, "just as I received it. The handkerchief is the sergeant's."

Thorndyke unrolled the handkerchief and took from it a large-sized Norwegian knife, which he looked at critically and then handed to me. While I was inspecting the blade, he shook out the handkerchief and, having looked it over on both sides, turned to the sergeant.

"At what time did you pick up this knife?" he asked.

"About seven-fifteen, sir; directly after the hounds had started. I was careful to pick it up by the ring, and I wrapped it in the handkerchief at once."

"Seven-fifteen," said Thorndyke. "Less than half-an-hour after the murder. That is very singular. Do you observe the state of this handkerchief? There is not a mark on it. Not a trace of any bloodstain; which proves that when the knife was picked up, the blood on it was already dry. But things dry slowly, if they dry at all, in the saturated air of an autumn evening. The appearances seem to suggest that the blood on the knife was dry when it was thrown down. By the way, sergeant, what do you scent your handkerchief with?"

"Scent, sir!" exclaimed the astonished officer in indignant accents; "me scent my handkerchief! No, sir, certainly not. Never used scent in my life, sir."

Thorndyke held out the handkerchief, and the sergeant sniffed at it incredulously. "It certainly does seem to smell of scent," he admitted, "but it must be the knife." The same idea having occurred to me, I applied the handle of the knife to my nose and instantly detected the sickly-sweet odour of musk.

"The question is," said the inspector, when the two articles had been tested by us all, "was it the knife that scented the Handkerchief or the handkerchief that scented the knife?"

"You heard what the sergeant said," replied Thorndyke. "There was no scent on the handkerchief when the knife was wrapped in it. Do you know, inspector, this scent seems to me to offer a very curious suggestion. Consider the facts of the case: the distinct trail leading straight to Ellis, who is, nevertheless, found to be without a scratch or a spot of blood; the inconsistencies in the case that I pointed out in the train, and now this knife, apparently dropped with dried blood on it and scented with musk. To me it suggests a carefully-planned, coolly-premeditated crime. The murderer knew about the general's bloodhounds and made use of them as a blind. He planted this knife, smeared with blood and tainted with musk, to furnish a scent. No doubt some object, also scented with musk, would be drawn over the ground to give the trail. It is only a suggestion, of course, but it is worth considering."

"But, sir," the inspector objected eagerly, "if the murderer had handled the knife, it would have scented him too."

"Exactly; so, as we are assuming that the man is not a fool, we may assume that he did not handle it. He will have left it here in readiness, hidden in some place whence he could knock it down, say, with a stick, without touching it."

"Perhaps in this very tree, sir," suggested the sergeant, pointing to the oak.

"No," said Thorndyke, "he would hardly have hidden in the tree where the knife had been. The hounds might have scented the place instead of following the trail at once. The most likely hiding-place for the knife is the one nearest the spot where it was found." He walked over to the stone that marked the spot, and looking round, continued: "You see, that hornbeam is much the nearest, and its flat crown would be very convenient for the purpose—easily reached even by a short man, as he appears to be. Let us see if there are any traces of it. Perhaps you will give me a 'back up', sergeant, as we haven't a ladder."

The sergeant assented with a faint grin, and stooping beside the tree in an attitude suggesting the game of leapfrog, placed his hands firmly on his knees. Grasping a stout branch, Thorndyke swung himself up on the sergeant's broad back, whence he looked down into the crown of the tree. Then, parting the branches, he stepped onto the ledge and disappeared into the central hollow.

When he re-appeared he held in his hands two very singular objects: a pair of iron crucible-tongs and an artist's brush-case of black-japanned tin. The former article he handed down to me, but the brush-case he held carefully by its wire handle as he dropped to the ground.

"The significance of these things is, I think, obvious," he said. "The tongs were used to handle the knife with and the case to carry it in, so that it should not scent his clothes or bag. It was very carefully planned."

"If that is so," said the inspector, "the inside of the case ought to smell of musk."

"No doubt," said Thorndyke; "but before we open it, there is a rather important matter to be attended to. Will you give me the Vitogen powder, Jervis?"

I opened the canvas-covered "research case" and took from it an object like a diminutive pepper-caster—an iodo-form dredger in fact—and handed it to him. Grasping the brush-case by its wire handle, he sprinkled the pale yellow powder from the dredger freely all round the pull-off lid, tapping the top with his knuckles to make the fine particles spread. Then he blew off the superfluous powder, and the two police officers gave a simultaneous gasp of joy; for now, on the black background, there stood out plainly a number of finger-prints, so clear and distinct that the ridge-pattern could be made out with perfect ease.

"These will probably be his right hand," said Thorndyke. "Now for the left." He treated the body of the case in the same way, and, when he had blown off the powder, the entire surface was spotted with yellow, oval impressions. "Now, Jervis," said he, "if you will put on a glove and pull off the lid, we can test the inside."

There was no difficulty in getting the lid off, for the shoulder of the case had been smeared with vaseline—apparently to produce an airtight joint—and, as it separated with a hollow sound, a faint, musky odour exhaled from its interior.

"The remainder of the inquiry," said Thorndyke, when I pushed the lid on again, "will be best conducted at the police station, where, also, we can photograph these fingerprints."

"The shortest way will be across the meadows," said Fox; "the way the hounds went."

By this route we accordingly travelled, Thorndyke carrying the brush-case tenderly by its handle.

"I don't quite see where Ellis comes in in this job," said the inspector, as we walked along, "if the fellow had a grudge against Pratt. They weren't chums."

"I think I do," said Thorndyke. "You say that both men were prison officers at Portland at the same time. Now doesn't it seem likely that this is the work of some old convict who had been identified—and perhaps blackmailed—by Pratt, and possibly by Ellis too? That is where the value of the finger-prints comes in. If he is an old 'lag' his prints will be at Scotland Yard. Otherwise they are not of much value as a clue."

"That's true, sir," said the inspector. "I suppose you want to see Ellis."

"I want to see that purse that you spoke of, first," replied Thorndyke. "That is probably the other end of the clue."

As soon as we arrived at the station, the inspector unlocked a safe and brought out a parcel. "These are Ellis's things," said he, as he unfastened it, "and that is the purse."

He handed Thorndyke a small pigskin pouch, which my colleague opened, and having smelt the inside, passed to me. The odour of musk was plainly perceptible, especially in the small compartment at the back.

"It has probably tainted the other contents of the parcel," said Thorndyke, sniffing at each article in turn, "but my sense of smell is not keen enough to detect any scent. They all seem odourless to me, whereas the purse smells quite distinctly. Shall we have Ellis in now?"

The sergeant took a key from a locked drawer and departed for the cells, whence he presently re-appeared accompanied by the prisoner—a stout, burly man, in the last stage of dejection.

"Come, cheer up, Ellis," said the inspector. "Here's Dr. Thorndyke come down to help us and he wants to ask you one or two questions."

Ellis looked piteously at Thorndyke, and exclaimed: "I know nothing whatever about this affair, sir, I swear to God I don't."

"I never supposed you did," said Thorndyke. "But there are one or two things that I want you to tell me. To begin with, that purse: where did you find it?"

"On the Thorpe road, sir. It was lying in the middle of the footway."

"Had any one else passed the spot lately? Did you meet or pass any one?"

"Yes, sir, I met a labourer about a minute before I saw the purse. I can't imagine why he didn't see it."

"Probably because it wasn't there," said Thorndyke. "Is there a hedge there?"

"Yes, sir; a hedge on a low bank."

"Ha! Well, now, tell me: is there any one about here whom you knew when you and Pratt were together at Portland? Any old lag—to put it bluntly—whom you and Pratt have been putting the screw on."

"No, sir, I swear there isn't. But I wouldn't answer for Pratt. He had a rare memory for faces."

Thorndyke reflected. "Were there any escapes from Portland in your time?" he asked.

"Only one—a man named Dobbs. He made off to the sea in a sudden fog and he was supposed to be drowned. His clothes washed up on the Bill, but not his body. At any rate, he was never heard of again."

"Thank you, Ellis. Do you mind my taking your fingerprints?"

"Certainly not, sir," was the almost eager reply; and the office inking-pad being requisitioned, a rough set of finger-prints was produced; and when Thorndyke had compared them with those on the brush-case and found no resemblance, Ellis returned to his cell in quite buoyant spirits.

Having made several photographs of the strange fingerprints, we returned to town that evening, taking the negatives with us; and while we waited for our train, Thorndyke gave a few parting injunctions to the inspector. "Remember," he said, "that the man must have washed his hands before he could appear in public. Search the banks of every pond, ditch and stream in the neighbourhood for footprints like those in the avenue; and, if you find any, search the bottom of the water thoroughly, for he is quite likely to have dropped the knife into the mud."

The photographs, which we handed in at Scotland Yard that same night, enabled the experts to identify the fingerprints as those of Francis Dobbs, an escaped convict. The two photographs—profile and full-face—which were attached to his record, were sent down to Baysford with a description of the man, and were, in due course, identified with a somewhat mysterious individual, who passed by the name of Rufus Pembury and who had lived in the neighbourhood as a private gentleman for some two years. But Rufus Pembury was not to be found either at his genteel house or elsewhere. All that was known was, that on the day after the murder, he had converted his entire "personalty" into "bearer securities," and then vanished from mortal ken. Nor has he ever been heard of to this day.

"And, between ourselves," said Thorndyke, when we were discussing the case some time after, "he deserved to escape. It was clearly a case of blackmail, and to kill a blackmailer—when you have no other defence against him—is hardly murder. As to Ellis, he could never have been convicted, and Dobbs, or Pembury, must have known it. But he would have been committed to the Assizes, and that would have given time for all traces to disappear. No, Dobbs was a man of courage, ingenuity and resource; and, above all, he knocked the bottom out of the great bloodhound superstition."

# CHAPTER III.

## THE ECHO OF A MUTINY

### PART I.
### DEATH ON THE GIRDLER

POPULAR belief ascribes to infants and the lower animals certain occult powers of divining character denied to the reasoning faculties of the human adult; and is apt to accept their judgment as finally overriding the pronouncements of mere experience.

Whether this belief rests upon any foundation other than the universal love of paradox it is unnecessary to inquire. It is very generally entertained, especially by ladies of a certain social status; and by Mrs. Thomas Solly it was loyally maintained as an article of faith.

"Yes," she moralized, "it's surprisin' how they know, the little children and the dumb animals. But they do. There's no deceivin' them. They can tell the gold from the dross in a moment, they can, and they reads the human heart like a book. Wonderful, I call it. I suppose it's instinct."

Having delivered herself of this priceless gem of philosophic thought, she thrust her arms elbow-deep into the foaming wash-tub and glanced admiringly at her lodger as he sat in the doorway, supporting on one knee an obese infant of eighteen months and on the other a fine tabby cat.

James Brown was an elderly seafaring man, small and slight in build and in manner suave, insinuating and perhaps a trifle sly. But he had all the sailor's love of children and animals, and the sailor's knack of making himself acceptable to them, for, as he sat with an empty pipe wobbling in the grasp of his toothless gums, the baby beamed with humid smiles, and the cat, rolled into a fluffy ball and purring like a stocking-loom, worked its fingers ecstatically as if it were trying on a new pair of gloves.

"It must be mortal lonely out at the lighthouse," Mrs. Solly resumed. "Only three men and never a neighbour to speak to; and, Lord! what a muddle they must be in with no woman to look after them and keep 'em tidy. But you won't be overworked, Mr. Brown, in these long days; daylight till past nine o'clock. I don't know what you'll do to pass the time."

"Oh, I shall find plenty to do, I expect," said Brown, "what with cleanin' the lamps and glasses and paintin' up the ironwork. And that reminds me," he added, looking round at the clock, "that time's getting on. High water at half-past ten, and here it's gone eight o'clock."

Mrs. Solly, acting on the hint, began rapidly to fish out the washed garments and wring them out into the form of short ropes. Then, having dried her hands on her apron, she relieved Brown of the protesting baby.

"Your room will be ready for you, Mr. Brown," said she, "when your turn comes for a spell ashore; and main glad me and Tom will be to see you back."

"Thank you, Mrs. Solly, ma'am," answered Brown, tenderly placing the cat on the floor; "you won't be more glad than what I will." He shook hands warmly with his landlady, kissed the baby, chucked the cat under the chin, and, picking up his little chest by its becket, swung it onto his shoulder and strode out of the cottage.

His way lay across the marshes, and, like the ships in the offing, he shaped his course by the twin towers of Reculver that stood up grotesquely on the rim of the land; and as he trod the springy turf, Tom Solly's fleecy charges looked up at him with vacant stares and valedictory bleatings. Once, at a dyke-gate, he paused to look back at the fair Kentish landscape: at the grey tower of St. Nicholas-at-Wade peeping above the trees and the faraway mill at Sarre, whirling slowly in the summer breeze; and, above all, at the solitary cottage where, for a brief spell in his stormy life, he had known the homely joys of domesticity and peace. Well, that was over for the present, and the lighthouse loomed ahead. With a half-sigh he passed through the gate and walked on towards Reculver.

Outside the whitewashed cottages with their official black chimneys a petty-officer of the coast-guard was adjusting the halyards of the flagstaff. He looked round as Brown approached, and hailed him cheerily.

"Here you are, then," said he, "all figged out in your new togs, too. But we're in a bit of a difficulty, d'ye see. We've got to pull up to Whitstable this morning, so I can't send a man out with you and I can't spare a boat."

"Have I got to swim out, then?" asked Brown.

The coast-guard grinned. "Not in them new clothes, mate," he answered. "No, but there's old Willett's boat; he isn't using her to-day; he's going over to Minster to see his daughter, and he'll let us have the loan of the boat. But there's no one to go with you, and I'm responsible to Willett."

"Well, what about it?" asked Brown, with the deep-sea sailor's (usually misplaced) confidence in his power to handle a sailing-boat. "D'ye think I can't manage a tub of a boat? Me what's used the sea since I was a kid of ten?"

"Yes," said the coast-guard; "but who's to bring her back?"

"Why, the man that I'm going to relieve," answered Brown. "He don't want to swim no more than what I do."

The coast-guard reflected with his telescope pointed at a passing barge. "Well, I suppose it'll be all right," he concluded; "but it's a pity they couldn't send the tender round. However, if you undertake to send the boat back, we'll get her afloat. It's time you were off."

He strolled away to the back of the cottages, whence he presently returned with two of his mates, and the four men proceeded along the shore to where Willett's boat lay just above high-water mark.

The Emily was a beamy craft of the type locally known as a "half-share skiff," solidly built of oak, with varnished planking and fitted with main and mizzen lugs. She was a good handful for four men, and, as she slid over the soft chalk rocks with a hollow rumble, the coast-guards debated the advisability of lifting out the bags of shingle with which she was ballasted. However, she was at length dragged down, ballast and all, to the water's edge, and then, while Brown stepped the mainmast, the petty-officer gave him his directions. "What you've got to do," said he, "is to make use of the flood-tide. Keep her nose nor'-east, and with this trickle of nor'-westerly breeze you ought to make the light-house in one board. Anyhow don't let her get east of the lighthouse, or, when the ebb sets in, you'll be in a fix."

To these admonitions Brown listened with jaunty indifference as he hoisted the sails and watched the incoming tide creep over the level shore. Then the boat lifted on the gentle swell. Putting out an oar, he gave a vigorous shove off that sent the boat, with a final scrape, clear of the beach, and then, having dropped the rudder onto its pintles, he seated himself and calmly belayed the main-sheet.

"There he goes," growled the coast-guard; "makin' fast his sheet. They will do it" (he invariably did it himself), "and that's how accidents happen. I hope old Willett'll see his boat back all right."

He stood for some time watching the dwindling boat as it sidled across the smooth water; then he turned and followed his mates towards the station.

Out on the south-western edge of the Girdler Sand, just inside the two-fathom line, the spindle-shanked lighthouse stood a-straddle on its long screw-piles like some uncouth red-bodied wading bird. It was now nearly half flood tide. The highest shoals were long since covered, and the lighthouse rose above the smooth sea as solitary as a slaver becalmed in the "middle passage."

On the gallery outside the lantern were two men, the entire staff of the building, of whom one sat huddled in a chair with his left leg propped up with pillows on another, while his companion rested a telescope on the rail and peered at the faint grey line of the distant land and the two tiny points that marked the twin spires of Reculver.

"I don't see any signs of the boat, Harry," said he.

The other man groaned. "I shall lose the tide," he complained, "and then there's another day gone."

"They can pull you down to Birchington and put you in the train," said the first man.

"I don't want no trains," growled the invalid. "The boat'll be bad enough. I suppose there's nothing coming our way, Tom?"

Tom turned his face eastward and shaded his eyes. "There's a brig coming across the tide from the north," he said. "Looks like a collier." He pointed his telescope at the approaching vessel, and added: "She's got two new cloths in her upper fore top-sail, one on each leech."

The other man sat up eagerly. "What's her trysail like, Tom?" he asked.

"Can't see it," replied Tom. "Yes, I can, now: it's tanned. Why, that'll be the old Utopia, Harry; she's the only brig I know that's got a tanned trysail."

"Look here, Tom," exclaimed the other, "If that's the Utopia, she's going to my home and I'm going aboard of her. Captain Mockett'll give me a passage, I know."

"You oughtn't to go until you're relieved, you know, Barnett," said Tom doubtfully; "it's against regulations to leave your station."

"Regulations be blowed!" exclaimed Barnett. "My leg's more to me than the regulations. I don't want to be a cripple all my life. Besides, I'm no good here, and this new chap, Brown, will be coming out presently. You run up the signal, Tom, like a good comrade, and hail the brig."

"Well, it's your look-out," said Tom, "and I don't mind saying that if I was in your place I should cut off home and see a doctor, if I got the chance." He sauntered off to the flag-locker, and, selecting the two code-flags, deliberately toggled them onto the halyards. Then, as the brig swept up within range, he hoisted the little balls of bunting to the flagstaff-head and jerked the halyards, when the two flags blew out making the signal "Need assistance."

Promptly a coal-soiled answering pennant soared to the brig's main-truck; less promptly the collier went about, and, turning her nose down stream, slowly drifted stern-forwards towards the lighthouse. Then a boat slid out through her gangway, and a couple of men plied the oars vigorously.

"Lighthouse ahoy!" roared one of them, as the boat came within hail. "What's amiss?"

"Harry Barnett has broke his leg," shouted the lighthouse keeper, "and he wants to know if Captain Mockett will give him a passage to Whitstable."

The boat turned back to the brig, and after a brief and bellowed consultation, once more pulled towards the lighthouse.

"Skipper says yus," roared the sailor, when he was within ear-shot, "and he says look alive, 'cause he don't want to miss his tide."

The injured man heaved a sigh of relief. "That's good news," said he, "though, how the blazes I'm going to get down the ladder is more than I can tell. What do you say, Jeffreys?"

"I say you'd better let me lower you with the tackle," replied Jeffreys. "You can sit in the bight of a rope and I'll give you a line to steady yourself with."

"Ah, that'll do, Tom," said Barnett; "but, for the Lord's sake, pay out the fall-rope gently."

The arrangements were made so quickly that by the time the boat was fast alongside everything was in readiness, and a minute later the injured man, dangling like a gigantic spider from the end of the tackle, slowly descended, cursing volubly to the accompaniment of the creaking of the blocks. His chest and kit-bag followed, and, as soon as these were unhooked from the tackle, the boat pulled off to the brig, which was now slowly creeping stern-foremost past the lighthouse. The sick man was hoisted up the side, his chest handed up after him, and then the brig was put on her course due south across the Kentish Flats.

Jeffreys stood on the gallery watching the receding vessel and listening to the voices of her crew as they grew small and weak in the increasing distance. Now that his gruff companion was gone, a strange loneliness had fallen on the lighthouse. The last of the homeward-bound ships had long since passed up the Princes Channel and left the calm sea desolate and blank. The distant buoys, showing as tiny black dots on the glassy surface, and the spindly shapes of the beacons which stood up from invisible shoals, but emphasized the solitude of the empty sea, and the tolling of the bell buoy on the Shivering Sand, stealing faintly down the wind, sounded weird and mournful. The day's work was already done. The lenses were polished, the lamps had been trimmed, and the little motor that worked the fog-horn had been cleaned and oiled. There were several odd jobs, it is true, waiting to be done, as there always are in a lighthouse; but, just now, Jeffreys was not in a working humour. A new comrade was coming into his life to-day, a stranger with whom he was to be shut up alone, night and day, for a month on end, and whose temper and tastes and habits might mean for him pleasant companionship or jangling and discord without end. Who was this man Brown? What had he been? and what was he like? These were the questions that passed, naturally enough, through the lighthouse keeper's mind and distracted him from his usual thoughts and occupations.

Presently a speck on the landward horizon caught his eye. He snatched up the telescope eagerly to inspect it. Yes, it was a boat; but not the coast-guard's cutter, for which he was looking. Evidently a fisherman's boat and with only one man in it. He laid down the telescope with a sigh of disappointment, and, filling his pipe, leaned on the rail with a dreamy eye bent on the faint grey line of the land.

Three long years had he spent in this dreary solitude, so repugnant to his active, restless nature: three blank, interminable years, with nothing to look back on but the endless succession of summer calms, stormy nights and the chilly fogs of winter, when the unseen steamers hooted from the void and the fog-horn bellowed its hoarse warning.

Why had he come to this God-forsaken spot? and why did he stay, when the wide world called to him? And then memory painted him a picture on which his mind's eye had often looked before and which once again arose before him, shutting out the vision of the calm sea and the distant land. It was a brightly-coloured picture. It showed a cloudless sky brooding over the deep blue tropic sea: and in the middle of the picture, see-sawing gently on the quiet swell, a white-painted barque.

Her sails were clewed up untidily, her swinging yards jerked at the slack braces and her untended wheel revolved to and fro to the oscillations of the rudder.

She was not a derelict, for more than a dozen men were on her deck; but the men were all drunk and mostly asleep, and there was never an officer among them.

Then he saw the interior of one of her cabins. The chart-rack, the tell-tale compass and the chronometers marked it as the captain's cabin. In it were four men, and two of them lay dead on the deck. Of the other two, one was a small, cunning-faced man, who was, at the moment, kneeling beside one of the corpses to wipe a knife upon its coat. The fourth man was himself.

Again, he saw the two murderers stealing off in a quarter-boat, as the barque with her drunken crew drifted towards the spouting surf of a river-bar. He saw the ship melt away in the surf like an icicle in the sunshine; and, later, two shipwrecked mariners, picked up in an open boat and set ashore at an American port.

That was why he was here. Because he was a murderer. The other scoundrel, Amos Todd, had turned Queen's Evidence and denounced him, and he had barely managed to escape. Since then he had hidden himself from the great world, and here he must continue to hide, not from the law—for his person was unknown now that his shipmates were dead—but from the partner of his crime. It was the fear of Todd that had changed him from Jeffrey Rorke to Tom Jeffreys and had sent him to the Girdler, a prisoner for life. Todd might die—might even now be dead—but he would never hear of it: would never hear the news of his release.

He roused himself and once more pointed his telescope at the distant boat. She was considerably nearer now and seemed to be heading out towards the lighthouse. Perhaps the man in her was bringing a message; at any rate, there was no sign of the coast-guard's cutter.

He went in, and, betaking himself to the kitchen, busied himself with a few simple preparations for dinner. But there was nothing to cook, for there remained the cold meat from yesterday's cooking, which he would make sufficient, with some biscuit in place of potatoes. He felt restless and unstrung; the solitude irked him, and the everlasting wash of the water among the piles jarred on his nerves.

When he went out again into the gallery the ebb-tide had set in strongly and the boat was little more than a mile distant; and now, through the glass, he could see that the man in her wore the uniform cap of the Trinity House. Then the man must be his future comrade, Brown; but this was very extraordinary. What were they to do with the boat? There was no one to take her back.

The breeze was dying away. As he watched the boat, he saw the man lower the sail and take to his oars; and something of hurry in the way the man pulled over the gathering tide, caused Jeffreys to look round the horizon. And then, for the first time, he noticed a bank of fog creeping up from the east and already so near that the beacon on the East Girdler had faded out of sight. He hastened in to start the little motor that compressed the air for the fog-horn and waited awhile to see that the mechanism was running properly. Then, as the deck vibrated to the roar of the horn, he went out once more into the gallery.

The fog was now all round the lighthouse and the boat was hidden from view. He listened intently. The enclosing wall of vapour seemed to have shut out sound as well as vision. At intervals the horn bellowed its note of warning, and then all was still save the murmur of the water among the piles below, and, infinitely faint and far away, the mournful tolling of the bell on the Shivering Sand.

At length there came to his ear the muffled sound of oars working in the holes; then, at the very edge of the circle of grey water that was visible, the boat appeared through the fog, pale and spectral, with a shadowy figure pulling furiously. The horn emitted a hoarse growl; the man looked round, perceived the lighthouse and altered his course towards it.

Jeffreys descended the iron stairway, and, walking along the lower gallery, stood at the head of the ladder earnestly watching the approaching stranger. Already he was tired of being alone. The yearning for human companionship had been growing ever since Barnett left. But what sort of comrade was this stranger who was coming into his life? And coming to occupy so dominant a place in it.

The boat swept down swiftly athwart the hurrying tide. Nearer it came and yet nearer: and still Jeffreys could catch no glimpse of his new comrade's face. At length it came fairly alongside and bumped against the fender-posts; the stranger whisked in an oar and grabbed a rung of the ladder, and Jeffreys dropped a coil of rope into the boat. And still the man's face was hidden.

Jeffreys leaned out over the ladder and watched him anxiously, as he made fast the rope, unhooked the sail from the traveller and unstepped the mast. When he had set all in order, the stranger picked up a small chest, and, swinging it over his shoulder, stepped onto the ladder. Slowly, by reason of his encumbrance, he mounted, rung by rung, with never an upward glance, and Jeffreys gazed down at the top of his head with growing curiosity. At last he reached the top of the ladder and Jeffreys stooped to lend him a hand. Then, for the first time, he looked up, and Jeffreys started back with a blanched face.

"God Almighty!" he gasped. "It's Amos Todd!"

As the newcomer stepped on the gallery, the fog-horn emitted a roar like that of some hungry monster. Jeffreys turned abruptly without a word, and walked to the stairs, followed by Todd, and the two men ascended with never a sound but the hollow clank of their footsteps on the iron plates. Silently Jeffreys stalked into the living-room and, as his companion followed, he turned and motioned to the latter to set down his chest.

"You ain't much of a talker, mate," said Todd, looking round the room in some surprise; "ain't you going to say 'good-morning'? We're going to be good comrades, I hope. I'm Jim Brown, the new hand, I am; what might your name be?"

Jeffreys turned on him suddenly and led him to the window. "Look at me carefully, Amos Todd," he said sternly, "and then ask yourself what my name is."

At the sound of his voice Todd looked up with a start and turned pale as death. "It can't be," he whispered, "it can't be Jeff Rorke!"

The other man laughed harshly, and leaning forward, said in a low voice: "Hast thou found me, O mine enemy!"

"Don't say that!" exclaimed Todd. "Don't call me your enemy, Jeff. Lord knows but I'm glad to see you, though I'd never have known you without your beard and with that grey hair. I've been to blame, Jeff, and I know it; but it ain't no use raking up old grudges. Let bygones be bygones, Jeff, and let us be pals as we used to be." He wiped his face with his handkerchief and watched his companion apprehensively.

"Sit down," said Rorke, pointing to a shabby rep-covered arm-chair; "sit down and tell me what you've done with all that money. You've blued it all, I suppose, or you wouldn't be here."

"Robbed, Jeff," answered Todd; "robbed of every penny. Ah! that was an unfortunate affair, that job on board the old Sea-flower. But it's over and done with and we'd best forget it. They're all dead but us, Jeff, so we're safe enough so long as we keep our mouths shut; all at the bottom of the sea—and the best place for 'em too."

"Yes," Rorke replied fiercely, "that's the best place for your shipmates when they know too much; at the bottom of the sea or swinging at the end of a rope." He paced up and down the little room with rapid strides, and each time that he approached Todd's chair the latter shrank back with an expression of alarm.

"Don't sit there staring at me," said Rorke. "Why don't you smoke or do something?"

Todd hastily produced a pipe from his pocket, and having filled it from a moleskin pouch, stuck it in his mouth while he searched for a match. Apparently he carried his matches loose in his pocket, for he presently brought one forth—a red-headed match, which, when he struck it on the wall, lighted with a pale-blue flame. He applied it to his pipe, sucking in his cheeks while he kept his eyes fixed on his companion. Rorke, meanwhile, halted in his walk to cut some shavings from a cake of hard tobacco with a large clasp-knife; and, as he stood, he gazed with frowning abstraction at Todd.

"This pipe's stopped," said the latter, sucking ineffectually at the mouthpiece. "Have you got such a thing as a piece of wire, Jeff?"

"No, I haven't," replied Rorke; "not up here. I'll get a bit from the store presently. Here, take this pipe till you can clean your own: I've got another in the rack there." The sailor's natural hospitality overcoming for the moment his animosity, he thrust the pipe that he had just filled towards Todd, who took it with a mumbled "Thank you" and an anxious eye on the open knife. On the wall beside the chair was a roughly-carved pipe-rack containing: several pipes, one of which Rorke lifted out; and, as he leaned over the chair to reach it, Todd's face went several shades paler.

"Well, Jeff," he said, after a pause, while Rorke cut a fresh "fill" of tobacco, "are we going to be pals same as what we used to be?"

Rorke's animosity lighted up afresh. "Am I going to be pals with the man that tried to swear away my life?" he said sternly; and after a pause he added: "That wants thinking about, that does; and meantime I must go and look at the engine."

When Rorke had gone the new hand sat, with the two pipes in his hands, reflecting deeply. Abstractedly he stuck the fresh pipe into his mouth, and, dropping the stopped one into the rack, felt for a match. Still with an air of abstraction he lit the pipe, and having smoked for a minute or two, rose from the chair and began softly to creep across the room, looking about him and listening intently. At the door he paused to look out into the fog, and then, having again listened attentively, he stepped on tip-toe out onto the gallery and along towards the stairway. Of a sudden the voice of Rorke brought him up with a start.

"Hallo, Todd! where are you off to?"

"I'm just going down to make the boat secure," was the reply.

"Never you mind about the boat," said Rorke. "I'll see to her."

"Right-o, Jeff," said Todd, still edging towards the stairway. "But, I say, mate, where's the other man—the man that I'm to relieve?"

"There ain't any other man," replied Rorke; "he went off aboard a collier."

Todd's face suddenly became grey and haggard. "Then there's no one here but us two!" he gasped; and then, with an effort to conceal his fear, he asked: "But who's going to take the boat back?"

"We'll see about that presently," replied Rorke; "you get along in and unpack your chest."

He came out on the gallery as he spoke, with a lowering frown on his face. Todd cast a terrified glance at him, and then turned and ran for his life towards the stairway.

"Come back!" roared Rorke, springing forward along the gallery; but Todd's feet were already clattering down the iron steps. By the time Rorke reached the head of the stairs, the fugitive was near the bottom; but here, in his haste, he stumbled, barely saving himself by the handrail, and when he recovered his balance Rorke was upon him. Todd darted to the head of the ladder, but, as he grasped the stanchion, his pursuer seized him by the collar. In a moment he had turned with his hand under his coat. There was a quick blow, a loud curse from Rorke, an answering yell from Todd, and a knife fell spinning through the air and dropped into the fore-peak of the boat below.

"You murderous little devil!" said Rorke in an ominously quiet voice, with his bleeding hand gripping his captive by the throat. "Handy with your knife as ever, eh? So you were off to give information, were you?"

"No, I wasn't Jeff," replied Todd in a choking voice; "I wasn't, s'elp me, God. Let go, Jeff. I didn't mean no harm. I was only—" With a sudden wrench he freed one hand and struck out frantically at his captor's face. But Rorke warded off the blow, and, grasping the other wrist, gave a violent push and let go. Todd staggered backward a few paces along the staging, bringing up at the extreme edge; and here, for a sensible time, he stood with wide-open mouth and starting eye-balls, swaying and clutching wildly at the air. Then, with a shrill scream, he toppled backwards and fell, striking a pile in his descent and rebounding into the water.

In spite of the audible thump of his head on the pile, he was not stunned, for when he rose to the surface, he struck out vigorously, uttering short, stifled cries for help. Rorke watched him with set teeth and quickened breath, but made no move. Smaller and still smaller grew the head with its little circle of ripples, swept away on the swift ebb-tide, and fainter the bubbling cries that came across the smooth water. At length as the small black spot began to fade in the fog, the drowning man, with a final effort, raised his head clear of the surface and sent a last, despairing shriek towards the lighthouse. The fog-horn sent back an answering bellow; the head sank below the surface and was seen no more; and in the dreadful stillness that settled down upon the sea there sounded faint and far away the muffled tolling of a bell.

Rorke stood for some minutes immovable, wrapped in thought. Presently the distant hoot of a steamer's whistle aroused him. The ebb-tide shipping was beginning to come down and the fog might lift at any moment; and there was the boat still alongside. She must be disposed of at once. No one had seen her arrive and no one must see her made fast to the lighthouse. Once get rid of the boat and all traces of Todd's visit would be destroyed. He ran down the ladder and stepped into the boat. It was simple. She was heavily ballasted, and would go down if she filled.

He shifted some of the bags of shingle, and, lifting the bottom boards, pulled out the plug. Instantly a large jet of water spouted up into the bottom. Rorke looked at it critically, and, deciding that it would fill her in a few minutes, replaced the bottom boards; and having secured the mast and sail with a few turns of the sheet round a thwart, to prevent them from floating away, he cast off the mooring-rope and stepped on the ladder.

As the released boat began to move away on the tide, he ran up and mounted to the upper gallery to watch her disappearance. Suddenly he remembered Todd's chest. It was still in the room below. With a hurried glance around into the fog, he ran down to the room, and snatching up the chest, carried it out on the lower gallery. After another nervous glance around to assure himself that no craft was in sight, he heaved the chest over the handrail, and, when it fell with a loud splash into the sea, he waited to watch it float away after its owner and the sunken boat. But it never rose; and presently he returned to the upper gallery.

The fog was thinning perceptibly now, and the boat remained plainly visible as she drifted away. But she sank more slowly than he had expected, and presently as she drifted farther away, he fetched the telescope and peered at her with growing anxiety. It would be unfortunate if any one saw her; if she should be picked up here, with her plug out, it would be disastrous.

He was beginning to be really alarmed. Through the glass he could see that the boat was now rolling in a sluggish, water-logged fashion, but she still showed some inches of free-board, and the fog was thinning every moment.

Presently the blast of a steamer's whistle sounded close at hand. He looked round hurriedly and, seeing nothing, again pointed the telescope eagerly at the dwindling boat. Suddenly he gave a gasp of relief. The boat had rolled gunwale under; had staggered back for a moment and then rolled again, slowly, finally, with the water pouring in over the submerged gunwale.

In a few more seconds she had vanished. Rorke lowered the telescope and took a deep breath. Now he was safe. The boat had sunk unseen. But he was better than safe: he was free. His evil spirit, the standing menace of his life, was gone, and the wide world, the world of life, of action, of pleasure, called to him.

In a few minutes the fog lifted. The sun shone brightly on the red-funnelled cattle-boat whose whistle had startled him just now, the summer blue came back to sky and sea, and the land peeped once more over the edge of the horizon.

He went in, whistling cheerfully, and stopped the motor; returned to coil away the rope that he had thrown to Todd; and, when he had hoisted a signal for assistance, he went in once more to eat his solitary meal in peace and gladness.

## PART II.
## "THE SINGING BONE"
## (RELATED BY CHRISTOPHER JERVIS, M.D.)

IN every kind of scientific work a certain amount of manual labour naturally appertains, labour that cannot be performed by the scientist himself, since art is long but life is short. A chemical analysis involves a laborious "clean up" of apparatus and laboratory, for which the chemist has no time; the preparation of a skeleton—the maceration, bleaching, "assembling," and riveting together of bones—must be carried out by someone whose time is not too precious. And so with other scientific activities. Behind the man of science with his outfit of knowledge is the indispensable mechanic with his outfit of manual skill.

Thorndyke's laboratory assistant, Polton, was a fine example of the latter type, deft, resourceful, ingenious and untiring. He was somewhat of an inventive genius, too; and it was one of his inventions that connected us with the singular case that I am about to record.

Though by trade a watchmaker, Polton was, by choice, an optician. Optical apparatus was the passion of his life; and when, one day, he produced for our inspection an improved prism for increasing the efficiency of gas-buoys, Thorndyke at once brought the invention to the notice of a friend at the Trinity House.

As a consequence, we three—Thorndyke, Polton and I—found ourselves early on a fine July morning making our way down Middle Temple Lane bound for the Temple Pier. A small oil-launch lay alongside the pontoon, and, as we made our appearance, a red-faced, white-whiskered gentleman stood up in the cockpit.

"Here's a delightful morning, doctor," he sang out in a fine, brassy, resonant, sea-faring voice; "sort of day for a trip to the lower river, hey? Hallo, Polton! Coming down to take the bread out of our mouths, are you? Ha, ha!" The cheery laugh rang out over the river and mingled with the throb of the engine as the launch moved off from the pier.

Captain Grumpass was one of the Elder Brethren of the Trinity House. Formerly a client of Thorndyke's he had subsided, as Thorndyke's clients were apt to do, into the position of a personal friend, and his hearty regard included our invaluable assistant.

"Nice state of things," continued the captain, with a chuckle, "when a body of nautical experts have got to be taught their business by a parcel of lawyers or doctors, what? I suppose trade's slack and 'Satan findeth mischief still,' hey, Polton?"

"There isn't much doing on the civil side, sir," replied Polton, with a quaint, crinkly smile, "but the criminals are still going strong."

"Ha! mystery department still flourishing, what? And, by Jove! talking of mysteries, doctor, our people have got a queer problem to work out; something quite in your line—quite. Yes, and, by the Lord Moses, since I've got you here, why shouldn't I suck your brains?"

"Exactly," said Thorndyke. "Why shouldn't you?"

"Well, then, I will," said the captain, "so here goes. All hands to the pump!" He lit a cigar, and, after a few preliminary puffs, began: "The mystery, shortly stated, is this: one of our lighthousemen has disappeared—vanished off the face of the earth and left no trace. He may have bolted, he may have been drowned accidentally or he may have been murdered. But I'd rather give you the particulars in order. At the end of last week a barge brought into Ramsgate a letter from the screw-pile lighthouse on the Girdler. There are only two men there, and it seems that one of them, a man named Barnett, had broken his leg, and he asked that the tender should be sent to bring him ashore. Well, it happened that the local tender, the Warden, was up on the slip in Ramsgate Harbour, having a scrape down, and wouldn't be available for a day or two, so, as the case was urgent, the officer at Ramsgate sent a letter to the lighthouse by one of the pleasure steamers saying that the man should be relieved by boat on the following morning, which was Saturday. He also wrote to a new hand who had just been taken on, a man named James Brown, who was lodging near Reculver, waiting his turn, telling him to go out on Saturday morning in the coast-guard's boat; and he sent a third letter to the coast-guard at Reculver asking him to take Brown out to the lighthouse and bring Barnett ashore. Well, between them, they made a fine muddle of it. The coast-guard couldn't spare either a boat or a man, so they borrowed a fisherman's boat, and in this the man Brown started off alone, like an idiot, on the chance that Barnett would be able to sail the boat back in spite of his broken leg.

"Meanwhile Barnett, who is a Whitstable man, had signalled a collier bound for his native town, and got taken off; so that the other keeper, Thomas Jeffreys, was left alone until Brown should turn up.

"But Brown never did turn up. The coast-guard helped him to put off and saw him well out to sea, and the keeper, Jeffreys, saw a sailing-boat with one man in her making for the lighthouse. Then a bank of fog came up and hid the boat, and when the fog cleared she was nowhere to be seen. Man and boat had vanished and left no sign."

"He may have been run down," Thorndyke suggested.

"He may," agreed the captain, "but no accident has been reported. The coast-guards think he may have capsized in a squall—they saw him make the sheet fast. But there weren't any squalls; the weather was quite calm."

"Was he all right and well when he put off?" inquired Thorndyke.

"Yes," replied the captain, "the coast-guards' report is highly circumstantial; in fact, it's full of silly details that have no bearing on anything. This is what they say." He pulled out an official letter and read: "'When last seen, the missing man was seated in the boat's stern to windward of the helm. He had belayed the sheet. He was holding a pipe and tobacco-pouch in his hands and steering with his elbow. He was filling the pipe from the tobacco-pouch.' There! 'He was holding the pipe in his hand,' mark you! not with his toes; and he was filling it from a tobacco-pouch, whereas you'd have expected him to fill it from a coalscuttle or a feeding-bottle. Bah!" The captain rammed the letter back in his pocket and puffed scornfully at his cigar.

"You are hardly fair to the coast-guard," said Thorndyke, laughing at the captain's vehemence. "The duty of a witness is to give all the facts, not a judicious selection."

"But, my dear sir," said Captain Grumpass, "what the deuce can it matter what the poor devil filled his pipe from?"

"Who can say?" answered Thorndyke. "It may turn out to be a highly material fact. One never knows beforehand. The value of a particular fact depends on its relation to the rest of the evidence."

"I suppose it does," grunted the captain; and he continued to smoke in reflective silence until we opened Black-wall Point, when he suddenly stood up.

"There's a steam trawler alongside our wharf," he announced. "Now what the deuce can she be doing there?" He scanned the little steamer attentively, and continued:

"They seem to be landing something, too. Just pass me those glasses, Polton. Why, hang me! it's a dead body! But why on earth are they landing it on our wharf? They must have known you were coming, doctor."

As the launch swept alongside the wharf, the captain sprang up lightly and approached the group gathered round the body. "What's this?" he asked. "Why have they brought this thing here?"

The master of the trawler, who had superintended the landing, proceeded to explain.

"It's one of your men, sir," said he. "We saw the body lying on the edge of the South Shingles Sand, close to the beacon, as we passed at low water, so we put off the boat and fetched it aboard. As there was nothing to identify the man by, I had a look in his pockets and found this letter."

He handed the captain an official envelope addressed to: "Mr. J. Brown, co Mr. Solly, Shepherd, Reculver, Kent."

"Why, this is the man we were speaking about, doctor," exclaimed Captain

Grumpass. "What a very singular coincidence. But what are we to do with the body?"

"You will have to write to the coroner," replied Thorndyke. "By the way, did you turn out all the pockets?" he asked, turning to the skipper of the trawler.

"No, sir," was the reply. "I found the letter in the first pocket that I felt in, so I didn't examine any of the others. Is there anything more that you want to know, sir?"

"Nothing but your name and address, for the coroner," replied Thorndyke, and the skipper, having given this information and expressed the hope that the coroner would not keep him "hanging about," returned to his vessel and pursued his way to Billingsgate.

"I wonder if you would mind having a look at the body of this poor devil, while Polton is showing us his contraptions," said Captain Grumpass.

"I can't do much without a coroner's order," replied Thorndyke; "but if it will give you any satisfaction, Jervis and I will make a preliminary inspection with pleasure."

"I should be glad if you would," said the captain. "We should like to know that the poor beggar met his end fairly."

The body was accordingly moved to a shed, and, as Polton was led away, carrying the black bag that contained his precious model, we entered the shed and commenced our investigation.

The deceased was a small, elderly man, decently dressed in a somewhat nautical fashion. He appeared to have been dead only two or three days, and the body, unlike the majority of sea-borne corpses, was uninjured by fish or crabs. There were no fractured bones or other gross injuries, and no wounds, excepting a rugged tear in the scalp at the back of the head.

"The general appearance of the body," said Thorndyke, when he had noted these particulars, "suggests death by drowning, though, of course, we can't give a definite opinion until a post mortem has been made."

"You don't attach any significance to that scalp-wound, then?" I asked.

"As a cause of death? No. It was obviously inflicted during life, but it seems to have been an oblique blow that spent its force on the scalp, leaving the skull uninjured. But it is very significant in another way."

"In what way?" I asked.

Thorndyke took out his pocket-case and extracted a pair of forceps. "Consider the circumstances," said he. "This man put off from the shore to go to the lighthouse, but never arrived there. The question is, where did he arrive?" As he spoke he stooped over the corpse and turned back the hair round the wound with the beak of the forceps. "Look at those white objects among the hair, Jervis, and inside the wound. They tell us something, I think."

I examined, through my lens, the chalky fragments to which he pointed.

"These seem to be bits of shells and the tubes of some marine worm," I said.

"Yes," he answered; "the broken shells are evidently those of the acorn barnacle, and the other fragments are mostly pieces of the tubes of the common serpula. The inference that these objects suggest is an important one. It is that this wound was produced by some body encrusted by acorn barnacles and serpula; that is to say, by a body that is periodically submerged. Now, what can that body be, and how can the deceased have knocked his head against it?"

"It might be the stem of a ship that ran him down," I suggested.

"I don't think you would find many serpulae on the stem of a ship," said Thorndyke. "The combination rather suggests some stationary object between tidemarks, such as a beacon. But one doesn't see how a man could knock his head against a beacon, while, on the other hand, there are no other stationary objects out in the estuary to knock against except buoys, and a buoy presents a flat surface that could hardly have produced this wound. By the way, we may as well see what there is in his pockets, though it is not likely that robbery had anything to do with his death."

"No," I agreed, "and I see his watch is in his pocket; quite a good silver one," I added, taking it out. "It has stopped at 12.13."

"That may be important," said Thorndyke, making a note of the fact; "but we had better examine the pockets one at a time, and put the things back when we have looked at them."

The first pocket that we turned out was the left hip-pocket of the monkey jacket. This was apparently the one that the skipper had rifled, for we found in it two letters, both bearing the crest of the Trinity House. These, of course, we returned without reading, and then passed on to the right pocket. The contents of this were common-place enough, consisting of a briar pipe, a moleskin pouch and a number of loose matches.

"Rather a casual proceeding, this," I remarked, "to carry matches loose in the pocket, and a pipe with them, too."

"Yes," agreed Thorndyke; "especially with these very inflammable matches. You notice that the sticks had been coated at the upper end with sulphur before the red phosphorous heads were put on. They would light with a touch, and would be very difficult to extinguish; which, no doubt, is the reason that this type of match is so popular among seamen, who have to light their pipes in all sorts of weather." As he spoke he picked up the pipe and looked at it reflectively, turning it over in his hand and peering into the bowl. Suddenly he glanced from the pipe to the dead man's face and then, with the forceps, turned back the lips to look into the mouth.

"Let us see what tobacco he smokes," said he.

I opened the sodden pouch and displayed a mass of dark, fine-cut tobacco. "It looks like shag," I said.

"Yes, it is shag," he replied; "and now we will see what is in the pipe. It has been only half-smoked out." He dug out the "dottle" with his pocket-knife onto a sheet of paper, and we both inspected it. Clearly it was not shag, for it consisted of coarsely-cut shreds and was nearly black.

"Shavings from a cake of 'hard,'" was my verdict, and Thorndyke agreed as he shot the fragments back into the pipe.

The other pockets yielded nothing of interest, except a pocket-knife, which Thorndyke opened and examined closely. There was not much money, though as much as one would expect, and enough to exclude the idea of robbery.

"Is there a sheath-knife on that strap?" Thorndyke asked, pointing to a narrow leather belt. I turned back the jacket and looked.

"There is a sheath," I said, "but no knife. It must have dropped out."

"That is rather odd," said Thorndyke. "A sailor's sheath-knife takes a deal of shaking out as a rule. It is intended to be used in working on the rigging when the man is aloft, so that he can get it out with one hand while he is holding on with the other. It has to be and usually is very secure, for the sheath holds half the handle as well as the blade. What makes one notice the matter in this case is that the man, as you see, carried a pocket-knife; and, as this would serve all the ordinary purposes of a knife, it seems to suggest that the sheath-knife was carried for defensive purposes: as a weapon, in fact. However, we can't get much further in the case without a post mortem, and here comes the captain."

Captain Grumpass entered the shed and looked down commiseratingly at the dead seaman.

"Is there anything, doctor, that throws any light on the man's disappearance?" he asked.

"There are one or two curious features in the case," Thorndyke replied; "but, oddly enough, the only really important point arises out of that statement of the coastguard's, concerning which you were so scornful."

"You don't say so!" exclaimed the captain.

"Yes," said Thorndyke; "the coast-guard states that when last seen deceased was filling his pipe from his tobacco-pouch. Now his pouch contains shag; but the pipe in his pocket contains hard cut."

"Is there no cake tobacco in any of the pockets?"

"Not a fragment. Of course, it is possible that he might have had a piece and used it up to fill the pipe; but there is no trace of any on the blade of his pocket-knife, and you know how this juicy black cake stains a knife-blade. His sheath-knife is missing, but he would hardly have used that to shred tobacco when he had a pocket-knife."

"No," assented the captain; "but are you sure he hadn't a second pipe?"

"There was only one pipe," replied Thorndyke, "and that was not his own."

"Not his own!" exclaimed the captain, halting by a huge, chequered buoy, to stare at my colleague. "How do you know it was not his own?"

"By the appearance of the vulcanite mouthpiece," said Thorndyke. "It showed deep tooth-marks; in fact, it was nearly bitten through. Now a man who bites through his pipe usually presents certain definite physical peculiarities, among which is, necessarily, a fairly good set of teeth. But the dead man had not a tooth in his head."

The captain cogitated a while, and then remarked: "I don't quite see the bearing of this."

"Don't you?" said Thorndyke. "It seems to me highly suggestive. Here is a man who, when last seen, was filling his pipe with a particular kind of tobacco. He is picked up dead, and his pipe contains a totally different kind of tobacco. Where did that tobacco come from? The obvious suggestion is that he had met someone."

"Yes, it does look like it," agreed the captain.

"Then," continued Thorndyke, "there is the fact that his sheath-knife is missing. That may mean nothing, but we have to bear it in mind. And there is another curious circumstance: there is a wound on the back of the head caused by a heavy bump against some body that was covered with acorn barnacles and marine worms. Now there are no piers or stages out in the open estuary. The question is, what could he have struck?"

"Oh, there is nothing in that," said the captain. "When a body has been washing about in a tide-way for close on three days—"

"But this is not a question of a body," Thorndyke interrupted. "The wound was made during life."

"The deuce it was!" exclaimed the captain. "Well, all I can suggest is that he must have fouled one of the beacons in the fog, stove in his boat and bumped his head, though, I must admit, that's rather a lame explanation." He stood for a minute gazing at his toes with a cogitative frown and then looked up at Thorndyke.

"I have an idea," he said. "From what you say, this matter wants looking into pretty carefully. Now, I am going down on the tender to-day to make inquiries on the spot. What do you say to coming with me as adviser—as a matter of business, of course—you and Dr. Jervis? I shall start about eleven; we shall be at the lighthouse by three o'clock, and you can get back to town to-night, if you want to. What do you say?"

"There's nothing to hinder us," I put in eagerly, for even at Bugsby's Hole the river looked very alluring on this summer morning.

"Very well," said Thorndyke, "we will come. Jervis is evidently hankering for a sea-trip, and so am I, for that matter."

"It's a business engagement, you know," the captain stipulated.

"Nothing of the kind," said Thorndyke; "it's unmitigated pleasure; the pleasure of the voyage and your high well-born society."

"I didn't mean that," grumbled the captain, "but, if you are coming as guests, send your man for your nightgear and let us bring you back to-morrow evening."

"We won't disturb Polton," said my colleague; "we can take the train from Blackwall and fetch our things ourselves. Eleven o'clock, you said?"

"Thereabouts," said Captain Grumpass; "but don't put yourselves out."

The means of communication in London have reached an almost undesirable state of perfection. With the aid of the snorting train and the tinkling, two-wheeled "gondola," we crossed and re-crossed the town with such celerity that it was barely eleven when we re-appeared on Trinity Wharf with a joint Gladstone and Thorndyke's little green case.

The tender had hauled out of Bow Creek, and now lay alongside the wharf with a great striped can buoy dangling from her derrick, and Captain Grumpass stood at the gangway, his jolly, red face beaming with pleasure. The buoy was safely stowed forward, the derrick hauled up to the mast, the loose shrouds re-hooked to the screw-lanyards, and the steamer, with four jubilant hoots, swung round and shoved her sharp nose against the incoming tide.

For near upon four hours the ever-widening stream of the "London River" unfolded its moving panorama. The smoke and smell of Woolwich Reach gave place to lucid air made soft by the summer haze; the grey huddle of factories fell away and green levels of cattle-spotted marsh stretched away to the high land bordering the river valley. Venerable training ships displayed their chequered hulls by the wooded shore, and whispered of the days of oak and hemp, when the tall three-decker, comely and majestic, with her soaring heights of canvas, like towers of ivory, had not yet given place to the mud-coloured saucepans that fly the white ensign now-a-days and devour the substance of the British taxpayer: when a sailor was a sailor and not a mere seafaring mechanic. Sturdily breasting the flood tide, the tender threaded her way through the endless procession of shipping; barges, billy-boys, schooners, brigs; lumpish Black-seamen, blue-funnelled China tramps, rickety Baltic barques with twirling windmills, gigantic liners, staggering under a mountain of top-hamper. Erith, Purfleet, Greenhithe, Grays greeted us and passed astern. The chimneys of Northfleet, the clustering roofs of Gravesend, the populous anchorage and the lurking batteries, were left behind, and, as we swung out of the Lower Hope, the wide expanse of sea reach spread out before us like a great sheet of blue-shot satin.

About half-past twelve the ebb overtook us and helped us on our way, as we could see by the speed with which the distant land slid past, and the freshening of the air as we passed through it.

But sky and sea were hushed in a summer calm. Balls of fleecy cloud hung aloft, motionless in the soft blue; the barges drifted on the tide with drooping sails, and a big, striped bell buoy—surmounted by a staff and cage and labelled, "Shivering Sand"—sat dreaming in the sun above its motionless reflection, to rouse for a moment as it met our wash, nod its cage drowsily, utter a solemn ding-dong, and fall asleep again.

It was shortly after passing the buoy that the gaunt shape of a screw-pile lighthouse began to loom up ahead, its dull-red paint turned to vermilion by the early afternoon sun. As we drew nearer, the name Girdler, painted in huge, white letters, became visible, and two men could be seen in the gallery around the lantern, inspecting us through a telescope.

"Shall you be long at the lighthouse, sir?" the master of the tender inquired of Captain Grumpass; "because we're going down, to the North-East Pan Sand to fix this new buoy and take up the old one."

"Then you'd better put us off at the lighthouse and come back for us when you've finished the job," was the reply. "I don't know how long we shall be."

The tender was brought to, a boat lowered, and a couple of hands pulled us across the intervening space of water.

"It will be a dirty climb for you in your shore-going clothes," the captain remarked—he was as spruce as a new pin himself, "but the stuff will all wipe off." We looked up at the skeleton shape. The falling tide had exposed some fifteen feet of the piles, and piles and ladder alike were swathed in sea-grass and encrusted with barnacles and worm-tubes. But we were not such town-sparrows as the captain seemed to think, for we both followed his lead without difficulty up the slippery ladder, Thorndyke clinging tenaciously to his little green case, from which he refused to be separated even for an instant.

"These gentlemen and I," said the captain, as we stepped on the stage at the head of the ladder, "have come to make inquiries about the missing man, James Brown. Which of you is Jeffreys?"

"I am, sir," replied a tall, powerful, square-jawed, beetle-browed man, whose left hand was tied up in a rough bandage.

"What have you been doing to your hand?" asked the captain.

"I cut it while I was peeling some potatoes," was the reply. "It isn't much of a cut, sir."

"Well, Jeffreys," said the captain, "Brown's body has been picked up and I want particulars for the inquest. You'll be summoned as a witness, I suppose, so come in and tell us all you know."

We entered the living-room and seated ourselves at the table. The captain opened a massive pocket-book, while Thorndyke, in his attentive, inquisitive fashion, looked about the odd, cabin-like room as if making a mental inventory of its contents.

Jeffreys' statement added nothing to what we already knew. He had seen a boat with one man in it making for the lighthouse. Then the fog had drifted up and he had lost sight of the boat. He started the fog-horn and kept a bright look-out, but the boat never arrived. And that was all he knew. He supposed that the man must have missed the lighthouse and been carried away on the ebb-tide, which was running strongly at the time.

"What time was it when you last saw the boat?" Thorndyke asked.

"About half-past eleven," replied Jeffreys.

"What was the man like?" asked the captain.

"I don't know, sir; he was rowing, and his back was towards me."

"Had he any kit-bag or chest with him?" asked Thorndyke.

"He'd got his chest with him," said Jeffreys.

"What sort of chest was it?" inquired Thorndyke.

"A small chest, painted green, with rope beckets."

"Was it corded?"

"It had a single cord round, to hold the lid down."

"Where was it stowed?"

"In the stern-sheets, sir."

"How far off was the boat when you last saw it?"

"About half-a-mile."

"Half-a-mile!" exclaimed the captain. "Why, how the deuce could you see that chest half-a-mile away?"

The man reddened and cast a look of angry suspicion at Thorndyke. "I was watching the boat through the glass, sir," he replied sulkily.

"I see," said Captain Grumpass. "Well, that will do, Jeffreys. We shall have to arrange for you to attend the inquest. Tell Smith I want to see him."

The examination concluded, Thorndyke and I moved our chairs to the window, which looked out over the sea to the east. But it was not the sea or the passing ships that engaged my colleague's attention. On the wall, beside the window, hung a rudely-carved pipe-rack containing five pipes. Thorndyke had noted it when we entered the room, and now, as we talked, I observed him regarding it from time to time with speculative interest.

"You men seem to be inveterate smokers," he remarked to the keeper, Smith, when the captain had concluded the arrangements for the "shift."

"Well, we do like our bit of 'baccy, sir, and that's a fact," answered Smith. "You see, sir," he continued, "it's a lonely life, and tobacco's cheap out here."

"How is that?" asked Thorndyke.

"Why, we get it given to us. The small craft from foreign, especially the Dutchmen, generally heave us a cake or two when they pass close. We're not ashore, you see, so there's no duty to pay."

"So you don't trouble the tobacconists much? Don't go in for cut tobacco?"

"No, sir; we'd have to buy it, and then the cut stuff wouldn't keep. No, it's hard-tack to eat out here and hard tobacco to smoke."

"I see you've got a pipe-rack, too, quite a stylish affair."

"Yes," said Smith, "I made it in my off-time. Keeps the place tidy and looks more ship-shape than letting the pipes lay about anywhere."

"Someone seems to have neglected his pipe," said Thorndyke, pointing to one at the end of the rack which was coated with green mildew.

"Yes; that's Parsons, my mate. He must have left it when he went off near a month ago. Pipes do go mouldy in the damp air out here."

"How soon does a pipe go mouldy if it is left untouched?" Thorndyke asked.

"It's according to the weather," said Smith. "When it's warm and damp they'll begin to go in about a week. Now here's Barnett's pipe that he's left behind—the man that broke his leg, you know, sir—it's just beginning to spot a little. He couldn't have used it for a day or two before he went."

"And are all these other pipes yours?"

"No, sir. This here one is mine. The end one is Jeffreys', and I suppose the middle one is his too, but I don't know it."

"You're a demon for pipes, doctor," said the captain, strolling up at this moment; "you seem to make a special study of them."

"'The proper study of mankind is man,'" replied Thorndyke, as the keeper retired, "and 'man' includes those objects on which his personality is impressed. Now a pipe is a very personal thing. Look at that row in the rack. Each has its own physiognomy which, in a measure, reflects the peculiarities of the owner. There is Jeffreys' pipe at the end, for instance. The mouth-piece is nearly bitten through, the bowl scraped to a shell and scored inside and the brim battered and chipped. The whole thing speaks of rude strength and rough handling. He chews the stem as he smokes, he scrapes the bowl violently, and he bangs the ashes out with unnecessary force. And the man fits the pipe exactly: powerful, square-jawed and, I should say, violent on occasion."

"Yes, he looks a tough customer, does Jeffreys," agreed the captain.

"Then," continued Thorndyke, "there is Smith's pipe, next to it; 'coked' up until the cavity is nearly filled and burnt all round the edge; a talker's pipe, constantly going out and being relit. But the one that interests me most is the middle one."

"Didn't Smith say that was Jeffreys' too?" I said.

"Yes," replied Thorndyke, "but he must be mistaken. It is the very opposite of Jeffreys' pipe in every respect. To begin with, although it is an old pipe, there is not a sign of any tooth-mark on the mouth-piece. It is the only one in the rack that is quite unmarked. Then the brim is quite uninjured: it has been handled gently, and the silver band is jet-black, whereas the band on Jeffreys' pipe is quite bright."

"I hadn't noticed that it had a band," said the captain. "What has made it so black?"

Thorndyke lifted the pipe out of the rack and looked at it closely. "Silver sulphide," said he, "the sulphur no doubt derived from something carried in the pocket."

"I see," said Captain Grumpass, smothering a yawn and gazing out of the window at the distant tender. "Incidentally it's full of tobacco. What moral do you draw from that?"

Thorndyke turned the pipe over and looked closely at the mouth-piece. "The moral is," he replied, "that you should see that your pipe is clear before you fill it." He pointed to the mouth-piece, the bore of which was completely stopped up with fine fluff.

"An excellent moral too," said the captain, rising with another yawn. "If you'll excuse me a minute I'll just go and see what the tender is up to. She seems to be crossing to the East Girdler." He reached the telescope down from its brackets and went out onto the gallery.

As the captain retreated, Thorndyke opened his pocket-knife, and, sticking the blade into the bowl of the pipe, turned the tobacco out into his hand.

"Shag, by Jove!" I exclaimed.

"Yes," he answered, poking it back into the bowl. "Didn't you expect it to be shag?"

"I don't know that I expected anything," I admitted. "The silver band was occupying my attention."

"Yes, that is an interesting point," said Thorndyke, "but let us see what the obstruction consists of." He opened the green case, and, taking out a dissecting needle, neatly extracted a little ball of fluff from the bore of the pipe. Laying this on a glass slide, he teased it out in a drop of glycerine and put on a cover-glass while I set up the microscope.

"Better put the pipe back in the rack," he said, as he laid the slide on the stage of the instrument. I did so and then turned, with no little excitement, to watch him as he examined the specimen. After a brief inspection he rose and waved his hand towards the microscope.

"Take a look at it, Jervis," he said.

I applied my eye to the instrument, and, moving the slide about, identified the constituents of the little mass of fluff. The ubiquitous cotton fibre was, of course, in evidence, and a few fibres of wool, but the most remarkable objects were two or three hairs—very minute hairs of a definite zigzag shape and having a flat expansion near the free end like the blade of a paddle.

"These are the hairs of some small animal," I said; "not a mouse or rat or any rodent, I should say. Some small insectivorous animal, I fancy. Yes! Of course! They are the hairs of a mole." I stood up, and, as the importance of the discovery flashed on me, I looked at my colleague in silence.

"Yes," he said, "they are unmistakable; and they furnish the keystone of the argument."

"You think that this is really the dead man's pipe, then?" I said.

"According to the law of multiple evidence," he replied, "it is practically a certainty. Consider the facts in sequence. Since there is no sign of mildew on it, this pipe can have been here only a short time, and must belong either to Barnett, Smith, Jeffreys or Brown. It is an old pipe, but it has no tooth-marks on it.

Therefore it has been used by a man who has no teeth. But Barnett, Smith and Jeffreys all have teeth and mark their pipes, whereas Brown has no teeth. The tobacco in it is shag. But these three men do not smoke shag, whereas Brown had shag in his pouch. The silver band is encrusted with sulphide; and Brown carried sulphur-tipped matches loose in his pocket with his pipe. We find hairs of a mole in the bore of the pipe; and Brown carried a moleskin pouch in the pocket in which he appears to have carried his pipe. Finally, Brown's pocket contained a pipe which was obviously not his and which closely resembled that of Jeffreys; it contained tobacco similar to that which Jeffreys smokes and different from that in Brown's pouch. It appears to me quite conclusive, especially when we add to this evidence the other items that are in our possession."

"What items are they?" I asked.

"First there is the fact that the dead man had knocked his head heavily against some periodically submerged body covered with acorn barnacles and serpulae. Now the piles of this lighthouse answer to the description exactly, and there are no other bodies in the neighbourhood that do: for even the beacons are too large to have produced that kind of wound. Then the dead man's sheath-knife is missing, and Jeffreys has a knife-wound on his hand. You must admit that the circumstantial evidence is overwhelming."

At this moment the captain bustled into the room with the telescope in his hand. "The tender is coming up towing a strange boat," he said. "I expect it's the missing one, and, if it is, we may learn something. You'd better pack up your traps and get ready to go on board."

We packed the green case and went out into the gallery, where the two keepers were watching the approaching tender; Smith frankly curious and interested, Jeffreys restless, fidgety and noticeably pale. As the steamer came opposite the lighthouse, three men dropped into the boat and pulled across, and one of them—the mate of the tender—came climbing up the ladder.

"Is that the missing boat?" the captain sang out.

"Yes, sir," answered the officer, stepping onto the staging and wiping his hands on the reverse aspect of his trousers, "we saw her lying on the dry patch of the East Girdler. There's been some hanky-panky in this job, sir."

"Foul play, you think, hey?"

"Not a doubt of it, sir. The plug was out and lying loose in the bottom, and we found a sheath-knife sticking into the kelson forward among the coils of the painter. It was stuck in hard as if it had dropped from a height."

"That's odd," said the captain. "As to the plug, it might have got out by accident."

"But it hadn't sir," said the mate. "The ballast-bags had been shifted along to get the bottom boards up. Besides, sir, a seaman wouldn't let the boat fill; he'd have put the plug back and baled out."

"That's true," replied Captain Grumpass; "and certainly the presence of the knife looks fishy. But where the deuce could it have dropped from, out in the open sea? Knives don't drop from the clouds—fortunately. What do you say, doctor?"

"I should say that it is Brown's own knife, and that it probably fell from this staging."

Jeffreys turned swiftly, crimson with wrath. "What d'ye mean?" he demanded. "Haven't I said that the boat never came here?"

"You have," replied Thorndyke; "but if that is so, how do you explain the fact that your pipe was found in the dead man's pocket and that the dead man's pipe is at this moment in your pipe-rack?"

The crimson flush on Jeffreys' face faded as quickly as it had come. "I don't know what you're talking about," he faltered.

"I'll tell you," said Thorndyke. "I will relate what happened and you shall check my statements. Brown brought his boat alongside and came up into the living-room, bringing his chest with him. He filled his pipe and tried to light it, but it was stopped and wouldn't draw. Then you lent him a pipe of yours and filled it for him. Soon afterwards you came out on this staging and quarrelled. Brown defended himself with his knife, which dropped from his hand into the boat. You pushed him off the staging and he fell, knocking his head on one of the piles. Then you took the plug out of the boat and sent her adrift to sink, and you flung the chest into the sea. This happened about ten minutes past twelve. Am I right?"

Jeffreys stood staring at Thorndyke, the picture of amazement and consternation; but he uttered no word in reply. "Am I right?" Thorndyke repeated.

"Strike me blind!" muttered Jeffreys. "Was you here, then? You talk as if you had been. Anyhow," he continued, recovering somewhat, "you seem to know all about it. But you're wrong about one thing. There was no quarrel. This chap, Brown, didn't take to me and he didn't mean to stay out here. He was going to put off and go ashore again and I wouldn't let him. Then he hit out at me with his knife and I knocked it out of his hand and he staggered backwards and went overboard."

"And did you try to pick him up?" asked the captain.

"How could I," demanded Jeffreys, "with the tide racing down and me alone on the station? I'd never have got back."

"But what about the boat, Jeffreys? Why did you scuttle her?"

"The fact is," replied Jeffreys, "I got in a funk, and I thought the simplest plan was to send her to the cellar and know nothing about it. But I never shoved him over. It was an accident, sir; I swear it!"

"Well, that sounds a reasonable explanation," said the captain. "What do you say, doctor?"

"Perfectly reasonable," replied Thorndyke, "and, as to its truth, that is no affair of ours."

"No. But I shall have to take you off, Jeffreys, and hand you over to the police.

You understand that?"

"Yes, sir, I understand," answered Jeffreys.

"That was a queer case, that affair on the Girdler," remarked Captain Grumpass, when he was spending an evening with us some six months later. "A pretty easy let off for Jeffreys, too—eighteen months, wasn't it?"

"Yes, it was a very queer case indeed," said Thorndyke. "There was something behind that 'accident,' I should say. Those men had probably met before."

"So I thought," agreed the captain. "But the queerest part of it to me was the way you nosed it all out. I've had a deep respect for briar pipes since then. It was a remarkable case," he continued. "The way in which you made that pipe tell the story of the murder seems to me like sheer enchantment."

"Yes," said I, "it spoke like the magic pipe—only that wasn't a tobacco-pipe—in the German folk-story of the 'Singing Bone.' Do you remember it? A peasant found the bone of a murdered man and fashioned it into a pipe. But when he tried to play on it, it burst into a song of its own—

*"'My brother slew me and buried my bones*
*Beneath the sand and under the stones.'"*

"A pretty story," said Thorndyke, "and one with an excellent moral. The inanimate things around us have each of them a song to sing to us if we are but ready with attentive ears."

# CHAPTER IV.

## A WASTREL'S ROMANCE

### PART I.
### THE SPINSTERS' GUEST

THE lingering summer twilight was fast merging into night as a solitary cyclist, whose evening-dress suit was thinly disguised by an overcoat, rode slowly along a pleasant country road. From time to time he had been overtaken and passed by a carriage, a car or a closed cab from the adjacent town, and from the festive garb of the occupants he had made shrewd guesses at their destination. His own objective was a large house, standing in somewhat extensive grounds just off the road, and the peculiar circumstances that surrounded his visit to it caused him to ride more and more slowly as he approached his goal.

Willowdale—such was the name of the house—was, tonight, witnessing a temporary revival of its past glories. For many months it had been empty and a notice-board by the gate-keeper's lodge had silently announced its forlorn state; but to-night, its rooms, their bare walls clothed in flags and draperies, their floors waxed or carpeted, would once more echo the sound of music and cheerful voices and vibrate to the tread of many feet. For on this night the spinsters of Raynesford were giving a dance; and chief amongst the spinsters was Miss Halliwell, the owner of Willowdale.

It was a great occasion. The house was large and imposing; the spinsters were many and their purses were long. The guests were numerous and distinguished, and included no less a person than Mrs. Jehu B. Chater. This was the crowning triumph of the function, for the beautiful American widow was the lion (or should we say lioness?) of the season. Her wealth was, if not beyond the dreams of avarice, at least beyond the powers of common British arithmetic, and her diamonds were, at once, the glory and the terror of her hostesses.

All these attractions notwithstanding, the cyclist approached the vicinity of Willowdale with a slowness almost hinting at reluctance; and when, at length, a curve of the road brought the gates into view, he dismounted and halted irresolutely. He was about to do a rather risky thing, and, though by no means a man of weak nerve, he hesitated to make the plunge.

The fact is, he had not been invited.

Why, then, was he going? And how was he to gain admittance? To which questions the answer involves a painful explanation.

Augustus Bailey lived by his wits. That is the common phrase, and a stupid phrase it is. For do we not all live by our wits, if we have any? And does it need any specially brilliant wits to be a common rogue? However, such as his wits were, Augustus Bailey lived by them, and he had not hitherto made a fortune.

The present venture arose out of a conversation overheard at a restaurant table and an invitation-card carelessly laid down and adroitly covered with the menu. Augustus had accepted the invitation that he had not received (on a sheet of Hotel Cecil notepaper that he had among his collection of stationery) in the name of Geoffrey Harrington-Baillie; and the question that exercised his mind at the moment was, would he or would he not be spotted? He had trusted to the number of guests and the probable inexperience of the hostesses. He knew that the cards need not be shown, though there was the awkward ceremony of announcement.

But perhaps it wouldn't get as far as that. Probably not, if his acceptance had been detected as emanating from an uninvited stranger.

He walked slowly towards the gates with growing discomfort. Added to his nervousness as to the present were certain twinges of reminiscence. He had once held a commission in a line regiment—not for long, indeed; his "wits" had been too much for his brother officers—but there had been a time when he would have come to such a gathering as this an invited guest. Now, a common thief, he was sneaking in under a false name, with a fair prospect of being ignominiously thrown out by the servants.

As he stood hesitating, the sound of hoofs on the road was followed by the aggressive bellow of a motor-horn. The modest twinkle of carriage lamps appeared round the curve and then the glare of acetylene headlights. A man came out of the lodge and drew open the gates; and Mr. Bailey, taking his courage in both hands, boldly trundled his machine up the drive.

Half-way up—it was quite a steep incline—the car whizzed by; a large Napier filled with a bevy of young men who economized space by sitting on the backs of the seats and on one another's knees. Bailey looked at them and decided that this was his chance, and, pushing forward, he saw his bicycle safely bestowed in the empty coach-house and then hurried on to the cloak-room. The young men had arrived there before him and, as he entered, were gaily peeling off their overcoats and flinging them down on a table. Bailey followed their example, and, in his eagerness to enter the reception-room with the crowd, let his attention wander from the business of the moment, and, as he pocketed the ticket and hurried away, he failed to notice that the bewildered attendant had put his hat with another man's coat and affixed his duplicate to them both.

"Major Podbury, Captain Barker-Jones, Captain Sparker, Mr. Watson, Mr. Goldsmith, Mr. Smart, Mr. Harrington-Baillie!"

As Augustus swaggered up the room, hugging the party of officers and quaking inwardly, he was conscious that his hostesses glanced from one man to another with more than common interest.

But at that moment the footman's voice rang out, sonorous and clear—

"Mrs. Chater, Colonel Grumpier!" and, as all eyes were turned towards the new arrivals, Augustus made his bow and passed into the throng. His little game of bluff had "come off," after all.

He withdrew modestly into the more crowded portion of the room, and there took up a position where he would be shielded from the gaze of his hostesses. Presently, he reflected, they would forget him, if they had really thought about him at all, and then he would see what could be done in the way of business. He was still rather shaky, and wondered how soon it would be decent to steady his nerves with a "refresher." Meanwhile he kept a sharp look-out over the shoulders of neighbouring guests, until a movement in the crowd of guests disclosed Mrs. Chater shaking hands with the presiding spinster. Then Augustus got a most uncommon surprise.

He knew her at the first glance. He had a good memory for faces, and Mrs. Chater's face was one to remember. Well did he recall the frank and lovely American girl with whom he had danced at the regimental ball years ago. That was in the old days when he was a subaltern, and before that little affair of the pricked court-cards that brought his military career to an end. They had taken a mutual liking, he remembered, that sweet-faced Yankee maid and he had danced many dances and had sat out others, to talk mystical nonsense which, in their innocence, they had believed to be philosophy. He had never seen her since. She had come into his life and gone out of it again, and he had forgotten her name, if he had ever known it. But here she was, middle-aged now, it was true, but still beautiful and a great personage withal. And, ye gods! what diamonds! And here was he, too, a common rogue, lurking in the crowd that he might, perchance, snatch a pendant or "pinch" a loose brooch.

Perhaps she might recognize him. Why not? He had recognized her. But that would never do. And thus reflecting, Mr. Bailey slipped out to stroll on the lawn and smoke a cigarette. Another man, somewhat older than himself, was pacing to and fro thoughtfully, glancing from time to time through the open windows into the brilliantly-lighted rooms. When they had passed once or twice, the stranger halted and addressed him.

"This is the best place on a night like this," he remarked; "it's getting hot inside already. But perhaps you're keen on dancing."

"Not so keen as I used to be," replied Bailey; and then, observing the hungry look that the other man was bestowing on his cigarette, he produced his case and offered it.

"Thanks awfully!" exclaimed the stranger, pouncing with avidity on the open case. "Good Samaritan, by Jove. Left my case in my overcoat. Hadn't the cheek to ask, though I was starving for a smoke." He inhaled luxuriously, and, blowing out a cloud of smoke, resumed: "These chits seem to be running the show pretty well, h'm? Wouldn't take it for an empty house to look at it, would you?"

"I have hardly seen it," said Bailey; "only just come, you know."

"We'll have a look round, if you like," said the genial stranger, "when we've finished our smoke, that is. Have a drink too; may cool us a bit. Know many people here?"

"Not a soul," replied Bailey. "My, hostess doesn't seem to have turned up."

"Well, that's easily remedied," said the stranger. "My daughter's one of the spinsters—Granby, my name; when we've had a drink, I'll make her find you a partner—that is, if you care for the light fantastic."

"I should like a dance or two," said Bailey, "though I'm getting a bit past it now, I suppose. Still, it doesn't do to chuck up the sponge prematurely."

"Certainly not," Granby agreed jovially; "a man's as young as he feels. Well, come and have a drink and then we'll hunt up my little girl." The two men flung away the stumps of their cigarettes and headed for the refreshments.

The spinsters' champagne was light, but it was well enough if taken in sufficient quantity; a point to which Augustus? and Granby too—paid judicious attention; and when he had supplemented the wine with a few sandwiches, Mr. Bailey felt in notably better spirits. For, to tell the truth, his diet, of late, had been somewhat meagre. Miss Granby, when found, proved to be a blonde and guileless "flapper" of some seventeen summers, childishly eager to play her part of hostess with due dignity; and presently Bailey found himself gyrating through the eddying crowd in company with a comely matron of thirty or thereabouts.

The sensations that this novel experience aroused rather took him by surprise. For years past he had been living a precarious life of mean and sordid shifts that oscillated between mere shabby trickery and downright crime; now conducting a paltry swindle just inside the pale of the law, and now, when hard pressed, descending to actual theft; consorting with shady characters, swindlers and knaves and scurvy rogues like himself; gambling, borrowing, cadging and, if need be, stealing, and always slinking abroad with an apprehensive eye upon "the man in blue."

And now, amidst the half-forgotten surroundings, once so familiar; the gaily-decorated rooms, the rhythmic music, the twinkle of jewels, the murmur of gliding feet and the rustle of costly gowns, the moving vision of honest gentlemen and fair ladies; the shameful years seemed to drop away and leave him to take up the thread of his life where it had snapped so disastrously. After all, these were his own people. The seedy knaves in whose steps he had walked of late were but aliens met by the way.

He surrendered his partner, in due course, with regret—which was mutual—to an inarticulate subaltern, and was meditating another pilgrimage to the refreshment-room, when he felt a light touch upon his arm. He turned swiftly. A touch on the arm meant more to him than to some men. But it was no wooden-faced plain-clothes man that he confronted; it was only a lady. In short, it was Mrs. Chater, smiling nervously and a little abashed by her own boldness.

"I expect you've forgotten me," she began apologetically, but Augustus interrupted her with an eager disclaimer.

"Of course I haven't," he said; "though I have forgotten your name, but I remember that Portsmouth dance as well as if it were yesterday; at least one incident in it—the only one that was worth remembering. I've often hoped that I might meet you again, and now, at last, it has happened."

"It's nice of you to remember," she rejoined. "I've often and often thought of that evening and all the wonderful things that we talked about. You were a nice boy then; I wonder what you are like now. What a long time ago it is!"

"Yes," Augustus agreed gravely, "it is a long time. I know it myself; but when I look at you, it seems as if it could only have been last season."

"Oh, fie!" she exclaimed. "You are not simple as you used to be. You didn't flatter then; but perhaps there wasn't the need." She spoke with gentle reproach, but her pretty face flushed with pleasure nevertheless, and there was a certain wistfulness in the tone of her concluding sentence.

"I wasn't flattering," Augustus replied, quite sincerely; "I knew you directly you entered the room and marvelled that Time had been so gentle with you. He hasn't been as kind to me."

"No. You have gotten a few grey hairs, I see, but after all, what are grey hairs to a man? Just the badges of rank, like the crown on your collar or the lace on your cuffs, to mark the steps of your promotion—for I guess you'll be a colonel by now."

"No," Augustus answered quickly, with a faint flush, "I left the army some years ago."

"My! what a pity!" exclaimed Mrs. Chater. "You must tell me all about it—but not now. My partner will be looking for me. We will sit out a dance and have a real gossip. But I've forgotten your name—never could recall it, in fact, though that didn't prevent me from remembering you; but, as our dear W. S. remarks, 'What's in a name—'"

"Ah, indeed," said Mr. Harrington-Baillie; and apropos of that sentiment, he added: "Mine is Rowland—Captain Rowland. You may remember it now."

Mrs. Chater did not, however, and said so. "Will number six do?" she asked, opening her programme; and, when Augustus had assented, she entered his provisional name, remarking complacently: "We'll sit out and have a right-down good talk, and you shall tell me all about yourself and if you still think the same about free-will and personal responsibility. You had very lofty ideals, I remember, in those days, and I hope you have still. But one's ideals get rubbed down rather faint in the friction of life. Don't you think so?"

"Yes, I am afraid you're right," Augustus assented gloomily. "The wear and tear of life soon fetches the gilt off the gingerbread. Middle age is apt to find us a bit patchy, not to say naked."

"Oh, don't be pessimistic," said Mrs. Chater; "that is the attitude of the disappointed idealist, and I am sure you have no reason, really, to be disappointed in yourself. But I must run away now. Think over all the things you have to tell me, and don't forget that it is number six." With a bright smile and a friendly nod she sailed away, a vision of glittering splendour, compared with which Solomon in all his glory was a mere matter of commonplace bullion.

The interview, evidently friendly and familiar, between the unknown guest and the famous American widow had by no means passed unnoticed; and in other circumstances, Bailey might have endeavoured to profit by the reflected glory that enveloped him. But he was not in search of notoriety; and the same evasive instinct that had led him to sink Mr. Harrington-Baillie in Captain Rowland, now advised him to withdraw his dual personality from the vulgar gaze. He had come here on very definite business. For the hundredth time he was "stony-broke," and it was the hope of picking up some "unconsidered trifles" that had brought him. But, somehow, the atmosphere of the place had proved unfavourable. Either opportunities were lacking or he failed to seize them. In any case, the game pocket that formed an unconventional feature of his dress-coat was still empty, and it looked as if a pleasant evening and a good supper were all that he was likely to get. Nevertheless, be his conduct never so blameless, the fact remained that he was an uninvited guest, liable at any moment to be ejected as an impostor, and his recognition by the widow had not rendered this possibility any the more remote.

He strayed out onto the lawn, whence the grounds fell away on all sides. But there were other guests there, cooling themselves after the last dance, and the light from the rooms streamed through the windows, illuminating their figures, and among them, that of the too-companionable Granby. Augustus quickly drew away from the lighted area, and, chancing upon a narrow path, strolled away along it in the direction of a copse or shrubbery that he saw ahead. Presently he came to an ivy-covered arch, lighted by one or two fairy lamps, and, passing through this, he entered a winding path, bordered by trees and shrubs and but faintly lighted by an occasional coloured lamp suspended from a branch.

Already he was quite clear of the crowd; indeed, the deserted condition of the pleasant retreat rather surprised him, until he reflected that to couples desiring seclusion there were whole ranges of untenanted rooms and galleries available in the empty house.

The path sloped gently downwards for some distance; then came a long flight of rustic steps and, at the bottom, a seat between two trees. In front of the seat the path extended in a straight line, forming a narrow terrace; on the right the ground sloped up steeply towards the lawn; on the left it fell away still more steeply towards the encompassing wall of the grounds; and on both sides it was covered with trees and shrubs.

Bailey sat down on the seat to think over the account of himself that he should present to Mrs. Chater. It was a comfortable seat, built into the trunk of an elm, which formed one end and part of the back. He leaned against the tree, and, taking out his silver case, selected a cigarette. But it remained unlighted between his fingers as he sat and meditated upon his unsatisfactory past and the melancholy tale of what might have been. Fresh from the atmosphere of refined opulence that pervaded the dancing-rooms, the throng of well-groomed men and dainty women, his mind travelled back to his sordid little flat in Bermondsey, encompassed by poverty and squalor, jostled by lofty factories, grimy with the smoke of the river and the reek from the great chimneys. It was a hideous contrast. Verily the way of the transgressor was not strewn with flowers.

At that point in his meditations he caught the sound of voices and footsteps on the path above and rose to walk on along the path. He did not wish to be seen wandering alone in the shrubbery. But now a woman's laugh sounded from somewhere down the path. There were people approaching that way too. He put the cigarette back in the case and stepped round behind the seat, intending to retreat in that direction, but here the path ended, and beyond was nothing but a rugged slope down to the wall thickly covered with bushes. And while he was hesitating, the sound of feet descending the steps and the rustle of a woman's dress left him to choose between staying where he was or coming out to confront the new-comers. He chose the former, drawing up close behind the tree to wait until they should have passed on.

But they were not going to pass on. One of them—a woman—sat down on the seat, and then a familiar voice smote on his ear.

"I guess I'll rest here quietly for a while; this tooth of mine is aching terribly; and, see here, I want you to go and fetch me something. Take this ticket to the cloak-room and tell the woman to give you my little velvet bag. You'll find in it a bottle of chloroform and a packet of cotton-wool."

"But I can't leave you here all alone, Mrs. Chater," her partner expostulated.

"I'm not hankering for society just now," said Mrs. Chater. "I want that chloroform. Just you hustle off and fetch it, like a good boy. Here's the ticket."

The young officer's footsteps retreated rapidly, and the voices of the couple advancing along the path grew louder. Bailey, cursing the chance that had placed him in his ridiculous and uncomfortable position, heard them approach and pass on up the steps; and then all was silent, save for an occasional moan from Mrs. Chater and the measured creaking of the seat as she rocked uneasily to and fro. But the young man was uncommonly prompt in the discharge of his mission, and in a very few minutes Bailey heard him approaching at a run along the path above and then bounding down the steps.

"Now I call that real good of you," said the widow gratefully. "You must have run like the wind. Cut the string of the packet and then leave me to wrestle with this tooth."

"But I can't leave you here all—"

"Yes, you can," interrupted Mrs. Chater. "There won't be any one about—the next dance is a waltz. Besides, you must go and find your partners."

"Well, if you'd really rather be alone," the subaltern began; but Mrs. Chater interrupted him.

"Of course I would, when I'm fixing up my teeth. Now go along, and a thousand thanks for your kindness."

With mumbled protestations the young officer slowly retired, and Bailey heard his reluctant feet ascending the steps. Then a deep silence fell on the place in which the rustle of paper and the squeak of a withdrawn cork seemed loud and palpable. Bailey had turned with his face towards the tree, against which he leaned with his lips parted scarcely daring to breathe. He cursed himself again and again for having thus entrapped himself for no tangible reason, and longed to get away. But there was no escape now without betraying himself. He must wait for the woman to go.

Suddenly, beyond the edge of the tree, a hand appeared holding an open packet of cotton-wool. It laid the wool down on the seat, and, pinching off a fragment, rolled it into a tiny ball. The fingers of the hand were encircled by rings, its wrist enclosed by a broad bracelet; and from rings and bracelet the light of the solitary fairy-lamp, that hung from a branch of the tree, was reflected in prismatic sparks. The hand was withdrawn and Bailey stared dreamily at the square pad of cotton-wool. Then the hand came again into view. This time it held a small phial which it laid softly on the seat, setting the cork beside it. And again the light flashed in many-coloured scintillations from the encrusting gems.

Bailey's knees began to tremble, and a chilly moisture broke out upon his forehead.

The hand drew back, but, as it vanished, Bailey moved his head silently until his face emerged from behind the tree. The woman was leaning back, her head resting against the trunk only a few inches away from his face. The great stones of the tiara flashed in his very eyes. Over her shoulder, he could even see the gorgeous pendant, rising and falling on her bosom with ever-changing fires; and both her raised hands were a mass of glitter and sparkle, only the deeper and richer for the subdued light.

His heart throbbed with palpable blows that drummed aloud in his ears. The sweat trickled clammily down his face, and he clenched his teeth to keep them from chattering. An agony of horror—of deadly fear—was creeping over him? a terror of the dreadful impulse that was stealing away his reason and his will.

The silence was profound. The woman's soft breathing, the creak of her bodice, were plainly—grossly—audible; and he checked his own breath until he seemed on the verge of suffocation.

Of a sudden through the night air was borne faintly the dreamy music of a waltz. The dance had begun. The distant sound but deepened the sense of solitude in this deserted spot.

Bailey listened intently. He yearned to escape from the invisible force that seemed to be clutching at his wrists, and dragging him forward inexorably to his doom.

He gazed down at the woman with a horrid fascination. He struggled to draw back out of sight—and struggled in vain.

Then, at last, with a horrible, stealthy deliberation, a clammy, shaking hand crept forward towards the seat. Without a sound it grasped the wool, and noiselessly, slowly drew back. Again it stole forth. The fingers twined snakily around the phial, lifted it from the seat and carried it back into the shadow.

After a few seconds it reappeared and softly replaced the bottle—now half empty. There was a brief pause. The measured cadences of the waltz stole softly through the quiet night and seemed to keep time with the woman's breathing. Other sound there was none. The place was wrapped in the silence of the grave.

Suddenly, from the hiding-place, Bailey leaned forward over the back of the seat. The pad of cotton-wool was in his hand.

The woman was now leaning back as if dozing, and her hands rested in her lap. There was a swift movement. The pad was pressed against her face and her head dragged back against the chest of the invisible assailant. A smothered gasp burst from her hidden lips as her hands flew up to clutch at the murderous arm; and then came a frightful struggle, made even more frightful by the gay and costly trappings of the writhing victim. And still there was hardly a sound; only muffled gasps, the rustle of silk, the creaking of the seat, the clink of the falling bottle and, afar off, with dreadful irony, the dreamy murmur of the waltz.

The struggle was but brief. Quite suddenly the jewelled hands dropped, the head lay resistless on the crumpled shirt-front, and the body, now limp and inert, began to slip forward off the seat. Bailey, still grasping the passive head, climbed over the back of the seat and, as the woman slid gently to the ground, he drew away the pad and stooped over her. The struggle was over now; the mad fury of the moment was passing swiftly into the chill of mortal fear.

He stared with incredulous horror into the swollen face, but now so comely, the sightless eyes that but a little while since had smiled into his with such kindly recognition.

He had done this! He, the sneaking wastrel, discarded of all the world, to whom this sweet woman had held out the hand of friendship. She had cherished his memory, when to all others he was sunk deep under the waters of oblivion. And he had killed her—for to his ear no breath of life seemed to issue from those purple lips.

A sudden hideous compunction for this irrevocable thing that he had done surged through him, and he stood up clutching at his damp hair with a hoarse cry that was like the cry of the damned.

The jewels passed straightaway out of his consciousness. Everything was forgotten now but the horror of this unspeakable thing that he had done. Remorse incurable and haunting fear were all that were left to him.

The sound of voices far away along the path aroused him, and the vague horror that possessed him materialized into abject bodily fear. He lifted the limp body to the edge of the path and let it slip down the steep declivity among the bushes. A soft, shuddering sigh came from the parted lips as the body turned over, and he paused a moment to listen. But there was no other sound of life. Doubtless that sigh was only the result of the passive movement.

Again he stood for an instant as one in a dream, gazing at the huddled shape half hidden by the bushes, before he climbed back to the path; and even then he looked back once more, but now she was hidden from sight. And, as the voices drew nearer, he turned, and ran up the rustic steps.

As he came out on the edge of the lawn the music ceased, and, almost immediately, a stream of people issued from the house. Shaken as he was, Bailey yet had wits enough left to know that his clothes and hair were disordered and that his appearance must be wild. Accordingly he avoided the dancers, and, keeping to the margin of the lawn, made his way to the cloak-room by the least frequented route. If he had dared, he would have called in at the refreshment-room, for he was deadly faint and his limbs shook as he walked. But a haunting fear pursued him and, indeed, grew from moment to moment. He found himself already listening for the rumour of the inevitable discovery.

He staggered into the cloak-room, and, flinging his ticket down on the table, dragged out his watch. The attendant looked at him curiously and, pausing with the ticket in his hand, asked sympathetically: "Not feeling very well, sir?"

"No," said Bailey. "So beastly hot in there."

"You ought to have a glass of champagne, sir, before you start," said the man.

"No time," replied Bailey, holding out a shaky hand for his coat. "Shall lose my train if I'm not sharp."

At this hint the attendant reached down the coat and hat, holding up the former for its owner to slip his arms into the sleeves. But Bailey snatched it from him, and, flinging it over his arm, put on his hat and hurried away to the coachhouse. Here, again, the attendant stared at him in astonishment, which was not lessened when Bailey, declining his offer to help him on with his coat, bundled the latter under his arm, clicked the lever of the "variable" on to the ninety gear, sprang onto the machine and whirled away down the steep drive, a grotesque vision of flying coat-tails.

"You haven't lit your lamp, sir," roared the attendant; but Bailey's ears were deaf to all save the clamour of the expected pursuit.

Fortunately the drive entered the road obliquely, or Bailey must have been flung into the opposite hedge. As it was, the machine, rushing down the slope, flew out into the road with terrific velocity; nor did its speed diminish then, for its rider, impelled by mortal terror, trod the pedals with the fury of a madman. And still, as the machine whizzed along the dark and silent road, his ears were strained to catch the clatter of hoofs or the throb of a motor from behind.

He knew the country well, in fact, as a precaution, he had cycled over the district only the day before; and he was ready, at any suspicious sound, to slip down any of the lanes or byways, secure of finding his way. But still he sped on, and still no sound from the rear came to tell him of the dread discovery.

When he had ridden about three miles, he came to the foot of a steep hill. Here he had to dismount and push his machine up the incline, which he did at such speed that he arrived at the top quite breathless. Before mounting again he determined to put on his coat, for his appearance was calculated to attract attention, if nothing more. It was only half-past eleven, and presently he would pass through the streets of a small town. Also he would light his lamp. It would be fatal to be stopped by a patrol or rural constable.

Having lit his lamp and hastily put on his coat he once more listened intently, looking back over the country that was darkly visible from the summit of the hill. No moving lights were to be seen, no ringing hoofs or throbbing engines to be heard, and, turning to mount, he instinctively felt in his overcoat pocket for his gloves.

A pair of gloves came out in his hand, but he was instantly conscious that they were not his. A silk muffler was there also; a white one. But his muffler was black.

With a sudden shock of terror he thrust his hand into the ticket-pocket, where he had put his latch-key. There was no key there; only an amber cigar-holder, which he had never seen before. He stood for a few moments in utter consternation. He had taken the wrong coat. Then he had left his own coat behind. A cold sweat of fear broke out afresh on his face as he realized this. His Yale latch-key was in its pocket; not that that mattered very much. He had a duplicate at home, and, as to getting in, well, he knew his own outside door and his tool-bag contained one or two trifles not usually found in cyclists' tool-bags. The question was whether that coat contained anything that could disclose his identity. And then suddenly he remembered, with a gasp of relief, that he had carefully turned the pockets out before starting.

No; once let him attain the sanctuary of his grimy little flat, wedged in as it was between the great factories by the river-side, and he would be safe: safe from everything but the horror of himself, and the haunting vision of a jewelled figure huddled up in a silken heap beneath the bushes.

With a last look round he mounted his machine, and, driving it over the brow of the hill, swept away into the darkness.

## PART II.
## MUNERA PULVERIS
## (RELATED BY CHRISTOPHER JERVIS, M.D.)

IT is one of the drawbacks of medicine as a profession that one is never rid of one's responsibilities. The merchant, the lawyer, the civil servant, each at the appointed time locks up his desk, puts on his hat and goes forth a free man with an interval of uninterrupted leisure before him. Not so the doctor. Whether at work or at play, awake or asleep, he is the servant of humanity, at the instant disposal of friend or stranger alike whose need may make the necessary claim.

When I agreed to accompany my wife to the spinsters' dance at Raynesford, I imagined that, for that evening, at least, I was definitely off duty; and in that belief I continued until the conclusion of the eighth dance. To be quite truthful, I was not sorry when the delusion was shattered. My last partner was a young lady of a slanginess of speech that verged on the inarticulate. Now it is not easy to exchange ideas in "pidgin" English; and the conversation of a person to whom all things are either "ripping" or "rotten" is apt to lack subtlety. In fact, I was frankly bored; and, reflecting on the utility of the humble sandwich as an aid to conversation, I was about to entice my partner to the refreshment-room when I felt someone pluck at my sleeve. I turned quickly and looked into the anxious and rather frightened face of my wife.

"Miss Halliwell is looking for you," she said. "A lady has been taken ill. Will you come and see what is the matter?" She took my arm and, when I had made my apologies to my partner, she hurried me on to the lawn.

"It's a mysterious affair," my wife continued. "The sick lady is a Mrs. Chater, a very wealthy American widow. Edith Halliwell and Major Podbury found her lying in the shrubbery all alone and unable to give any account of herself. Poor Edith is dreadfully upset. She doesn't know what to think."

"What do you mean?" I began; but at this moment Miss Halliwell, who was waiting by an ivy-covered rustic arch, espied us and ran forward.

"Oh, do hurry, please, Dr. Jervis," she exclaimed; "such a shocking thing has happened. Has Juliet told you?" Without waiting for an answer, she darted through the arch and preceded us along a narrow path at the curious, flat-footed, shambling trot common to most adult women. Presently we descended a flight of rustic steps which brought us to a seat, from whence extended a straight path cut like a miniature terrace on a steep slope, with a high bank rising to the right and declivity falling away to the left. Down in the hollow, his head and shoulders appearing above the bushes, was a man holding in his hand a fairy-lamp that he had apparently taken down from a tree. I climbed down to him, and, as I came round the bushes, I perceived a richly-dressed woman lying huddled on the ground. She was not completely insensible, for she moved slightly at my approach, muttering a few words in thick, indistinct accents. I took the lamp from the man, whom I assumed to be Major Podbury, and, as he delivered it to me with a significant glance and a faint lift of the eyebrows, I understood Miss Halliwell's agitation. Indeed—for one horrible moment I thought that she was right—that the prostrate woman was intoxicated. But when I approached nearer, the flickering light of the lamp made visible a square reddened patch on her face, like the impression of a mustard plaster, covering the nose and mouth; and then I scented mischief of a more serious kind.

"We had better carry her up to the seat," I said, handing the lamp to Miss Halliwell. "Then we can consider moving her to the house." The major and I lifted the helpless woman and, having climbed cautiously up to the path, laid her on the seat.

"What is it, Dr. Jervis?" Miss Halliwell whispered.

"I can't say at the moment," I replied; "but it's not what you feared."

"Thank God for that!" was her fervent rejoinder. "It would have been a shocking scandal."

I took the dim lamp and once more bent over the half-conscious woman.

Her appearance puzzled me not a little. She looked like a person recovering from an anaesthetic, but the square red patch on her face, recalling, as it did, the

Burke murders, rather suggested suffocation. As I was thus reflecting, the light of the lamp fell on a white object lying on the ground behind the seat, and holding the lamp forward, I saw that it was a square pad of cotton-wool. The coincidence of its shape and size with that of the red patch on the woman's face instantly struck me, and I stooped down to pick it up; and then I saw, lying under the seat, a small bottle. This also I picked up and held in the lamplight. It was a one-ounce phial, quite empty, and was labelled "Methylated Chloroform." Here seemed to be a complete explanation of the thick utterance and drunken aspect; but it was an explanation that required, in its turn, to be explained. Obviously no robbery had been committed, for the woman literally glittered with diamonds. Equally obviously she had not administered the chloroform to herself.

There was nothing for it but to carry her indoors and await her further recovery, so, with the major's help, we conveyed her through the shrubbery and kitchen garden to a side door, and deposited her on a sofa in a half-furnished room.

Here, under the influence of water dabbed on her face and the plentiful use of smelling salts, she quickly revived, and was soon able to give an intelligible account of herself.

The chloroform and cotton-wool were her own. She had used them for an aching tooth; and she was sitting alone on the seat with the bottle and the wool beside her when the incomprehensible thing had happened. Without a moment's warning a hand had come from behind her and pressed the pad of wool over her nose and mouth. The wool was saturated with chloroform, and she had lost consciousness almost immediately.

"You didn't see the person, then?" I asked.

"No, but I know he was in evening dress, because I felt my head against his shirt-front."

"Then," said I, "he is either here still or he has been to the cloak-room. He couldn't have left the place without an overcoat."

"No, by Jove!" exclaimed the major; "that's true. I'll go and make inquiries." He strode away all agog, and I, having satisfied myself that Mrs. Chater could be left safely, followed him almost immediately.

I made my way straight to the cloak-room, and here I found the major and one or two of his brother officers putting on their coats in a flutter of gleeful excitement.

"He's gone," said Podbury, struggling frantically into his overcoat; "went off nearly an hour ago on a bicycle. Seemed in a deuce of a stew, the attendant says, and no wonder. We're goin' after him in our car. Care to join the hunt?"

"No, thanks. I must stay with the patient. But how do you know you're after the right man?"

"Isn't any other. Only one Johnnie's left. Besides—here, confound it! you've given me the wrong coat!" He tore off the garment and handed it back to the attendant, who regarded it with an expression of dismay.

"Are you sure, sir?" he asked.

"Perfectly," said the major. "Come, hurry up, my man."

"I'm afraid, sir," said the attendant, "that the gentleman who has gone has taken your coat. They were on the same peg, I know. I am very sorry, sir."

The major was speechless with wrath. What the devil was the good of being sorry; and how the deuce was he to get his coat back—

"But," I interposed, "if the stranger has got your coat, then this coat must be his."

"I know," said Podbury; "but I don't want his beastly coat."

"No," I replied, "but it may be useful for identification."

This appeared to afford the bereaved officer little consolation, but as the car was now ready, he bustled away, and I, having directed the man to put the coat away in a safe place, went back to my patient.

Mrs. Chater was by now fairly recovered, and had developed a highly vindictive interest in her late assailant. She even went so far as to regret that he had not taken at least some of her diamonds, so that robbery might have been added to the charge of attempted murder, and expressed the earnest hope that the officers would not be foolishly gentle in their treatment of him when they caught him.

"By the way, Dr. Jervis," said Miss Halliwell, "I think I ought to mention a rather curious thing that happened in connection with this dance. We received an acceptance from a Mr. Harrington-Baillie, who wrote from the Hotel Cecil. Now I am certain that no such name was proposed by any of the spinsters."

"But didn't you ask them?" I inquired.

"Well, the fact is," she replied, "that one of them, Miss Waters, had to go abroad suddenly, and we had not got her address; and as it was possible that she might have invited him, I did not like to move in the matter. I am very sorry I didn't now. We may have let in a regular criminal? though why he should have wanted to murder Mrs. Chater I cannot imagine."

It was certainly a mysterious affair, and the mystery was in no wise dispelled by the return of the search party an hour later. It seemed that the bicycle had been tracked for a couple of miles towards London, but then, at the cross-roads, the tracks had become hopelessly mixed with the impressions of other machines and the officers, after cruising about vaguely for a while, had given up the hunt and returned.

"You see, Mrs. Chater," Major Podbury explained apologetically, "the fellow must have had a good hour's start, and that would have brought him pretty close to London."

"Do you mean to tell me," exclaimed Mrs. Chater, regarding the major with hardly-concealed contempt, "that that villain has got off scot-free?"

"Looks rather like it," replied Podbury, "but if I were you I should get the man's description from the attendants who saw him and go up to Scotland Yard to-morrow. They may know the Johnny there, and they may even recognize the coat if you take it with you."

"That doesn't seem very likely," said Mrs. Chater, and it certainly did not; but since no better plan could be suggested the lady decided to adopt it; and I supposed that I had heard the last of the matter.

In this, however, I was mistaken. On the following day, just before noon, as I was drowsily considering the points in a brief dealing with a question of survivorship, while Thorndyke drafted his weekly lecture, a smart rat-tat at the door of our chambers announced a visitor. I rose wearily—I had had only four hours' sleep—and opened the door, whereupon there sailed into the room no less a person than Mrs. Chater, followed by Superintendent Miller, with a grin on his face and a brown-paper parcel under his arm.

The lady was not in the best of tempers, though wonderfully lively and alert considering the severe shock that she had suffered so recently, and her disapproval of Miller was frankly obvious.

"Dr. Jervis has probably told you about the attempt to murder me last night," she said, when I had introduced her to my colleague. "Well, now, will you believe it? I have been to the police, I have given them a description of the murderous villain, and I have even shown them the very coat that he wore, and they tell me that nothing can be done. That, in short, this scoundrel must be allowed to go his way free and unmolested."

"You will observe, doctor," said Miller, "that this lady has given us a description that would apply to fifty per cent, of the middle-class men of the United Kingdom, and has shown us a coat without a single identifying mark of any kind on it, and expects us to lay our hands on the owner without a solitary clue to guide us. Now we are not sorcerers at the Yard; we're only policemen. So I have taken the liberty of referring Mrs. Chater to you." He grinned maliciously and laid the parcel on the table.

"And what do you want me to do?" Thorndyke asked quietly.

"Why sir," said Miller, "there is a coat. In the pockets were a pair of gloves, a muffler, a box of matches, a tram-ticket and a Yale key. Mrs. Chater would like to know whose coat it is." He untied the parcel with his eye cocked at our rather disconcerted client, and Thorndyke watched him with a faint smile.

"This is very kind of you, Miller," said he, "but I think a clairvoyant would be more to your purpose."

The superintendent instantly dropped his facetious manner.

"Seriously, sir," he said, "I should be glad if you would take a look at the coat. We have absolutely nothing to go on, and yet we don't want to give up the case. I have gone through it most thoroughly and can't find any clue to guide us. Now I know that nothing escapes you, and perhaps you might notice something that I have overlooked; something that would give us a hint where to start on, our inquiry. Couldn't you turn the microscope on it, for instance?" he added, with a deprecating smile.

Thorndyke reflected, with an inquisitive eye on the coat. I saw that the problem was not without its attractions to him; and when the lady seconded Miller's request with persuasive eagerness, the inevitable consequence followed.

"Very well," he said. "Leave the coat with me for an hour or so and I will look it over. I am afraid there is not the remotest chance of our learning anything from it, but even so, the examination will have done no harm. Come back at two o'clock; I shall be ready to report my failure by then."

He bowed our visitors out and, returning to the table, looked down with a quizzical smile on the coat and the large official envelope containing articles from the pockets.

"And what does my learned brother suggest?" he asked, looking up at me.

"I should look at the tram-ticket first," I replied, "and then—well, Miller's suggestion wasn't such a bad one; to explore the surface with the microscope."

"I think we will take the latter measure first," said he. "The tram-ticket might create a misleading bias. A man may take a tram anywhere, whereas the indoor dust on a man's coat appertains mostly to a definite locality."

"Yes," I replied; "but the information that it yields is excessively vague."

"That is true," he agreed, taking up the coat and envelope to carry them to the laboratory, "and yet, you know, Jervis, as I have often pointed out, the evidential value of dust is apt to be under-estimated. The naked-eye appearances? which are the normal appearances—are misleading. Gather the dust, say, from a table-top, and what have you? A fine powder of a characterless grey, just like any other dust from any other table-top. But, under the microscope, this grey powder is resolved into recognizable fragments of definite substances, which fragments may often be traced with certainty to the masses from which they have been detached. But you know all this as well as I do."

"I quite appreciate the value of dust as evidence in certain circumstances," I replied, "but surely the information that could be gathered from dust on the coat of an unknown man must be too general to be of any use in tracing the owner."

"I am afraid you are right," said Thorndyke, laying the coat on the laboratory bench; "but we shall soon see, if Polton will let us have his patent dust-extractor."

The little apparatus to which my colleague referred was the invention of our ingenious laboratory assistant, and resembled in principle the "vacuum cleaners" used for restoring carpets. It had, however, one special feature: the receiver was made to admit a microscope-slide, and on this the dust-laden air was delivered from a jet.

The "extractor" having been clamped to the bench by its proud inventor, and a wetted slide introduced into the receiver, Thorndyke applied the nozzle of the instrument to the collar of the coat while Polton worked the pump. The slide was then removed and, another having been substituted, the nozzle was applied to the right sleeve near the shoulder, and the exhauster again worked by Polton. By repeating this process, half-a-dozen slides were obtained charged with dust from different parts of the garment, and then, setting up our respective microscopes, we proceeded to examine the samples.

A very brief inspection showed me that this dust contained matter not usually met with—at any rate, in appreciable quantities. There were, of course, the usual fragments of wool, cotton and other fibres derived from clothing and furniture, particles of straw, husk, hair, various mineral particles and, in fact, the ordinary constituents of dust from clothing. But, in addition to these, and in much greater quantity, were a number of other bodies, mostly of vegetable origin and presenting well-defined characters in considerable variety, and especially abundant were various starch granules.

I glanced at Thorndyke and observed he was already busy with a pencil and a slip of paper, apparently making a list of the objects visible in the field of the microscope. I hastened to follow his example, and for a time we worked on in silence. At length my colleague leaned back in his chair and read over his list.

"This is a highly interesting collection, Jervis," he remarked. "What do you find on your slides out of the ordinary?"

"I have quite a little museum here," I replied, referring to my list. "There is, of course, chalk from the road at Raynesford. In addition to this I find various starches, principally wheat and rice, especially rice, fragments of the cortices of several seeds, several different stone-cells, some yellow masses that look like turmeric, black pepper resin-cells, one 'port wine' pimento cell, and one or two particles of graphite."

"Graphite!" exclaimed Thorndyke. "I have found no graphite, but I have found traces of cocoa—spiral vessels and starch grains—and of hops—one fragment of leaf and several lupulin glands. May I see the graphite?"

I passed him the slide and he examined it with keen interest. "Yes," he said, "this is undoubtedly graphite, and no less than six particles of it. We had better go over the coat systematically. You see the importance of this?"

"I see that this is evidently factory dust and that it may fix a locality, but I don't see that it will carry us any farther."

"Don't forget that we have a touchstone," said he; and, as I raised my eyebrows inquiringly, he added, "The Yale latchkey. If we can narrow the locality down sufficiently, Miller can make a tour of the front doors."

"But can we?" I asked incredulously. "I doubt it."

"We can try," answered Thorndyke. "Evidently some of the substances are distributed over the entire coat, inside and out, while others, such as the graphite, are present only on certain parts. We must locate those parts exactly and then consider what this special distribution means." He rapidly sketched out on a sheet of paper a rough diagram of the coat, marking each part with a distinctive letter, and then, taking a number of labelled slides, he wrote a single letter on each. The samples of dust taken on the slides could thus be easily referred to the exact spots whence they had been obtained.

Once more we set to work with the microscope, making, now and again, an addition to our lists of discoveries, and, at the end of nearly an hour's strenuous search, every slide had been examined and the lists compared.

"The net result of the examination," said Thorndyke, "is this. The entire coat, inside and out, is evenly powdered with the following substances: Rice-starch in abundance, wheat-starch in less abundance, and smaller quantities of the starches of ginger, pimento and cinnamon; bast fibre of cinnamon, various seed cortices, stone-cells of pimento, cinnamon, cassia and black pepper, with other fragments of similar origin, such as resin-cells and ginger pigment—not turmeric. In addition there are, on the right shoulder and sleeve, traces of cocoa and hops, and on the back below the shoulders a few fragments of graphite. Those are the data; and now, what are the inferences? Remember this is not mere surface dust, but the accumulation of months, beaten into the cloth by repeated brushing—dust that nothing but a vacuum apparatus could extract."

"Evidently," I said, "the particles that are all over the coat represent dust that is floating in the air of the place where the coat habitually hangs. The graphite has obviously been picked up from a seat and the cocoa and hops from some factories that the man passes frequently, though I don't see why they are on the right side only."

"That is a question of time," said Thorndyke, "and incidentally throws some light on our friend's habits. Going from home, he passes the factories on his right; returning home, he passes them on his left, but they have then stopped work. However, the first group of substances is the more important as they indicate the locality of his dwelling—for he is clearly not a workman or factory employee. Now rice-starch, wheat-starch and a group of substances collectively designated 'spices' suggest a rice-mill, a flour-mill and a spice factory. Polton, may I trouble you for the Post Office Directory?"

He turned over the leaves of the "Trades" section and resumed: "I see there are four rice-mills in London, of which the largest is Carbutt's at Dockhead. Let us look at the spice-factories." He again turned over the leaves and read down the list of names. "There are six spice-grinders in London," said he. "One of them, Thomas Williams & Co., is at Dockhead. None of the others is near any rice-mill. The next question is as to the flour-mill. Let us see. Here are the names of several flour millers, but none of them is near either a rice-mill or a spice-grinder, with one exception: Seth Taylor's, St. Saviour's Flour Mills, Dockhead."

"This is really becoming interesting," said I.

"It has become interesting," Thorndyke retorted. "You observe that at Dockhead we find the peculiar combination of factories necessary to produce the composite dust in which this coat has hung; and the directory shows us that this particular combination exists nowhere else in London. Then the graphite, the cocoa and the hops tend to confirm the other suggestions. They all appertain to industries of the locality. The trams which pass Dockhead, also, to my knowledge, pass at no great distance from the black-lead works of Pearce Duff & Co. in Rouel Road, and will probably collect a few particles of black-lead on the seats in certain states of the wind. I see, too, that there is a cocoa factory—Payne's—in Goat Street, Horsleydown, which lies to the right of the tram line going west, and I have noticed several hop warehouses on the right side of Southwark Street, going west. But these are mere suggestions; the really important data are the rice and flour mills and the spice-grinders, which seem to point unmistakably to Dockhead."

"Are there any private houses at Dockhead?" I asked.

"We must look up the 'Street' list," he replied. "The Yale latch-key rather suggests a flat, and a flat with a single occupant, and the probable habits of our absent friend offer a similar suggestion." He ran his eye down the list and presently turned to me with his finger on the page.

"If the facts that we have elicited—the singular series of agreements with the required conditions—are only a string of coincidences, here is another. On the south side of Dockhead, actually next door to the spice-grinders and opposite to Carbutt's rice-mills, is a block of workmen's flats, Hanover Buildings. They fulfil the conditions exactly. A coat hung in a room in those flats, with the windows open (as they would probably be at this time of year), would be exposed to the air containing a composite dust of precisely the character of that which we have found. Of course, the same conditions obtain in other dwellings in this part of Dockhead, but the probability is in favour of the buildings. And that is all that we can say. It is no certainty. There may be some radical fallacy in our reasoning. But, on the face of it, the chances are a thousand to one that the door that that key will open is in some part of Dockhead, and most probably in Hanover Buildings. We must leave the verification to Miller."

"Wouldn't it be as well to look at the tram-ticket?" I asked.

"Dear me!" he exclaimed. "I had forgotten the ticket. Yes, by all means." He opened the envelope and, turning its contents out on the bench, picked up the dingy slip of paper. After a glance at it he handed it to me. It was punched for the journey from Tooley Street to Dockhead.

"Another coincidence," he remarked; "and by yet another, I think I hear Miller knocking at our door."

It was the superintendent, and, as we let him into the room, the hum of a motor-car entering from Tudor Street announced the arrival of Mrs. Chater. We waited for her at the open door, and, as she entered, she held out her hands impulsively.

"Say, now, Dr. Thorndyke," she exclaimed, "have you gotten something to tell us?"

"I have a suggestion to make," replied Thorndyke. "I think that if the superintendent will take this key to Hanover Buildings, Dockhead, Bermondsey, he may possibly find a door that it will fit."

"The deuce!" exclaimed Miller. "I beg your pardon, madam; but I thought I had gone through that coat pretty completely. What was it that I had overlooked, sir? Was there a letter hidden in it, after all?"

"You overlooked the dust on it, Miller; that is all," said Thorndyke.

"Dust!" exclaimed the detective, staring round-eyed at my colleague. Then he chuckled softly. "Well," said he, "as I said before, I'm not a sorcerer; I'm only a policeman." He picked up the key and asked: "Are you coming to see the end of it, sir?"

"Of course he is coming," said Mrs. Chater, "and Dr. Jervis too, to identify the man. Now that we have gotten the villain we must leave him no loophole for escape."

Thorndyke smiled dryly. "We will come if you wish it, Mrs. Chater," he said, "but you mustn't look upon our quest as a certainty. We may have made an entire miscalculation, and I am, in fact, rather curious to see if the result works out correctly. But even if we run the man to earth, I don't see that you have much evidence against him. The most that you can prove is that he was at the house and that he left hurriedly."

Mrs. Chater regarded my colleague for a moment in scornful silence, and then, gathering up her skirts, stalked out of the room. If there is one thing that the average woman detests more than another, it is an entirely reasonable man.

The big car whirled us rapidly over Blackfriars Bridge into the region of the Borough, whence we presently turned down Tooley Street towards Bermondsey.

As soon as Dockhead came into view, the detective, Thorndyke and I, alighted and proceeded on foot, leaving our client, who was now closely veiled, to follow at a little distance in the car. Opposite the head of St. Saviour's Dock, Thorndyke halted and, looking over the wall, drew my attention to the snowy powder that had lodged on every projection on the backs of the tall buildings and on the decks of the barges that were loading with the flour and ground rice. Then, crossing the road, he pointed to the wooden lantern above the roof of the spice works, the louvres of which were covered with greyish-buff dust.

"Thus," he moralized, "does commerce subserve the ends of justice—at least, we hope it does," he added quickly, as Miller disappeared into the semi-basement of the buildings.

We met the detective returning from his quest as we entered the building.

"No go there," was his report. "We'll try the next floor."

This was the ground-floor, or it might be considered the first floor. At any rate, it yielded nothing of interest, and, after a glance at the doors that opened on the landing, he strode briskly up the stone stairs. The next floor was equally unrewarding, for our eager inspection disclosed nothing but the gaping keyhole associated with the common type of night-latch.

"What name was you wanting?" inquired a dusty knight of industry who emerged from one of the flats.

"Muggs," replied Miller, with admirable promptness.

"Don't know 'im," said the workman. "I expect it's farther up."

Farther up we accordingly went, but still from each door the artless grin of the invariable keyhole saluted us with depressing monotony. I began to grow uneasy, and when the fourth floor had been explored with no better result, my anxiety became acute. A mare's nest may be an interesting curiosity, but it brings no kudos to its discoverer.

"I suppose you haven't made any mistake, sir?" said Miller, stopping to wipe his brow.

"It's quite likely that I have." replied Thorndyke, with unmoved composure. "I only proposed this search as a tentative proceeding, you know."

The superintendent grunted. He was accustomed—as was I too, for that matter—to regard Thorndyke's "tentative suggestions" as equal to another man's certainties.

"It will be an awful suck-in for Mrs. Chater if we don't find him after all," he growled as we climbed up the last flight. "She's counted her chickens to a feather." He paused at the head of the stairs and stood for a few moments looking round the landing. Suddenly he turned eagerly, and, laying his hand on Thorndyke's arm, pointed to a door in the farthest corner.

"Yale lock!" he whispered impressively.

We followed him silently as he stole on tip-toe across the landing, and watched him as he stood for an instant with the key in his land looking gloatingly at the brass disc. We saw him softly apply the nose of the fluted key-blade to the crooked slit in the cylinder, and, as we watched, it slid noiselessly up to the shoulder. The detective looked round with a grin of triumph, and, silently withdrawing the key, stepped back to us.

"You've run him to earth, sir," he whispered, "but I don't think Mr. Fox is at home. He can't have got back yet."

"Why not?" asked Thorndyke.

Miller waved his hand towards the door. "Nothing has been disturbed," he replied. "There's not a mark on the paint. Now he hadn't got the key, and you can't pick a Yale lock. He'd have had to break in, and he hasn't broken in."

Thorndyke stepped up to the door and softly pushed in the flap of the letter-slit, through which he looked into the flat.

"There's no letter-box," said he. "My dear Miller, I would undertake to open that door in five minutes with a foot of wire and a bit of resined string."

Miller shook his head and grinned once more. "I am glad you're not on the lay, sir; you'd be one too many for us. Shall we signal to the lady?"

I went out onto the gallery and looked down at the waiting car. Mrs. Chater was staring intently up at the building, and the little crowd that the car had collected stared alternately at the lady and at the object of her regard. I wiped my face with my handkerchief—the signal agreed upon—and she instantly sprang out of the car, and in an incredibly short time she appeared on the landing, purple and gasping, but with the fire of battle flashing from her eyes.

"We've found his flat, madam," said Miller, "and we're going to enter. You're not intending to offer any violence, I hope," he added, noting with some uneasiness the lady's ferocious expression.

"Of course I'm not," replied Mrs. Chater. "In the States ladies don't have to avenge insults themselves. If you were American men you'd hang the ruffian from his own bedpost."

"We're not American men, madam," said the superintendent stiffly. "We are law-abiding Englishmen, and, moreover, we are all officers of the law. These gentlemen are barristers and I am a police officer."

With this preliminary caution, he once more inserted the key, and as he turned it and pushed the door open, we all followed him into the sitting-room.

"I told you so, sir," said Miller, softly shutting the door; "he hasn't come back yet."

Apparently he was right. At any rate, there was no one in the flat, and we proceeded unopposed on our tour of inspection. It was a miserable spectacle, and, as we wandered from one squalid room to another, a feeling of pity for the starving wretch into whose lair we were intruding stole over me and began almost to mitigate the hideousness of his crime. On all sides poverty—utter, grinding poverty—stared us in the face. It looked at us hollow-eyed in the wretched sitting-room, with its bare floor, its solitary chair and tiny deal table; its unfurnished walls and windows destitute of blind or curtain. A piece of Dutch cheese-rind on the table, scraped to the thinness of paper, whispered of starvation; and famine lurked in the gaping cupboard, in the empty bread-tin, in the tea-caddy with its pinch of dust at the bottom, in the jam-jar, wiped clean, as a few crumbs testified, with a crust of bread. There was not enough food in the place to furnish a meal for a healthy mouse.

The bedroom told the same tale, but with a curious variation. A miserable truckle-bed with a straw mattress and a cheap jute rug for bed-clothes, an orange-case, stood on end, for a dressing-table, and another, bearing a tin washing-bowl, formed the wretched furniture. But the suit that hung from a couple of nails was well-cut and even fashionable, though shabby; and another suit lay on the floor, neatly folded and covered with a newspaper; and, most incongruous of all, a silver cigarette-case reposed on the dressing-table.

"Why on earth does this fellow starve," I exclaimed, "when he has a silver case to pawn?"

"Wouldn't do," said Miller. "A man doesn't pawn the implements of his trade."

Mrs. Chater, who had been staring about her with the mute amazement of a wealthy woman confronted, for the first time, with abject poverty, turned suddenly to the superintendent. "This can't be the man!" she exclaimed. "You have made some mistake. This poor creature could never have made his way into a house like Willowdale."

Thorndyke lifted the newspaper. Beneath it was a dress suit with the shirt, collar and tie all carefully smoothed out and folded. Thorndyke unfolded the shirt and pointed to the curiously crumpled front. Suddenly he brought it close to his eye and then, from the sham diamond stud, he drew a single hair—a woman's hair.

"That is rather significant," said he, holding it up between his finger and thumb; and Mrs. Chater evidently thought so too, for the pity and compunction suddenly faded from her face, and once more her eyes flashed with vindictive fire.

"I wish he would come," she exclaimed viciously. "Prison won't be much hardship to him after this, but I want to see him in the dock all the same."

"No," the detective agreed, "it won't hurt him much to swap this for Portland. Listen!"

A key was being inserted into the outer door, and as we all stood like statues, a man entered and closed the door after him. He passed the door of the bedroom without seeing us, and with the dragging steps of a weary, dispirited man. Almost immediately we heard him go to the kitchen and draw water into some vessel. Then he went back to the sitting-room.

"Come along," said Miller, stepping silently towards the door. We followed closely, and as he threw the door open, we looked in over his shoulder.

The man had seated himself at the table, on which now lay a hunk of household bread resting on the paper in which he had brought it, and a tumbler of water. He half rose as the door opened, and as if petrified remained staring at Miller with a dreadful expression of terror upon his livid face.

At this moment I felt a hand on my arm, and Mrs. Chater brusquely pushed past me into the room. But at the threshold she stopped short; and a singular change crept over the man's ghastly face, a change so remarkable that I looked involuntarily from him to our client. She had turned, in a moment, deadly pale, and her face had frozen into an expression of incredulous horror.

The dramatic silence was broken by the matter-of-fact voice of the detective.

"I am a police officer," said he, "and I arrest you for—?"

A peal of hysterical laughter from Mrs. Chater interrupted him, and he looked at her in astonishment. "Stop, stop!" she cried in a shaky voice. "I guess we've made a ridiculous mistake. This isn't the man. This gentleman is Captain Rowland, an old friend of mine."

"I'm sorry he's a friend of yours," said Miller, "because I shall have to ask you to appear against him."

"You can ask what you please," replied Mrs. Chater. "I tell you he's not the man."

The superintendent rubbed his nose and looked hungrily at his quarry. "Do I understand, madam," he asked stiffly, "that you refuse to prosecute?"

"Prosecute!" she exclaimed. "Prosecute my friends for offences that I know they have not committed? Certainly I refuse."

The superintendent looked at Thorndyke, but my colleague's countenance had congealed into a state of absolute immobility and was as devoid of expression as the face of a Dutch clock.

"Very well," said Miller, looking sourly at his watch. "Then we have had our trouble for nothing. I wish you good afternoon, madam."

"I am sorry I troubled you, now," said Mrs. Chater.

"I am sorry you did," was the curt reply; and the superintendent, flinging the key on the table, stalked out of the room.

As the outer door slammed the man sat down with an air of bewilderment; and then, suddenly flinging his arms on the table, he dropped his head on them and burst into a passion of sobbing.

It was very embarrassing. With one accord Thorndyke and I turned to go, but Mrs. Chater motioned us to stay. Stepping over to the man, she touched him lightly on the arm.

"Why did you do it?" she asked in a tone of gentle reproach.

The man sat up and flung out one arm in an eloquent gesture that comprehended the miserable room and the yawning cupboard.

"It was the temptation of a moment," he said. "I was penniless, and those accursed diamonds were thrust in my face; they were mine for the taking. I was mad, I suppose."

"But why didn't you take them?" she said. "Why didn't you?"

"I don't know. The madness passed; and then—when I saw you lying there—? Oh, God! Why don't you give me up to the police?" He laid his head down and sobbed afresh.

Mrs. Chater bent over him with tears standing in her pretty grey eyes. "But tell me," she said, "why didn't you take the diamonds? You could if you'd liked, I suppose?"

"What good were they to me?" he demanded passionately. "What did anything matter to me? I thought you were dead."

"Well, I'm not, you see," she said, with a rather tearful smile; "I'm just as well as an old woman like me can expect to be. And I want your address, so that I can write and give you some good advice."

The man sat up and produced a shabby cardcase from his pocket, and, as he took out a number of cards and spread them out like the "hand" of a whist player, I caught a twinkle in Thorndyke's eye.

"My name is Augustus Bailey," said the man. He selected the appropriate card, and, having scribbled his address on it with a stump of lead pencil, relapsed into his former position.

"Thank you," said Mrs. Chater, lingering for a moment by the table. "Now we'll go. Good-bye, Mr. Bailey. I shall write to-morrow, and you must attend seriously to the advice of an old friend."

I held open the door for her to pass out and looked back before I turned to follow. Bailey still sat sobbing quietly, with his hand resting on his arms; and a little pile of gold stood on the corner of the table.

"I expect, doctor," said Mrs. Chater, as Thorndyke handed her into the car, "you've written me down a sentimental fool."

Thorndyke looked at her with an unwonted softening of his rather severe face and answered quietly, "It is written: Blessed are the Merciful."

# CHAPTER V.

## THE OLD LAG

### PART I.
### THE CHANGED IMMUTABLE

AMONG the minor and purely physical pleasures of life, I am disposed to rank very highly that feeling of bodily comfort that one experiences on passing from the outer darkness of a wet winter's night to a cheerful interior made glad by mellow lamplight and blazing hearth. And so I thought when, on a dreary November night, I let myself into our chambers in the Temple and found my friend smoking his pipe in slippered ease, by a roaring fire, and facing an empty armchair evidently placed in readiness for me.

As I shed my damp overcoat, I glanced inquisitively at my colleague, for he held in his hand an open letter, and I seemed to perceive in his aspect something meditative and self-communing—something, in short, suggestive of a new case.

"I was just considering," he said, in answer to my inquiring look, "whether I am about to become an accessory after the fact. Read that and give me your opinion."

He handed me the letter, which I read aloud.

> *"Dear sir,—I am in great danger and distress. A warrant has been issued for my arrest on a charge of which I am entirely innocent. Can I come and see you, and will you let me leave in safety? The bearer will wait for a reply."*

"I said 'Yes,' of course; there was nothing else to do," said Thorndyke. "But if I let him go, as I have promised to do, I shall be virtually conniving at his escape."

"Yes, you are taking a risk," I answered. "When is he coming?"

"He was due five minutes ago—and I rather think—yes, here he is."

A stealthy tread on the landing was followed by a soft tapping on the outer door.

Thorndyke rose and, flinging open the inner door, unfastened the massive "oak."

"Dr. Thorndyke?" inquired a breathless, quavering voice.

"Yes, come in. You sent me a letter by hand?"

"I did, sir," was the reply; and the speaker entered, but at the sight of me he stopped short.

"This is my colleague, Dr. Jervis," Thorndyke explained. "You need have no—?"

"Oh, I remember him," our visitor interrupted in a tone of relief. "I have seen you both before, you know, and you have seen me too—though I don't suppose you recognize me," he added, with: a sickly smile.

"Frank Belfield?" asked Thorndyke, smiling also.

Our visitor's jaw fell and he gazed at my colleague in sudden dismay.

"And I may remark," pursued Thorndyke, "that for a man in your perilous position, you are running most unnecessary risks. That wig, that false beard and those spectacles—through which you obviously cannot see—are enough to bring the entire police force at your heels. It is not wise for a man who is wanted by the police to make up as though he had just escaped from a comic opera."

Mr. Belfield seated himself with a groan, and, taking off his spectacles, stared stupidly from one of us to the other.

"And now tell us about your little affair," said Thorndyke. "You say that you are innocent?"

"I swear it, doctor," replied Belfield; adding, with great earnestness, "And you may take it from me, sir, that if I was not, I shouldn't be here. It was you that convicted me last time, when I thought myself quite safe, so I know your ways too well to try to gammon you."

"If you are innocent," rejoined Thorndyke, "I will do what I can for you; and if you are not—well, you would have been wiser to stay away."

"I know that well enough," said Belfield, "and I am only afraid that you won't believe what I am going to tell you."

"I shall keep an open mind, at any rate," replied Thorndyke.

"If you only will," groaned Belfield, "I shall have a look in, in spite of them all. You know, sir, that I have been on the crook, but I have paid in full. That job when you tripped me up was the last of it—it was, sir, so help me. It was a woman that changed me—the best and truest woman on God's earth. She said she would marry me when I came out if I promised her to go straight and live an honest life. And she kept her promise—and I have kept mine. She found me work as clerk in a warehouse and I have stuck to it ever since, earning fair wages and building up a good character as an honest, industrious man. I thought all was going well, and that I was settled for life, when only this very morning the whole thing comes tumbling about my ears like a house of cards."

"What happened this morning, then?" asked Thorndyke.

"Why, I was on my way to work when, as I passed the police station, I noticed a bill with the heading 'Wanted' and a photograph. I stopped for a moment to look at it, and you may imagine my feelings when I recognized my own portrait—taken at Holloway—and read my own name and description. I did not stop to read the bill through, but ran back home and told my wife, and she ran down to the station and read the bill carefully. Good God, sir! What do you think I am wanted for?" He paused for a moment, and then replied in breathless tones to his own question: "The Camberwell murder!"

Thorndyke gave a low whistle.

"My wife knows I didn't do it," continued Belfield, "because I was at home all the evening and night; but what use is a man's wife to prove an alibi?"

"Not much, I fear," Thorndyke admitted; "and you have no other witness?"

"Not a soul. We were alone all the evening."

"However," said Thorndyke, "if you are innocent—as I am assuming—the evidence against you must be entirely circumstantial and your alibi may be quite sufficient. Have you any idea of the grounds of suspicion against you?"

"Not the faintest. The papers said that the police had an excellent clue, but they did not say what it was. Probably someone has given false information for the—?"

A sharp rapping at the outer door cut short the explanation, and our visitor rose, trembling and aghast, with beads of sweat standing upon his livid face.

"You had better go into the office, Belfield, while we see who it is," said Thorndyke. "The key is on the inside."

The fugitive wanted no second bidding, but hurried into the empty apartment, and, as the door closed, we heard the key turn in the lock.

As Thorndyke threw open the outer door, he cast a meaning glance at me over his shoulder which I understood when the newcomer entered the room; for it was none other than Superintendent Miller of Scotland Yard.

"I have just dropped in," said the superintendent, in his brisk, cheerful way, "to ask you to do me a favour. Good-evening, Dr. Jervis. I hear you are reading for the bar; learned counsel soon, sir, hey? Medico-legal expert. Dr. Thorndyke's mantle going to fall on you, sir?"

"I hope Dr. Thorndyke's mantle will continue to drape his own majestic form for many a long year yet," I answered; "though he is good enough to spare me a corner—but what on earth have you got there?" For during this dialogue the superintendent had been deftly unfastening a brown-paper parcel, from which he now drew a linen shirt, once white, but now of an unsavoury grey.

"I want to know what this is," said Miller, exhibiting a brownish-red stain on one sleeve. "Just look at that, sir, and tell me if it is blood, and, if so, is it human blood?"

"Really, Miller," said Thorndyke, with a smile, "you flatter me; but I am not like the wise woman of Bagdad who could tell you how many stairs the patient had tumbled down by merely looking at his tongue. I must examine this very thoroughly. When do you want to know?"

"I should like to know to-night," replied the detective.

"Can I cut a piece out to put under the microscope?"

"I would rather you did not," was the reply.

"Very well; you shall have the information in about an hour."

"It's very good of you, doctor," said the detective; and he was taking up his hat preparatory to departing, when Thorndyke said suddenly—"By the way, there is a little matter that I was going to speak to you about. It refers to this Camberwell murder case. I understand you have a clue to the identity of the murderer?"

"Clue!" exclaimed the superintendent contemptuously. "We have spotted our man all right, if we could only lay hands on him; but he has given us the slip for the moment."

"Who is the man?" asked Thorndyke.

The detective looked doubtfully at Thorndyke for some seconds and then said, with evident reluctance: "I suppose there is no harm in telling you—especially as you probably know already"—this with a sly grin; "it's an old crook named Belfield."

"And what is the evidence against him?"

Again the superintendent looked doubtful and again relented.

"Why, the case is as clear as—as cold Scotch," he said (here Thorndyke in illustration of this figure of speech produced a decanter, a syphon and a tumbler, which he pushed towards the officer). "You see, sir, the silly fool went and stuck his sweaty hand on the window; and there we found the marks—four fingers and a thumb, as beautiful prints as you could wish to see. Of course we cut out the piece of glass and took it up to the Finger-print Department; they turned up their files and out came Mr. Belfield's record, with his finger-prints and photograph all complete."

"And the finger-prints on the window-pane were identical with those on the prison form?"

"Identical."

"H'm!" Thorndyke reflected for a while, and the superintendent watched him foxily over the edge of his tumbler.

"I guess you are retained to defend Belfield," the latter observed presently.

"To look into the case generally," replied Thorndyke.

"And I expect you know where the beggar is hiding," continued the detective.

"Belfield's address has not yet been communicated to me," said Thorndyke. "I am merely to investigate the case—and there is no reason, Miller, why you and I should be at cross purposes. We are both working at the case; you want to get a conviction and you want to convict the right man."

"That's so—and Belfield's the right man—but what do you want of us, doctor?"

"I should like to see the piece of glass with the finger-prints on it, and the prison form, and take a photograph of each. And I should like to examine the room in which the murder took place—you have it locked up, I suppose?"

"Yes, we have the keys. Well, it's all rather irregular, letting you see the things. Still, you've always played the game fairly with us, so we might stretch a point. Yes, I will. I'll come back in an hour for your report and bring the glass and the form. I can't let them go out of my custody, you know. I'll be off now—no, thank you, not another drop."

The superintendent caught up his hat and strode away, the personification of mental alertness and bodily vigour.

No sooner had the door closed behind him than Thorndyke's stolid calm changed instantaneously into feverish energy. Darting to the electric bell that rang into the laboratories above, he pressed the button while he gave me my directions.

"Have a look at that blood-stain, Jervis, while I am finishing with Belfield. Don't wet it; scrape it into a drop of warm normal saline solution."

I hastened to reach down the microscope and set out on the table the necessary apparatus and reagents, and, as I was thus occupied, a latch-key turned in the outer door and our invaluable helpmate, Polton, entered the room in his habitual silent, unobtrusive fashion.

"Let me have the finger-print apparatus, please, Polton," said Thorndyke; "and have the copying camera ready by nine o'clock. I am expecting Mr. Miller with some documents."

As his laboratory assistant departed, Thorndyke rapped at the office door.

"It's all clear, Belfield," he called; "you can come out."

The key turned and the prisoner emerged, looking ludicrously woebegone in his ridiculous wig and beard.

"I am going to take your finger-prints, to compare with some that the police found on the window."

"Finger-prints!" exclaimed Belfield, in a tone of dismay. "They don't say they're my finger-prints, do they, sir?"

"They do indeed," replied Thorndyke, eyeing the man narrowly. "They have compared them with those taken when you were at Holloway, and they say that they are identical."

"Good God!" murmured Belfield, collapsing into a chair, faint and trembling. "They must have made some awful mistake. But are mistakes possible with finger-prints?"

"Now look here, Belfield," said Thorndyke. "Were you in that house that night, or were you not? It is of no use for you to tell me any lies."

"I was not there, sir; I swear to God I was not."

"Then they cannot be your finger-prints, that is obvious." Here he stepped to the door to intercept Polton, from whom he received a substantial box, which he brought in and placed on the table.

"Tell me all you know about this case," he continued, as he set out the contents of the box on the table.

"I know nothing about it whatever," replied Belfield; "nothing, at least, except—?"

"Except what?" demanded Thorndyke, looking up sharply as he squeezed a drop from a tube of finger-print ink onto a smooth copper plate.

"Except that the murdered man, Caldwell, was a retired fence."

"A fence, was he?" said Thorndyke in a tone of interest.

"Yes; and I suspect he was a 'nark' too. He knew more than was wholesome for a good many."

"Did he know anything about you?"

"Yes; but nothing that the police don't know."

With a small roller Thorndyke spread the ink upon the plate into a thin film. Then he laid on the edge of the table a smooth white card and, taking Belfield's right hand, pressed the forefinger firmly but quickly, first on the inked plate and then on the card, leaving on the latter a clear print of the finger-tip. This process he repeated with the other fingers and thumb, and then took several additional prints of each.

"That was a nasty injury to your forefinger, Belfield," said Thorndyke, holding the finger to the light and examining the tip carefully. "How did you do it?"

"Stuck a tin-opener into it—a dirty one, too. It was bad for weeks; in fact, Dr. Sampson thought at one time that he would have to amputate the finger."

"How long ago was that?"

"Oh, nearly a year ago, sir."

Thorndyke wrote the date of the injury by the side of the finger-print and then, having rolled up the inking plate afresh, laid on the table several larger cards. "I am now going to take the prints of the four fingers and the thumb all at once," he said.

"They only took the four fingers at once at the prison," said Belfield. "They took the thumb separately."

"I know," replied Thorndyke; "but I am going to take the impression just as it would appear on the window glass."

He took several impressions thus, and then, having looked at his watch, he began to repack the apparatus in its box. While doing this, he glanced, from time to time, in meditative fashion, at the suspected man who sat, the living picture of misery and terror, wiping the greasy ink from his trembling fingers with his handkerchief.

"Belfield," he said at length, "you have sworn to me that you are an innocent man and are trying to live an honest life. I believe you; but in a few minutes I shall know for certain."

"Thank God for that, sir," exclaimed Belfield, brightening up wonderfully.

"And now," said Thorndyke, "you had better go back into the office, for I am expecting Superintendent Miller, and he may be here at any moment."

Belfield hastily slunk back into the office, locking the door after him, and Thorndyke, having returned the box to the laboratory and deposited the cards bearing the finger-prints in a drawer, came round to inspect my work. I had managed to detach a tiny fragment of dried clot from the blood-stained garment, and this, in a drop of normal saline solution, I now had under the microscope.

"What do you make out, Jervis?" my colleague asked.

"Oval corpuscles with distinct nuclei," I answered.

"Ah," said Thorndyke, "that will be good hearing for some poor devil. Have you measured them?"

"Yes. Long diameter one twenty-one hundredth of an inch; short diameter about one thirty-four hundredth of an inch."

Thorndyke reached down an indexed note-book from a shelf of reference volumes and consulted a table of histological measurements.

"That would seem to be the blood of a pheasant, then, or it might, more probably, be that of a common fowl." He applied his eye to the microscope and, fitting in the eyepiece micrometer, verified my measurements. He was thus employed when a sharp tap was heard on the outer door, and rising to open it he admitted the superintendent.

"I see you are at work on my little problem, doctor," said the latter, glancing at the microscope. "What do you make of that stain?"

"It is the blood of a bird—probably a pheasant, or perhaps a common fowl."

The superintendent slapped his thigh. "Well, I'm hanged!" he exclaimed. "You're a regular wizard, doctor, that's what you are. The fellow said he got that stain through handling a wounded pheasant and here are you able to tell us yes or no without a hint from us to help you. Well, you've done my little job for me, sir, and I'm much obliged to you; now I'll carry out my part of the bargain." He opened a hand-bag and drew forth a wooden frame and a blue foolscap envelope and laid them with extreme care on the table.

"There you are, sir," said he, pointing to the frame; "you will find Mr. Belfield's trade-mark very neatly executed, and in the envelope is the finger-print sheet for comparison."

Thorndyke took up the frame and examined it. It enclosed two sheets of glass, one being the portion of the window-pane and the other a cover-glass to protect the fingerprints. Laying a sheet of white paper on the table, where the light was strongest, Thorndyke held the frame over it and gazed at the glass in silence, but with that faint lighting up of his impassive face which I knew so well and which meant so much to me. I walked round, and looking over his shoulder saw upon the glass the beautifully distinct imprints of four fingers and a thumb—the finger-tips, in fact, of an open hand.

After regarding the frame attentively for some time, Thorndyke produced from his pocket a little wash-leather bag, from which he extracted a powerful doublet lens, and with the aid of this he again explored the finger-prints, dwelling especially upon the print of the forefinger.

"I don't think you will find much amiss with those finger-prints, doctor," said the superintendent, "they are as clear as if he made them on purpose."

"They are indeed," replied Thorndyke, with an inscrutable smile, "exactly as if he had made them on purpose. And how beautifully clean the glass is—as if he had polished it before making the impression."

The superintendent glanced at Thorndyke with quick suspicion; but the smile had faded and given place to a wooden immobility from which nothing could be gleaned.

When he had examined the glass exhaustively, Thorndyke drew the finger-print form from its envelope and scanned it quickly, glancing repeatedly from the paper to the glass and from the glass to the paper. At length he laid them both on the table, and turning to the detective looked him steadily in the face.

"I think, Miller," said he, "that I can give you a hint."

"Indeed, sir? And what might that be?"

"It is this: you are after the wrong man."

The superintendent snorted—not a loud snort, for that would have been rude, and no officer could be more polite than Superintendent Miller. But it conveyed a protest which he speedily followed up in words.

"You don't mean to say that the prints on that glass are not the finger-prints of Frank Belfield?"

"I say that those prints were not made by Frank Belfield," Thorndyke replied firmly.

"Do you admit, sir, that the finger-prints on the official form were made by him?"

"I have no doubt that they were."

"Well, sir, Mr. Singleton, of the Finger-print Department, has compared the prints on the glass with those on the form and he says they are identical; and I have examined them and I say they are identical."

"Exactly," said Thorndyke; "and I have examined them and I say they are identical—and that therefore those on the glass cannot have been made by Belfield."

The superintendent snorted again—somewhat louder this time—and gazed at Thorndyke with wrinkled brows.

"You are not pulling my leg, I suppose, sir?" he asked, a little sourly.

"I should as soon think of tickling a porcupine," Thorndyke answered, with a suave smile.

"Well," rejoined the bewildered detective, "if I didn't know you, sir, I should say you were talking confounded nonsense. Perhaps you wouldn't mind explaining what you mean."

"Supposing," said Thorndyke, "I make it clear to you that those prints on the window-pane were not made by Belfield. Would you still execute the warrant?"

"What do you think?" exclaimed Miller. "Do you suppose we should go into court to have you come and knock the bottom out of our case, like you did in that Hornby affair? By the way, that was a finger-print case too, now I come to think of it," and the superintendent suddenly became thoughtful.

"You have often complained," pursued Thorndyke, "that I have withheld information from you and sprung unexpected evidence on you at the trial. Now I am going to take you into my confidence, and when I have proved to you that this clue of yours is a false one, I shall expect you to let this poor devil Belfield go his way in peace."

The superintendent grunted—a form of utterance that committed him to nothing.

"These prints," continued Thorndyke, taking up the frame once more, "present several features of interest, one of which, at least, ought not to have escaped you and Mr. Singleton, as it seems to have done. Just look at that thumb."

The superintendent did so, and then pored over the official paper.

"Well," he said, "I don't see anything the matter with it. It's exactly like the print on the paper."

"Of course it is," rejoined Thorndyke, "and that is just the point. It ought not to be. The print of the thumb on the paper was taken separately from the fingers. And why? Because it was impossible to take it at the same time. The thumb is in a different plane from the fingers; when the hand is laid flat on any surface—as this window-pane, for instance—the palmar surfaces of the fingers touch it, whereas it is the side of the thumb which comes in contact and not the palmar surface. But in this"—he tapped the framed glass with his finger—"the prints show the palmar surfaces of all the five digits in contact at once, which is an impossibility. Just try to put your own thumb in that position and you will see that it is so."

The detective spread out his hand on the table and immediately perceived the truth of my colleague's statement.

"And what does that prove?" he asked.

"It proves that the thumb-print on the window-pane was not made at the same time as the finger-prints—that it was added separately; and that fact seems to prove that the prints were not made accidentally, but—as you ingeniously suggested just now—were put there for a purpose."

"I don't quite see the drift of all this," said the superintendent, rubbing the back of his head perplexedly; "and you said a while back that the prints on the glass can't be Belfield's because they are identical with the prints on the form. Now that seems to me sheer nonsense, if you will excuse my saying so."

"And yet," replied Thorndyke, "it is the actual fact. Listen: these prints"—here he took up the official sheet—"were taken at Holloway six years ago. These"—pointing to the framed glass—"were made within the present week. The one is, as regards the ridge-pattern, a perfect duplicate of the other. Is that not so?"

"That is so, doctor," agreed the superintendent.

"Very well. Now suppose I were to tell you that within the last twelve months something had happened to Belfield that made an appreciable change in the ridge-pattern on one of his fingers?"

"But is such a thing possible?"

"It is not only possible but it has happened. I will show you."

He brought forth from the drawer the cards on which Belfield had made his finger-prints, and laid them before the detective.

"Observe the prints of the forefinger," he said, indicating them; "there are a dozen, in all, and you will notice in each a white line crossing the ridges and dividing them. That line is caused by a scar, which has destroyed a portion of the ridges, and is now an integral part of Belfield's finger-print. And since no such blank line is to be seen in this print on the glass—in which the ridges appear perfect, as they were before the injury—it follows that that print could not have been made by Belfield's finger."

"There is no doubt about the injury, I suppose?"

"None whatever. There is the scar to prove it, and I can produce the surgeon who attended Belfield at the time."

The officer rubbed his head harder than before, and regarded Thorndyke with puckered brows.

"This is a teaser," he growled, "it is indeed. What you say, sir, seems perfectly sound, and yet—there are those finger-prints on the window-glass. Now you can't get fingerprints without fingers, can you?"

"Undoubtedly you can," said Thorndyke.

"I should want to see that done before I could believe even you, sir," said Miller.

"You shall see it done now," was the calm rejoinder. "You have evidently forgotten the Hornby case—the case of the Red Thumb-mark, as the newspapers called it."

"I only heard part of it," replied Miller, "and I didn't really follow the evidence in that."

"Well, I will show you a relic of that case," said Thorndyke. He unlocked a cabinet and took from one of the shelves a small box labelled "Hornby," which, being opened, was seen to contain a folded paper, a little red-covered oblong book and what looked like a large boxwood pawn.

"This little book," Thorndyke continued, "is a 'thumb-ograph'—a sort of finger-print album—I dare say you know the kind of thing."

The superintendent nodded contemptuously at the little volume.

"Now while Dr. Jervis is finding us the print we want, I will run up to the laboratory for an inked slab."

He handed me the little book and, as he left the room, I began to turn over the leaves—not without emotion, for it was this very "thumbograph" that first introduced me to my wife, as is related elsewhere—glancing at the various prints above the familiar names and marvelling afresh at the endless variations of pattern that they displayed. At length I came upon two thumb-prints of which one—the left—was marked by a longitudinal white line—evidently the trace of a scar; and underneath them was written the signature "Reuben Hornby."

At this moment Thorndyke re-entered the room carrying the inked slab, which he laid on the table, and seating himself between the superintendent and me, addressed the former.

"Now, Miller, here are two thumb-prints made by a gentleman named Reuben Hornby. Just glance at the left one; it is a highly characteristic print."

"Yes," agreed Miller, "one could swear to that from memory, I should think."

"Then look at this." Thorndyke took the paper from the box and, unfolding it, handed it to the detective. It bore a pencilled inscription, and on it were two blood-smears and a very distinct thumb-print in blood. "What do you say to that thumb-print?"

"Why," answered Miller, "it's this one, of course; Reuben Hornby's left thumb."

"Wrong, my friend," said Thorndyke. "It was made by an ingenious gentleman named Walter Hornby (whom you followed from the Old Bailey and lost on Ludgate Hill); but not with his thumb."

"How, then?" demanded the superintendent incredulously.

"In this way." Thorndyke took the boxwood "pawn" from its receptacle and pressed its flat base onto the inked slab; then lifted it and pressed it onto the back of a visiting-card, and again raised it; and now the card was marked by a very distinct thumb-print.

"My God!" exclaimed the detective, picking up the card and viewing it with a stare of dismay, "this is the very devil, sir. This fairly knocks the bottom out of finger-print identification. May I ask, sir, how you made that stamp—for I suppose you did make it?"

"Yes, we made it here, and the process we used was practically that used by photo-engravers in making line blocks; that is to say, we photographed one of

Mr. Hornby's thumb-prints, printed it on a plate of chrome-gelatine, developed the plate with hot water and this"—here he touched the embossed surface of the stamp—"is what remained. But we could have done it in various other ways; for instance, with common transfer paper and lithographic stone; indeed, I assure you, Miller, that there is nothing easier to forge than a finger-print, and it can be done with such perfection that the forger himself cannot tell his own forgery from a genuine original, even when they are placed side by side."

"Well, I'm hanged," grunted the superintendent, "you've fairly knocked me, this time, doctor." He rose gloomily and prepared to depart. "I suppose," he added, "your interest in this case has lapsed, now Belfield's out of it?"

"Professionally, yes; but I am disposed to finish the case for my own satisfaction. I am quite curious as to who our too-ingenious friend may be."

Miller's face brightened. "We shall give you every facility, you know—and that reminds me that Singleton gave me these two photographs for you, one of the official paper and one of the prints on the glass. Is there anything more that we can do for you?"

"I should like to have a look at the room in which the murder took place."

"You shall, doctor; to-morrow, if you like; I'll meet you there in the morning at ten, if that will do."

It would do excellently, Thorndyke assured him, and with this the superintendent took his departure in renewed spirits.

We had only just closed the door when there came a hurried and urgent tapping upon it, whereupon I once more threw it open, and a quietly-dressed woman in a thick veil, who was standing on the threshold, stepped quickly past me into the room.

"Where is my husband?" she demanded, as I closed the door; and then, catching sight of Thorndyke, she strode up to him with a threatening air and a terrified but angry face.

"What have you done with my husband, sir?" she repeated. "Have you betrayed him, after giving your word? I met a man who looked like a police officer on the stairs."

"Your husband, Mrs. Belfield, is here and quite safe," replied Thorndyke. "He has locked himself in that room," indicating the office.

Mrs. Belfield darted across and rapped smartly at the door. "Are you there, Frank?" she called.

In immediate response the key turned, the door opened and Belfield emerged looking very pale and worn.

"You have kept me a long time in there, sir," he said.

"It took me a long time to prove to Superintendent Miller that he was after the wrong man. But I succeeded, and now, Belfield, you are free. The charge against you is withdrawn."

Belfield stood for a while as one stupefied, while his wife, after a moment of silent amazement, flung her arms round his neck and burst into tears. "But how did you know I was innocent, sir?" demanded the bewildered Belfield.

"Ah! how did I? Every man to his trade, you know. Well, I congratulate you, and now go home and have a square meal and get a good night's rest."

He shook hands with his clients—vainly endeavouring to prevent Mrs. Belfield from kissing his hand—and stood at the open door listening until the sound of their retreating footsteps died away.

"A noble little woman, Jervis," said he, as he closed the door. "In another moment she would have scratched my face—and I mean to find out the scoundrel who tried to wreck her happiness."

## PART II.
## THE SHIP OF THE DESERT

THE case which I am now about to describe has always appeared to me a singularly instructive one, as illustrating the value and importance of that fundamental rule in the carrying out of investigations which Thorndyke had laid down so emphatically—the rule that all facts, in any way relating to a case, should be collected impartially and without reference to any theory, and each fact, no matter how trivial or apparently irrelevant, carefully studied. But I must not anticipate the remarks of my learned and talented friend on this subject which I have to chronicle anon; rather let me proceed to the case itself.

I had slept at our chambers in King's Bench Walk—as I commonly did two or three nights a week—and on coming down to the sitting-room, found Thorndyke's man, Polton, putting the last touches to the breakfast-table, while Thorndyke himself was poring over two photographs of fingerprints, of which he seemed to be taking elaborate measurements with a pair of hair-dividers. He greeted me with his quiet, genial smile and, laying down the dividers, took his seat at the breakfast-table.

"You are coming with me this morning, I suppose," said he; "the Camberwell murder case, you know."

"Of course I am if you will have me, but I know practically nothing of the case. Could you give me an outline of the facts that are known?"

Thorndyke looked at me solemnly, but with a mischievous twinkle. "This," he said, "is the old story of the fox and the crow; you 'bid me discourse,' and while I 'enchant thine ear,' you claw to windward with the broiled ham. A deep-laid plot, my learned brother."

"And such," I exclaimed, "is the result of contact with the criminal classes!"

"I am sorry that you regard yourself in that light," he retorted, with a malicious smile. "However, with regard to this case. The facts are briefly these: The murdered man, Caldwell, who seems to have been formerly a receiver of stolen goods and probably a police spy as well, lived a solitary life in a small house with only an elderly woman to attend him.

"A week ago this woman went to visit a married daughter and stayed the night with her, leaving Caldwell alone in the house. When she returned on the following morning she found her master lying dead on the floor of his office, or study, in a small pool of blood.

"The police surgeon found that he had been dead about twelve hours. He had been killed by a single blow, struck from behind, with some heavy implement, and a jemmy which lay on the floor beside him fitted the wound exactly. The deceased wore a dressing-gown and no collar, and a bedroom candlestick lay upside down on the floor, although gas was laid on in the room; and as the window of the office appears to have been forced with the jemmy that was found, and there were distinct footprints on the flower-bed outside the window, the police think that the deceased was undressing to go to bed when he was disturbed by the noise of the opening window; that he went down to the office and, as he entered, was struck down by the burglar who was lurking behind the door. On the window-glass the police found the greasy impression of an open right hand, and, as you know, the finger-prints were identified by the experts as those of an old convict named Belfield. As you also know, I proved that those finger-prints were, in reality, forgeries, executed with rubber or gelatine stamps. That is an outline of the case."

The close of this recital brought our meal to an end, and we prepared for our visit to the scene of the crime. Thorndyke slipped into his pocket his queer outfit—somewhat like that of a field geologist—locked up the photographs, and we set forth by way of the Embankment.

"The police have no clue, I suppose, to the identity of the murderer, now that the finger-prints have failed?" I asked, as we strode along together.

"I expect not," he replied, "though they might have if they examined their material. I made out a rather interesting point this morning, which is this: the man who made those sham finger-prints used two stamps, one for the thumb and the other for the four fingers; and the original from which those stamps were made was the official finger-print form."

"How did you discover that?" I inquired.

"It was very simple. You remember that Mr. Singleton of the Finger-print Department sent me, by Superintendent Miller, two photographs, one of the prints on the window and one of the official form with Belfield's finger-prints on it. Well, I have compared them and made the most minute measurements of each, and they are obviously duplicates. Not only are all the little imperfections on the form—due to defective inking—reproduced faithfully on the window-pane, but the relative positions of the four fingers on both cases agree to the hundredth of an inch. Of course the thumb stamp was made by taking an oval out of the rolled impression on the form."

"Then do you suggest that this murder was committed by someone connected with the Finger-print Department at Scotland Yard?"

"Hardly. But someone has had access to the forms. There has been leakage somewhere."

When we arrived at the little detached house in which the murdered man had lived, the door was opened by an elderly woman, and our friend, Superintendent Miller, greeted us in the hall.

"We are all ready for you, doctor," said he. "Of course, the things have all been gone over once, but we are turning them out more thoroughly now." He led the way into the small, barely-furnished office in which the tragedy had occurred. A dark stain on the carpet and a square hole in one of the window-panes furnished memorials of the crime, which were supplemented by an odd assortment of objects laid out on the newspaper-covered table. These included silver teaspoons, watches, various articles of jewellery, from which the stones had been removed—none of them of any considerable value—and a roughly-made jemmy.

"I don't know why Caldwell should have kept all these odds and ends," said the detective superintendent. "There is stuff here, that I can identify, from six different burglaries—and not a conviction among the six."

Thorndyke looked over the collection with languid interest; he was evidently disappointed at finding the room so completely turned out.

"Have you any idea what has been taken?" he asked.

"Not the least. We don't even know if the safe was opened. The keys were on the writing-table, so I suppose he went through everything, though I don't see why he left these things if he did. We found them all in the safe."

"Have you powdered the jemmy?"

The superintendent turned very red. "Yes," he growled, "but some half-dozen blithering idiots had handled the thing before I saw it—been trying it on the window, the blighters—so, of course, it showed nothing but the marks of their beastly paws."

"The window had not really been forced, I suppose?" said Thorndyke.

"No," replied Miller, with a glance of surprise at my colleague, "that was a plant; so were the footprints. He must have put on a pair of Caldwell's boots and gone out and made them—unless Caldwell made them himself, which isn't likely."

"Have you found any letter or telegram?"

"A letter making an appointment for nine o'clock on the night of the murder. No signature or address, and the handwriting evidently disguised."

"Is there anything that furnishes any sort of clue?"

"Yes, sir, there is. There's this, which we found in the safe." He produced a small parcel which he proceeded to unfasten, looking somewhat queerly at Thorndyke the while. It contained various odds and ends of jewellery, and a smaller parcel formed of a pocket-handkerchief tied with tape. This the detective also unfastened, revealing half-a-dozen silver teaspoons, all engraved with the same crest, two salt-cellars and a gold locket bearing a monogram. There was also a half-sheet of note-paper on which was written, in a manifestly disguised hand: "These are the goods I told you about. F. B." But what riveted Thorndyke's attention and mine was the handkerchief itself (which was not a very clean one and was sullied by one or two small blood-stains), for it was marked in one corner with the name "F. Belfield," legibly printed in marking-ink with a rubber stamp.

Thorndyke and the superintendent looked at one another and both smiled.

"I know what you are thinking, sir," said the latter.

"I am sure you do," was the reply, "and it is useless to pretend that you don't agree with me."

"Well, sir," said Miller doggedly, "if that handkerchief has been put there as a plant, it's Belfield's business to prove it. You see, doctor," he added persuasively, "it isn't this job only that's affected. Those spoons, those salt-cellars and that locket are part of the proceeds of the Winchmore Hill burglary, and we want the gentleman who did that crack—we want him very badly."

"No doubt you do," replied Thorndyke, "but this handkerchief won't help you. A sharp counsel—Mr. Anstey, for instance—would demolish it in five minutes. I assure you, Miller, that handkerchief has no evidential value whatever, whereas it might prove an invaluable instrument of research. The best thing you can do is to hand it over to me and let me see what I can learn from it."

The superintendent was obviously dissatisfied, but he eventually agreed, with manifest reluctance, to Thorndyke's suggestion.

"Very well, doctor," he said; "you shall have it for a day or two. Do you want the spoons and things as well?"

"No. Only the handkerchief and the paper that was in it."

The two articles were accordingly handed to him and deposited in a tin box which he usually carried in his pocket, and, after a few more words with the disconsolate detective, we took our departure.

"A very disappointing morning," was Thorndyke's comment as we walked away. "Of course the room ought to have been examined by an expert before anything was moved."

"Have you picked up anything in the way of information?" I asked.

"Very little excepting confirmation of my original theory. You see, this man Caldwell was a receiver and evidently a police spy. He gave useful information to the police, and they, in return, refrained from inconvenient inquiries. But a spy, or 'nark,' is nearly always a blackmailer too, and the probabilities in this case are that some crook, on whom Caldwell was putting the screw rather too tightly, made an appointment for a meeting when the house was empty, and just knocked Caldwell on the head. The crime was evidently planned beforehand, and the murderer came prepared to kill several birds with one stone. Thus he brought with him the stamps to make the sham finger-prints on the window, and I have no doubt that he also brought this handkerchief and the various oddments of plate and jewellery from those burglaries that Miller is so keen about, and planted them in the safe. You

noticed, I suppose, that none of the things were of any value, but all were capable of easy identification?"

"Yes, I noticed that. His object, evidently, was to put those burglaries as well as the murder onto poor Belfield."

"Exactly. And you see what Miller's attitude is; Belfield is the bird in the hand, whereas the other man—if there is another—is still in the bush; so Belfield is to be followed up and a conviction obtained if possible. If he is innocent, that is his affair, and it is for him to prove it."

"And what shall you do next?" I asked.

"I shall telegraph to Belfield to come and see us this evening. He may be able to tell us something about this handkerchief that, with the clue we already have, may put us on the right track. What time is your consultation?"

"Twelve-thirty—and here comes my 'bus. I shall be in to lunch." I sprang onto the footboard, and as I took my seat on the roof and looked back at my friend striding along with an easy swing, I knew that he was deep in thought, though automatically attentive to all that was happening. My consultation—it was a lunacy case of some importance—was over in time to allow of my return to our chambers punctually at the luncheon hour; and as I entered, I was at once struck by something new in Thorndyke's manner—a certain elation and gaiety which I had learned to associate with a point scored successfully in some intricate and puzzling case. He made no confidences, however, and seemed, in fact, inclined to put away, for a time, all his professional cares and business.

"Shall we have an afternoon off, Jervis?" he said gaily. "It is a fine day and work is slack just now. What say you to the Zoo? They have a splendid chimpanzee and several specimens of that remarkable fish Periophthalmos Kolreuteri. Shall we go?"

"By all means," I replied; "and we will mount the elephant, if you like, and throw buns to the grizzly bear and generally renew our youth like the eagle."

But when, an hour later, we found ourselves in the gardens, I began to suspect my friend of some ulterior purpose in this holiday jaunt; for it was not the chimpanzee or even the wonderful fish that attracted his attention. On the contrary, he hung about the vicinity of the lamas and camels in a way that I could not fail to notice; and even there it appeared to be the sheds and houses rather than the animals themselves that interested him.

"Behold, Jervis," he said presently, as a saddled camel of seedy aspect was led towards its house, "behold the ship of the desert, with raised saloon-deck amidships, fitted internally with watertight compartments and displaying the effects of rheumatoid arthritis in his starboard hip-joint. Let us go and examine him before he hauls into dock." We took a cross-path to intercept the camel on its way to its residence, and Thorndyke moralized as we went.

"It is interesting," he remarked, "to note the way in which these specialized animals, such as the horse, the reindeer and the camel, have been appropriated by man, and their special character made to subserve human needs. Think, for instance, of the part the camel has played in history, in ancient commerce—and modern too, for that matter—and in the diffusion of culture; and of the role he has enacted in war and conquest from the Egyptian campaign of Cambyses down to that of Kitchener. Yes, the camel is a very remarkable animal, though it must be admitted that this particular specimen is a scurvy-looking beast."

The camel seemed to be sensible of these disparaging remarks, for as it approached it saluted Thorndyke with a supercilious grin and then turned away its head.

"Your charge is not as young as he used to be," Thorndyke observed to the man who was leading the animal.

"No, sir, he isn't; he's getting old, and that's the fact. He shows it too."

"I suppose," said Thorndyke, strolling towards the house by the man's side, "these beasts require a deal of attention?"

"You're right, sir; and nasty-tempered brutes they are."

"So I have heard; but they are interesting creatures, the camels and lamas. Do you happen to know if complete sets of photographs of them are to be had here?"

"You can get a good many at the lodge, sir," the man replied, "but not all, I think. If you want a complete set, there's one of our men in the camel-house that could let you have them; he takes the photos himself, and very clever he is at it, too. But he isn't here just now."

"Perhaps you could give me his name so that I could write to him," said Thorndyke.

"Yes, sir. His name is Woodthorpe—Joseph Woodthorpe. He'll do anything for you to order. Thank you, sir; good-afternoon, sir;" and pocketing an unexpected tip, the man led his charge towards its lair.

Thorndyke's absorbing interest in the camels seemed now suddenly to become extinct, and he suffered me to lead him to any part of the gardens that attracted me, showing an imperial interest in all the inmates from the insects to the elephants, and enjoying his holiday—if it was one—with the gaiety and high spirits of a schoolboy. Yet he never let slip a chance of picking up a stray hair or feather, but gathered up each with care, wrapped it in its separate paper, on which was written its description, and deposited it in his tin collecting-box.

"You never know," he remarked, as we turned away from the ostrich enclosure, "when a specimen for comparison may be of vital importance. Here, for instance, is a small feather of a cassowary, and here the hair of a wapiti deer; now the recognition of either of those might, in certain circumstances, lead to the detection of a criminal or save the life of an innocent man. The thing has happened repeatedly, and may happen again to-morrow."

"You must have an enormous collection of hairs in your cabinet," I remarked, as we walked home.

"I have," he replied, "probably the largest in the world. And as to other microscopical objects of medico-legal interest, such as dust and mud from different localities and from special industries and manufactures, fibres, food-products and drugs, my collection is certainly unique."

"And you have found your collection useful in your work?" I asked.

"Constantly. Over and over again I have obtained, by reference to my specimens, the most unexpected evidence, and the longer I practise, the more I become convinced that the microscope is the sheet-anchor of the medical jurist."

"By the way," I said, "you spoke of sending a telegram to Belfield. Did you send it?"

"Yes. I asked him to come to see me to-night at half-past eight, and, if possible, bring his wife with him. I want to get to the bottom of that handkerchief mystery."

"But do you think he will tell you the truth about it?"

"That is impossible to judge; he will be a fool if he does not. But I think he will; he has a godly fear of me and my methods."

As soon as our dinner was finished and cleared away, Thorndyke produced the "collecting-box" from his pocket, and began to sort out the day's "catch," giving explicit directions to Polton for the disposal of each specimen. The hairs and small feathers were to be mounted as microscopic objects, while the larger feathers were to be placed, each in its separate labelled envelope, in its appropriate box. While these directions were being given, I stood by the window absently gazing out as I listened, gathering many a useful hint in the technique of preparation and preservation, and filled with admiration alike at my colleague's exhaustive knowledge of practical detail and the perfect manner in which he had trained his assistant. Suddenly I started, for a well-known figure was crossing from Crown Office Row and evidently bearing down on our chambers.

"My word, Thorndyke," I exclaimed, "here's a pretty mess!"

"What is the matter?" he asked, looking up anxiously.

"Superintendent Miller heading straight for our doorway. And it is now twenty minutes past eight."

Thorndyke laughed. "It will be a quaint position," he remarked, "and somewhat of a shock for Belfield. But it really doesn't matter; in fact, I think, on the whole, I am rather pleased that he should have come."

The superintendent's brisk knock was heard a few moments later, and when he was admitted by Polton, he entered and looked round the room a little, sheepishly.

"I am ashamed to come worrying you like this, sir," he began apologetically.

"Not at all," replied Thorndyke, serenely slipping the cassowary's feather into an envelope, and writing the name, date and locality on the outside. "I am your servant in this case, you know. Polton, whisky and soda for the superintendent."

"You see, sir," continued Miller, "our people are beginning to fuss about this case, and they don't approve of my having handed that handkerchief and the paper over to you as they will have to be put in evidence."

"I thought they might object," remarked Thorndyke.

"So did I, sir; and they do. And, in short, they say that I have got to get them back at once. I hope it won't put you out, sir."

"Not in the least," said Thorndyke. "I have asked Belfield to come here tonight—I expect him in a few minutes—and when I have heard what he has to say I shall have no further use for the handkerchief."

"You're not going to show it to him!" exclaimed the detective, aghast.

"Certainly I am."

"You mustn't do that, sir. I can't sanction it; I can't indeed."

"Now, look you here, Miller," said Thorndyke, shaking his forefinger at the officer; "I am working for you in this case, as I have told you. Leave the matter in my hands. Don't raise silly objections; and when you leave here tonight you will take with you not only the handkerchief and the paper, but probably also the name and address of the man who committed this murder and those various burglaries that you are so keen about."

"Is that really so, sir?" exclaimed the astonished detective. "Well, you haven't let the grass grow under your feet. Ah!" as a gentle rap at the door was heard, "here's Belfield, I suppose."

It was Belfield—accompanied by his wife—and mightily disturbed they were when their eyes lighted on our visitor.

"You needn't be afraid of me, Belfield," said Miller, with ferocious geniality; "I am not here after you." Which was not literally true, though it served to reassure the affrighted ex-convict.

"The superintendent dropped in by chance," said Thorndyke; "but it is just as well that he should hear what passes. I want you to look at this handkerchief and tell me if it is yours. Don't be afraid, but just tell us the simple truth."

He took the handkerchief out of a drawer and spread it on the table; and I now observed that a small square had been cut out of one of the bloodstains.

Belfield took the handkerchief in his trembling hands, and as his eye fell on the stamped name in the corner he turned deadly pale.

"It looks like mine," he said huskily. "What do you say, Liz?" he added, passing it to his wife.

Mrs. Belfield examined first the name and then the hem. "It's yours, right enough, Frank," said she. "It's the one that got changed in the wash. You see, sir," she continued, addressing Thorndyke, "I bought him half-a-dozen new ones about six months ago, and I got a rubber stamp made and marked them all. Well, one day when I was looking over his things I noticed that one of his handkerchiefs had got no mark on it. I spoke to the laundress about it, but she couldn't explain it, so as the right one never came back, I marked the one that we got in exchange."

"How long ago was that?" asked Thorndyke.

"About two months ago I noticed it."

"And you know nothing more about it."

"Nothing whatever, sir. Nor you, Frank, do you?"

Her husband shook his head gloomily, and Thorndyke replaced the handkerchief in the drawer.

"And now," said he, "I am going to ask you a question on another subject. When you were at Holloway there was a warder—or assistant warder—there, named Woodthorpe. Do you remember him?"

"Yes, sir, very well indeed; in fact, it was him that—?"

"I know," interrupted Thorndyke. "Have you seen him since you left Holloway?"

"Yes, sir, once. It was last Easter Monday. I met him at the Zoo; he is a keeper there now in the camel-house" (here a sudden light dawned upon me and I chuckled aloud, to Belfield's great astonishment). "He gave my little boy a ride on one of the camels and made himself very pleasant."

"Do you remember anything else happening?" Thorndyke inquired.

"Yes, sir. The camel had a little accident; he kicked out—he was an ill-tempered beast—and his leg hit a post; there happened to be a nail sticking out from that post, and it tore up a little flap of skin. Then Woodthorpe got out his handkerchief to tie up the wound, but as it was none of the cleanest, I said to him: 'Don't use that, Woodthorpe; have mine,' which was quite a clean one. So he took it and bound up the camel's leg, and he said to me: 'I'll have it washed and send it to you if you give me your address.' But I told him there was no need for that; I should be passing the camel-house on my way out and I would look in for the handkerchief. And I did: I looked in about an hour later, and Woodthorpe gave me my handkerchief, folded up but not washed."

"Did you examine it to see if it was yours?" asked Thorndyke.

"No, sir. I just slipped it in my pocket as it was."

"And what became of it afterwards?"

"When I got home I dropped it into the dirty-linen basket."

"Is that all you know about it?"

"Yes, sir; that is all I know."

"Very well, Belfield, that will do. Now you have no reason to be uneasy. You will soon know all about the Camberwell murder—that is, if you read the papers."

The ex-convict and his wife were obviously relieved by this assurance and departed in quite good spirits. When they were gone, Thorndyke produced the handkerchief and the half-sheet of paper and handed them to the superintendent, remarking—"This is highly satisfactory, Miller; the whole case seems to join up very neatly indeed. Two months ago the wife first noticed the substituted handkerchief, and last Easter Monday—a little over two months ago—this very significant incident took place in the Zoological Gardens."

"That is all very well, sir," objected the superintendent, "but we've only their word for it, you know."

"Not so," replied Thorndyke. "We have excellent corroborative evidence. You noticed that I had cut a small piece out of the blood-stained portion of the handkerchief?"

"Yes; and I was sorry you had done it. Our people won't like that."

"Well, here it is, and we will ask Dr. Jervis to give us his opinion of it."

From the drawer in which the handkerchief had been hidden he brought forth a microscope slide, and setting the microscope on the table, laid the slide on the stage.

"Now, Jervis," he said, "tell us what you see there."

I examined the edge of the little square of fabric (which had been mounted in a fluid reagent) with a high-power objective, and was, for a time, a little puzzled by the appearance of the blood that adhered to it.

"It looks like bird's blood," I said presently, with some hesitation, "but yet I can make out no nuclei." I looked again, and then, suddenly, "By Jove!" I exclaimed, "I have it; of course! It's the blood of a camel!"

"Is that so, doctor?" demanded the detective, leaning forward in his excitement.

"That is so," replied Thorndyke. "I discovered it after I came home this morning. You see," he explained, "it is quite unmistakable. The rule is that the blood corpuscles of mammals are circular; the one exception is the camel family, in which the corpuscles are elliptical."

"Why," exclaimed Miller, "that seems to connect Woodthorpe with this Camberwell job."

"It connects him with it very conclusively," said Thorndyke. "You are forgetting the finger-prints."

The detective looked puzzled. "What about them?" he asked.

"They were made with stamps—two stamps, as a matter of fact—and those stamps were made by photographic process from the official finger-print form. I can prove that beyond all doubt."

"Well, suppose they were. What then?"

Thorndyke opened a drawer and took out a photograph, which he handed to Miller. "Here," he said, "is the photograph of the official finger-print form which you were kind enough to bring me. What does it say at the bottom there?" and he pointed with his finger.

The superintendent read aloud: "Impressions taken by Joseph Woodthorpe. Rank, Warder; Prison, Holloway." He stared at the photograph for a moment, and then exclaimed—"Well, I'm hanged! You have worked this out neatly, doctor! and so quick too. We'll have Mr. Woodthorpe under lock and key the first thing to-morrow morning. But how did he do it, do you think?"

"He might have taken duplicate finger-prints and kept one form; the prisoners would not know there was anything wrong; but he did not in this case. He must have contrived to take a photograph of the form before sending it in—it would take a skilful photographer only a minute or two with a suitable hand-camera placed on a table at the proper distance from the wall; and I have ascertained that he is a skilful photographer. You will probably find the apparatus, and the stamps too, when you search his rooms."

"Well, well. You do give us some surprises, doctor. But I must be off now to see about this warrant. Good-night, sir, and many thanks for your help."

When the superintendent had gone we sat for a while looking at one another in silence. At length Thorndyke spoke. "Here is a case, Jervis," he said, "which, simple as it is, teaches a most invaluable lesson—a lesson which you should take well to heart. It is this: The evidential value of any fact is an unknown quantity until the fact has been examined. That seems a self-evident truth, but like many other self-evident truths, it is constantly overlooked in practice. Take this present case. When I left Caldwell's house this morning the facts in my possession were these: (1) The man who murdered Caldwell was directly or indirectly connected with the Finger-print Department. (2) He was almost certainly a skilled photographer. (3) He probably committed the Winchmore Hill and the other burglaries. (4) He was known to Caldwell, had had professional dealings with him and was probably being blackmailed. This was all; a very vague clue, as you see.

"There was the handkerchief, planted, as I had no doubt; but could not prove; the name stamped on it was Belfield's, but any one can get a rubber stamp made. Then it was stained with blood, as handkerchiefs often are; that blood might or might not be human blood; it did not seem to matter a straw whether it was or not. Nevertheless, I said to myself: If it is human, or at least mammalian blood, that is a fact; and if it is not human blood, that is also a fact. I will have that fact, and then I shall know what its value is. I examined the stain when I reached home, and behold! it was camel's blood; and immediately this insignificant fact swelled up into evidence of primary importance. The rest was obvious. I had seen Woodthorpe's name on the form, and I knew several other officials. My business was to visit all places in London where there were camels, to get the names of all persons connected with them and to ascertain if any among them was a photographer. Naturally I went first to the Zoo, and at the very first cast hooked Joseph Woodthorpe. Wherefore I say again: Never call any fact irrelevant until you have examined it."

The remarkable evidence given above was not heard at the trial, nor did Thorndyke's name appear among the witnesses; for when the police searched Woodthorpe's rooms, so many incriminating articles were found (including a pair of fingerprint stamps which exactly answered to Thorndyke's description of them, and a number of photographs of finger-print forms) that his guilt was put beyond all doubt; and society was shortly after relieved of a very undesirable member.

**Lector House believes that a society develops through a two-fold approach of continuous learning and adaptation, which is derived from the study of classic literary works spread across the historic timeline of literature records. Therefore, we aim at reviving, repairing and redeveloping all those inaccessible or damaged but historically as well as culturally important literature across subjects so that the future generations may have an opportunity to study and learn from past works to embark upon a journey of creating a better future.**

**This book is a result of an effort made by Lector House towards making a contribution to the preservation and repair of original ancient works which might hold historical significance to the approach of continuous learning across subjects.**

**HAPPY READING & LEARNING!**

**LECTOR HOUSE LLP**
**E-MAIL: lectorpublishing@gmail.com**

9 789353 446345

Lightning Source UK Ltd.
Milton Keynes UK
UKHW011253061021
391760UK00003B/328

9 789353 446345